BETRAYED

HOSTAGE RESCUE TEAM SERIES

KAYLEA CROSS

BETRAYED

Copyright © 2016
by Kaylea Cross

* * * * *

Cover Art & Formatting by
Sweet 'N Spicy Designs

* * * * *

ISBN: 978-1532861307

Dedication

To Kara and Stacey. Thanks for not only coming to Hawaii with me, but for also introducing me to the joys of the beach umbrella. Who knew that was the secret to filling in plot holes? Here's to more tropical plotting sessions in our future! Love you guys.

(Also, women who practice room-clearing techniques with coat hangers while wearing cocktail dresses are totally *BADASS*. Just saying.)

Kaylea xoxo

Author's Note

This one's for all of you HRT fans who fell in love with Bautista as hard as I did in *Exposed*. If there was ever a villain who deserved a chance at redemption and a happy ending, it's him.

Up next will be Blackwell's story, the final book of the HRT series (*sniffle*) and I plan to make it gut-wrenching. Better buckle up!

Happy reading!

Kaylea Cross

Chapter One

Miguel "el Santo" Bautista stayed perfectly still as he read the last section of the amended contract before him, aware of the man and woman staring at him from across the table.

At first he'd thought it was some kind of joke when the NSA had approached him for recruitment three weeks ago. They'd offered him what amounted to a fancy reduced sentence in exchange for his services but he'd smelled their desperation and upped the ante by demanding a full pardon. Among other things.

Negotiations had been ongoing ever since, and against all odds, they were offering him everything he'd wanted in this final contract. He'd lost most of his assets, of course, which were seized and frozen by the IRS.

But not all of them. The government hadn't found them all, and his resourcefulness, along with his background in business and economics, had allowed him to bury his investments well. From what he could tell, he still had a sizeable sum in the Caymans that had thus far gone undiscovered.

He didn't say a word as he finished reading, kept his

expression blank to hide his surprise. His military background and work as a contract killer had taught him how to mask his emotions. Emotion made a person weak, could get a man killed in this business.

He'd thought this through carefully. On the one hand, he didn't want to aid the NSA in capturing the mysterious Georgia Randall. On the other, he desperately wanted to see her again. And working with the NSA was the only way to make that happen.

In the end, the driving need to see her won out.

Satisfied by the terms—though unsure at this point if he would fulfill the length of the term specified in the contract—he picked up the pen and signed his name on the line, then slid the document back to the man opposite him. Alex Rycroft, a former SF soldier and renowned NSA agent in his early fifties.

Those piercing eyes, more silver than gray in this light, locked on Bautista and the corner of his mouth lifted in a hint of a smile. "Glad to have you on board."

Before he could answer, Rycroft nodded at another male agent, standing at the rear of the room. The man approached Bautista and removed first the ankle restraints, then the ones around his wrists. But the tracking device, wherever they'd implanted it on him during his last surgery, remained in place. A hidden reminder that they didn't trust him, that they owned him.

He rubbed his wrists, flexed them. It felt so strange to have the cuffs off after wearing them for the past four months, even while recovering from the bullet wounds that should have killed him.

Well, technically he *had* died that day back in June, flat lining twice. The medical staff had brought him back each time. For months he'd resented their efforts, hating that they'd saved him just to subject him to a lifetime of misery, but now he realized he'd lived for a reason. *This.*

To see Georgia again.

"So, down to business?" Briar Jones said. The young woman slid another folder across to him.

Even though he already suspected what it contained, a jolt still shot through him when he saw Georgia's ice-blue eyes staring back at him from the photograph. Looking at her was like a punch to the gut, and he struggled to mask his reaction. His memories of her had haunted him for months.

Back in Miami he'd known and fallen for her as Julia. But had he really known her at all? The caring volunteer he'd met at his grandmother's nursing home and the cool-headed operator he'd seen during that boat chase and shootout in Miami were two totally different people.

Which made sense, considering it turned out she was a government-trained assassin. A trained killer, just like him.

God, he still couldn't believe she'd fooled him so completely.

Now the NSA was planning to use him as the lure to draw her out of hiding. Counting on the fact that she would care about him enough to reveal herself when she learned he was alive, that he was searching for her.

Seemed like a huge gamble to him, and he knew there had to be more to the big picture than the NSA merely wanting to bring Georgia in to recruit her for the agency. But once they located her, he wanted to find out just how much of what they'd shared had been real, and how much had been pure lies and manipulation on her part. Because not knowing that was eating him up inside.

If she'd lied, he'd walk away without a backward glance. He didn't forgive, and he never forgot.

And yet...some part of him stubbornly refused to believe it had all been a scam. There had been a true emotional connection between them, he was sure of it. The part that scared him most was the prospect of finding out he was wrong about that.

He quickly read the notes someone had compiled on Georgia. She was wanted for questioning regarding several open cases involving former government agents and people linked with the Fuentes cartel.

All murders.

Reading that part wasn't a shock now that he knew her true identity, but it helped fill in some of the blanks when he thought back to the way she'd handled herself in Miami. So brave, especially considering she'd suffered a gunshot wound to the forearm.

He looked up at Briar, met her dark brown stare. She knew Georgia personally, had been trained with her. That's all he knew. Did the agency have a lead? "When was this reported?"

"That last part, yesterday at sixteen-hundred hours. We don't have a confirmed sighting of her yet but our latest intel suggests she's likely in the D.C. area."

He hated not knowing the details. One of the reasons he'd been so good at what he did was because of the meticulous research and prep he put into each and every op. His reputation as the most ruthless enforcer in the cartel was well earned.

"Who is she after?" he asked, his voice rough as sandpaper. The bullet scar beneath the base of his throat had given him a permanent rasp that made him sound as sinister as his rep.

"Word is she's targeting two remaining people on her hit list, who for whatever reason she thinks are involved with the murder of her former handler. Based on the possible targets we've compiled, we've narrowed our focus to five people. One is a former trainer of ours who lives in the D.C. area. Two are other men involved in the program we were part of, and the remaining two are linked to the Fuentes cartel. My money's on the trainer. The second target, I'm not so sure about. But I'm betting you'd have a pretty good idea about who she might be after in the Fuentes cartel."

Considering that he'd been the enforcer for one of Fuentes's top lieutenants, yeah, he'd bet so too. But he sensed she was about to press him for information he wasn't willing to give.

"I'm not discussing Perez again," he said flatly. "That wasn't part of the deal and it's not on the table for negotiations." As far as he knew, his former boss and the man's family had gone into hiding when Bautista was taken into custody, and he hoped Perez stayed off the government's radar. He refused to turn on the man who'd been his mentor and most loyal friend throughout the past turbulent seven years.

Briar exchanged a glance with Rycroft before looking back at him. "He's going to come up as part of the investigation."

"And if you refuse to cooperate you'll be in breach of contract, according to section 32.6 of the document you just signed," Rycroft added.

Bautista didn't answer. He'd read the section. It was worded just vaguely enough to allow for a loophole about disclosure of knowledge, but whether it held up in court would depend on which judge's desk it landed on. He was willing to risk it.

After a moment of tense silence, Briar spoke. "Back to the matter at hand. We start recon tonight."

He studied his new teammates in silence. He'd worked alone for so long, preferred it that way. No need to worry about whether he could trust others during an operation.

He'd had total freedom of movement and choice of action. It had been years since he'd operated as part of a team, back in his military days. The idea of being constrained by rules and regulations chafed but he'd known it was coming and didn't have a choice at this point anyway.

Besides, he was only doing this for the expunged record, and for the chance to see Georgia again.

"You and I will stake out a fundraising event the former trainer is attending," she continued, "while Alex monitors the situation from another location with his team."

"And what about the threat against her? Have you found anything?"

"Nothing specific. But the people she's targeting know she's out there and will want her taken out before she can attack," Rycroft said.

He was lying. They knew something.

It irritated him that Rycroft didn't explain more or give names, even though Bautista understood his refusal to share details. They'd purposely left him in the dark about Georgia's agenda until now, and most of her history was still a huge blank. He was on a need to know basis and they made sure to remind him of that at every opportunity.

Briar nodded, her dark brown hair shining in the fluorescent lights overhead. "We've got to bring her in before someone else finds her, and before she racks up an even higher body count that will put her behind bars for the rest of her life." She paused a moment. "It's not too late for her to get her life back."

The line shouldn't have tugged at the heartstrings he liked to pretend he didn't have, but it did. Despite all his suspicion and questions about Georgia, his gut told him it hadn't all been a lie. That she *had* cared about him. Hell, it had to be. He'd seen the way she'd grieved when she thought he was dying in front of her.

He straightened. If there was any shred of truth to the feelings he'd thought she had for him, then he had to protect her, bring her in safely before anything happened to her. "I'm gonna need some equipment."

Briar gave him a slow smile. "We've got you covered."

****

Georgia Randall raced up the concrete steps to the motel room and checked the anti-intruder devices she'd placed on the door. Finding them still intact, she jammed the key into the lock.

The moment she opened the door to her room, a wave of stale, cigarette smoke-tinged air hit her. Quickly shutting and locking the door behind her, she rushed to the closet and hauled out her gear: a go bag and her weapons.

A warning prickle at her nape amplified the sense of urgency driving her.

Hurry. Go, go!

She'd bought herself some time with a little evasive maneuver, but she didn't know how much.

She hefted the guitar case holding her sniper rifle, pulled on a new pair of gloves, grabbed her duffel and crossed back to the door. There was no sign of danger outside the peephole but that meant nothing. She knew someone was out there. They'd been following her for at least two days now, maybe more. And she needed to lose them fast because her target would be on the move shortly.

Outside, the cool October night air carried the scent of damp leaves and wet pavement. This time she hurried down a different set of steps that led to the parking lot out back. She'd left her rental car close to the exit. There were no signs that it had been tampered with but out of habit she checked for explosives and tracking devices regardless before opening the door.

All clear.

After setting the guitar case on the floorboards of the

backseat and her duffel on the passenger seat, she slid behind the wheel and started the engine. Traffic behind the motel was sparse. She didn't notice anything suspicious as she steered out of the lot and quickly drove away from the seedy part of town, taking random turns to ensure she wasn't being followed.

The prickling at her nape had subsided but her gut told her that her shadow was still out there somewhere.

One problem at a time.

She glanced at her watch. She had plenty of time to make the drive, but didn't dare linger here a moment longer. Soon she'd ditch the car for something else. Her life depended on remaining undetected.

Turning east, she headed for Alexandria. Fifteen minutes later she had reached her destination in one of the city's oldest and wealthiest neighborhoods.

Here well-tended oaks and maples showed off their fall colors in bursts of scarlet and amber. Expensive brick and clapboard homes lined the quiet street, the warm yellow glow from the old-fashioned lampposts reflecting off the wet cobblestones and puddles from the rainstorms that had fallen on and off throughout the day.

As she neared the second house from the end she crouched down slightly behind the wheel and continued past the wrought-iron gate at the bottom of the curving driveway. Perched on top of a rise in the center of the historic district, the Colonial-style brick mansion loomed over the property, warm yellow light spilling from the bank of large windows lining the front.

It looked like something out of a Thomas Kincade painting, all cozy and welcoming. But the beautiful exterior was merely a façade. Because evil lurked within the stately home's historic walls.

The rest of the country might see the homeowner as a patriot. An all-American hero. Georgia knew differently.

The magnificent wrought-iron gate began to open. She pressed down a little more on the accelerator, kept watch in her rearview mirror as she continued up the street. A black Escalade pulled out behind her. It was armor plated, she knew, and she could make out the silhouettes of both the driver and a passenger in the front seat.

A bodyguard. Because her target never traveled with fewer than two security personnel at all times.

She turned right at the next intersection, watched as the SUV continued on straight, then doubled back around the block and followed it at a safe distance. As expected, the vehicle drove to a posh hotel in downtown D.C. where a charity benefit for the children of SOF members killed in the line of duty was being held.

Georgia set her jaw. Five days now she'd been watching him, looking for patterns in his movements, something that would give her an advantage. She'd found none, except for this gala tonight. Not surprising given his SOF and intelligence agency background. This benefit might be her best chance of killing him.

She parked in the far corner of the lot to observe what was going on. Because of her prior recon she already knew the layout of the building, but the security measures were still somewhat of a question mark.

From her vantage point she could see uniformed private security guards stationed throughout the lot and in front of the entrance. There would be more inside, along with others dressed in civilian clothing.

Going inside was too risky. She'd done hits like that before, up close and personal. The femme fatal routine while dressed in a killer gown, when she'd cozy up to the victim and slip something into his drink. Or follow him to the bathroom and take him out with a knife or a shot to the head while he had his fly open and his dick in his hand.

None of that would work now. There were dangerous

people looking for her. Even wearing her current disguise she'd be too visible. She'd have to wait until her target left the hotel, make her move then.

Georgia watched as the man exited the Escalade, flanked by his bodyguards, and entered the lobby. He still wore that unmistakable military bearing, and his ego was even broader than the wide shoulders filling out the jacket of his custom-fitted tux.

Observing him, she was surprised to realize that she felt…nothing. No tingle of excitement at the thought of meting out the justice he deserved. No sense of relief that this could end tonight. Where once the bright fire of promised retribution had burned inside her, now there was only emptiness.

The thought made her frown. This man had known her once upon a time. Had helped shape her into the deadly weapon she'd become. But then he'd turned on her, helped frame her. She knew he'd been aware of the hit on Frank, the man who'd been the closest thing she'd ever had to a father, and done nothing to stop it. Worse, he'd helped cover it up.

His willingness to look the other way while good officers were murdered in cold blood to cover the sins of others made him just as guilty as the killer in her eyes.

A vague tingling at the back of her neck warned her that she wasn't safe here. Whoever was following her must be close.

No way. She'd been too careful, living like a ghost these past four months, rarely staying in the same place for more than a night. She wore disguises everywhere she went and changed them several times a day whenever she went out. Facial recognition software was getting better all the time but making sure her ears were covered and her nose altered would help stymy most efforts to identify her.

But not all.

She took a covert look around, couldn't see anyone

in the immediate area watching her, but she knew they were out there. Getting close. She didn't know who it was, but there were only two real possibilities.

A contract killer from the CIA, or an enforcer from the Fuentes cartel. Both equally dangerous, both highly skilled and lethal.

And both had good reason to kill her.

Georgia wasn't scared of dying. Not anymore. As long as she finished her mission, she didn't care what happened to her after that. Death would actually come as a relief at this point.

That burning need for revenge that had once eclipsed everything was gone, a once roaring blaze now banked to glowing embers. Its residual heat was all that drove her now. That inner fire was all that made her get out of bed during the rare times she was actually able to sleep, which amounted to only a few hours every other day or so.

She couldn't go on like this much longer. Didn't want to. Because losing the only men she'd ever cared about had changed her. Damaged her irreparably.

When the tingling at her nape increased to a warning buzz, she drove out of the parking lot to a secluded spot she'd picked out the day before, after circling the block a couple times to make sure she didn't have a tail. A few blocks up, she found the perfect vehicle for the next part of this op.

Away from the lights, out of range of the CCTV cameras mounted on the nearby power poles, she stepped out into the cool night air. The disabled dome light kept the interior dark as the crisp breeze ruffled the fallen leaves strewn along the shoulder of the road, its chilly edge caressing her face. From the backseat she pulled out the guitar case holding the components of her custom-made sniper rifle, then grabbed her duffel.

She approached the older model car, its age allowing her to steal it much more easily, took one last look around, then used her special Leatherman tool to jimmy the door open. A minute later she was driving back to the hotel. This time she chose a spot across the street, with good views of the hotel entrance. She opened the guitar case, took out her rifle.

With practiced motions she assembled it quickly and adjusted the scope. The feel of the perfectly calibrated weapon in her grip was familiar, comforting.

A sense of calm overtook her. *Almost over.*

She'd bide her time now, lay across the backseat and hide her rifle beneath the blanket she'd brought in her bag, set up her shot through the side window. Then she'd wait. As long as it took for her target to come out, she'd wait. And if tonight didn't pan out, just like the two previous nights had not, then she'd follow him and try again tomorrow. One pull of the trigger and it would be done.

Then only one more to go.

If she killed the two remaining men responsible for all her suffering, then she could die at peace. There would be no one to mourn her anyway.

Georgia kept her eye on her scope, watching that front entrance. She'd gone off the grid four months ago. Cut off from everything and everyone she'd ever cared about, she had no one to rely on but herself.

It was better this way. To operate without emotion. But how ironic that her next victim had inadvertently turned her into something that his training session all those years ago had failed to—a stone cold killer.

She was twice as lethal as she had been before she'd found Frank's body lying on his living room floor. Before Miguel had died right in front of her.

Her targets would pay for that with their lives.

The loneliness was a small price to pay in order to see this through. Revenge was all she had left to live for. The only two men she'd ever cared for would get their justice. Then…well, she'd accept whatever fate dealt her.

Chapter Two

Something was up. Briar never texted him to meet up with her in the middle of the afternoon on a workday, but she'd done just that two hours ago, saying something about having a late night work meeting later on.

Stepping out onto the private shooting range, Supervisory Special Agent Matt DeLuca paused to enjoy the sight that greeted him. A dozen yards away Briar lay stretched out on her stomach, sniper rifle to her shoulder, eyes on target downrange.

It was a difficult shot, at least eight hundred yards away down a rise, the air was heavy with the promise of more rain and the wind was gusting. He took a moment to admire her form, let his gaze travel down the length of her body to linger on the firm curve of her ass and the length of her sexy legs now encased in camo cargo pants.

She'd been such a surprise. He hadn't been looking for a relationship last December, much less a partner, but then she'd blindsided him and knocked his world off-center, stolen his heart with her courage and loyalty. Not to mention her insane skills as an operator.

Briar was almost thirty but looked much younger than that. People who didn't know her had no clue what she was capable of. They saw only her youthful face and slender build, dismissed her as a threat. Some might even think she was delicate or vulnerable. He knew firsthand just how wrong they were.

Briar was lethal. Deadly with any number of weapons, but especially a sniper rifle. And he still thought that was the hottest fucking thing in the universe. As a former Marine Scout/Sniper, he guessed that made some kind of twisted sense.

He crossed his arms and stood there watching her settle into the shot. Without a doubt she knew he was there. Might have known it even before he'd stepped out from behind the twelve-foot yew hedge that served as a screen, blocking the view of the range from prying eyes. Even after all these months of working on-the-books ops for the NSA, she still hadn't lost the sharp edge that came with working years of solo covert ops.

Her lithe body was completely still, her ribs barely moving with her calm breaths, butt of the rifle tight against her shoulder, cheek pressed to the stock. But he saw the moment she exhaled all the air from her lungs, knew she was about to pull the trigger.

A heartbeat later the report of the big rifle cracked through the air as it recoiled against her shoulder.

Matt reached over and picked up a pair of binos resting on the wooden bench beside him. Aiming them toward the target downrange, he tightened the focus and checked the paper target.

A single hole marked the target a few inches from dead center.

His lips curled upward in amusement and pride. She never ceased to amaze him. *That's my girl.*

"Yep, you've still got it," he murmured, lowering the binos and walking toward her.

Briar turned her head toward him, gave him a smug smile. "Want a turn?" She waggled her eyebrows as she stroked a hand along the rifle's barrel in a possessive caress. She didn't let just anyone fire her baby.

He chuckled. "Nah, I'm good. But I'll spot you for a while."

Lowering himself to his belly beside her, he stretched out and picked out a new target, gave her the range, elevation and windage. An afternoon at the range might not be most people's idea of an ideal date, but it was for him. It had been a couple months at least since they'd last gone on a date, and spending time at the range was a favorite way to unwind.

Other than sex, he quickly amended, already looking forward to going home after this. With the demands of their jobs, they didn't get a lot of downtime together. He'd been traveling a lot recently and she'd been off on various ops. For the next few hours, however, she was all his.

And he intended to make every second count. She was a slippery little thing. Whenever he tried to pin her down about getting married or planning for the future together, having kids one day, she evaded him. It drove him nuts. He desperately wanted that sense of permanency and commitment with her but for whatever reason she wasn't ready yet.

Briar was dead still beside him, eyes on target. After a long moment, she squeezed the trigger. Matt watched through the binos as the round punched through the target, this time damn near dead center. "Good hit," he murmured, filled with pride at this incredible woman.

"Gimme another."

That was another thing he loved about her—her work ethic. Briar drove herself hard, expected more of herself than anyone he'd ever met.

After another forty-five minutes of shooting she propped up on her elbows and looked over at him with a smile that told him she was no longer in shooter mode. "I needed that, thanks."

"Anytime."

That dark gaze roved over his face and lingered on his lips before darting back up to his eyes. "I'm hungry. You hungry?" The heat in her gaze made it clear she didn't mean for food.

He was so on board with that. "Starving."

In the parking lot Matt caught her up against the passenger door of his truck, pinning her there with his weight, and took her face between his hands. She gave him a heated smile and threaded her fingers into his hair, going pliant as he brought his mouth down on hers.

The way she melted into him set him on fire. He didn't feel the rain or the wind, all he felt was her heat and the desire humming between them. She tasted of honey, her tongue twining with his as a soft hum of enjoyment issued from her throat.

Hard and throbbing for her, he rolled his hips against her once before lifting his head. They were both breathing faster and her eyes were dilated.

Truck. Now.

Suppressing a growl of frustration, he opened her door, leaned in for one more blistering kiss before rounding the hood and climbing behind the wheel. He was glad she'd gotten a ride here; he couldn't wait to drive her home to their place.

Briar immediately reached for his hand, linked their fingers together over the cushioned center console. The gesture pleased him not only because it showed just how comfortable she'd become in expressing affection, but because the move rang with possessiveness. He squeezed her hand, rubbed his thumb over the back of hers, impatient to get home so he could get her naked and underneath him.

Or on top of him, he wasn't fussy.

Rain pattered against the windshield as he drove through the light traffic. "So the work thing I told you I have tonight," she began with a slight edge of hesitance that pinged his internal radar. "It's not exactly a meeting."

Frowning, he glanced over at her. "So what is it?"

She was looking straight at him but he could sense her reluctance about answering. "It's an op." A beat passed before she continued. "With Bautista."

At the mention of that name, every muscle in Matt's body pulled tight. His fingers clenched around the wheel. "What?" he asked in a low voice that sounded strained even to his own ears.

She pushed out a sigh. "Rycroft and I got him to agree to a deal. He's going to help us bring Georgia in."

The hell he was. More like he'd bide his time until the moment was right, then try to kill her and Rycroft before escaping.

Matt bit back the words, tried to calm his thudding heart. Bautista had earned his reputation as the cartel's most dangerous enforcer for good reason. He was a killer, and wouldn't hesitate to eliminate anyone who got in his way. Hell, he'd even used one of Matt's agent's better half as a human shield to avoid being killed or captured in Miami.

And Georgia had been right there with him. She'd had no problem letting an innocent woman get hurt if it served her purposes.

"The op's a go for tonight."

Matt had to consciously relax his jaw in order to respond. "Not him," he grated out, unable to stop the impulsive words.

She turned to stare out the windshield and shook her head, her expression exasperated. "This is why I didn't want to tell you."

That stung, but it didn't change his reaction or opinion. "He's a stone cold killer, Briar. You can't trust him."

She swung her head around, her glare as sharp as a blade. "Really? And here I thought that because he signed the agreement, it meant he'd suddenly turned into a nice guy."

Her sarcasm scraped over his suddenly raw nerve endings. "It's too dangerous."

Her jaw flexed once. "*Not* my first op."

He goddamn knew it wasn't. That wasn't the point. What the hell was Rycroft thinking, asking her to take this on?

Matt realized she was a well-trained operative, but he didn't give a shit about that right now. All he cared about was her safety. He knew how men like Bautista operated. "He'll turn on you. And he'll do it when you least expect it."

The anger in her gaze suddenly turned icy. "I'm not stupid, Matt."

Then why do this? He barely kept from blurting it out, fought to curb his own anger.

"Is she worth dying for?" he demanded instead. "For chrissake, until she came *hunting* you last year, you hadn't even seen or heard from her in two decades, and since then she's dropped out of your life completely. She disappeared after that op in Miami for a reason. She doesn't want to be found and she's sure as hell not worth you risking your life over."

He knew he wasn't acting rationally, but he couldn't make himself care about that or the fact that he was being a colossal hypocrite at the moment. He'd risked his life on a daily basis, for complete strangers, for *years*, yet knowing Briar was about to take this on triggered an innate protectiveness he couldn't contain.

An icy silence enveloped the interior for a long moment before Briar spoke again, her voice quiet but cold. "She and Trinity were the closest thing I ever had to family, aside from Janaia."

Her former handler, who had been murdered in cold blood last year.

"We were roommates during our initial training in the program. There's a bond between us that I can't ignore." She shook her head. "Georgia risked her life to help me bring down a dirty CIA officer, and I can't turn my back on her now that she's got enemies gunning for her. I *won't*."

She paused to pull in a steadying breath. "And she still thinks Bautista is dead. Once she finds out he's not and that he's looking for her, she'll come out of hiding. When she does, I need to be there to bring her in safely."

Matt didn't answer, knowing that whatever came out of his mouth right now would be the equivalent of gas on a fire. The idea of Briar going on this op, trying to find and bring in Georgia while other killers were targeting her, was bad enough. But to add Bautista's volatility into the mix? It twisted his guts into a giant knot of fear.

Neither of them spoke for the remainder of the drive, the tension between them mounting with every minute. When he parked in the garage she got out and stormed into the house without a backward glance.

Matt turned off the engine and sat alone for a few minutes, until the worst of his temper had burned itself out, leaving only that gnawing fear in its place. Once Briar cooled off a little he would talk to her again, try to get her to see reason.

This was insane, and though he'd liked and respected Rycroft up until now, the man was a fucking bastard for asking this of her. And all for the sake of recruiting another agent for the NSA.

When he entered the quiet kitchen he heard Briar moving around upstairs in their bedroom. He found her in their walk-in closet, angrily shoving things into a duffel on the floor. He knew she was fully aware that he was standing ten feet behind her, but she refused to acknowledge him in any way.

A trickle of guilt slid through him. He hadn't meant to start a fight, he'd simply been reacting out of concern for her welfare. And he didn't want to leave things like this between them right before she walked out the door to go on an op like this.

But the dread had taken root inside him and it wasn't easing up. Throughout his service in the Corps and with the FBI, he'd routinely gone into harm's way over and over again. He realized it was a double standard, but knowing Briar was about to do the same triggered something primal inside him that he had no control over.

It didn't matter that he'd just been reminded of how skilled she was with a rifle. It didn't matter that he'd seen her in action and knew how capable an operator she was. She was still the woman he loved, the woman who held his heart in her hands. The protective part of him couldn't handle the thought of anything happening to her.

If he lost her, he didn't know if he'd survive it. To have her walk away from him like this, with this anger and resentment between them…

No. He'd learned once already how fleeting and fragile life was. It was a lesson he'd never forget. But that same lesson placed him in direct conflict with Briar now. To him, it didn't matter that he'd understood from day one that she was an operator. Didn't matter that he respected it, even supported it as best he could. In the time they'd been together he'd never once tried to interfere or dissuade her from anything to do with her job.

Until now.

Because his gut was screaming at him that this time was different. That something terrible would happen to her if she did this, and he couldn't shake the feeling no matter how hard he tried. His reaction had nothing to do with him not trusting her ability on the job. It was about watching the woman he loved jeopardizing her life by placing her trust in the wrong people.

Briar continued to ignore him as she packed, each movement rigid, the silence thick enough to cut. He hated the silent treatment more than anything, which she knew.

Steeling himself, he stepped up close behind her and settled his hands on her hips. She stilled instantly, her entire body rigid before she twisted out of his grip with a tight, angry motion.

Matt ignored it and slid his arms around her waist, drew her back firmly against his chest. Again she stilled, and he could feel her irritation in every taut line of her delectable body. He understood why she was so angry, and some part of him acknowledged that he would react the same way if their roles in this situation had been reversed. Still, he couldn't stop himself from trying to protect her.

Fighting the apprehension beating inside him, he pressed his face into the curve of her neck, his lips against her soft skin. Her pulse beat just beneath the surface, steady but so damn vulnerable despite her strength and all her training.

"Don't go," he whispered finally, not knowing what else to do to make her listen, how to reach her. He was irrationally afraid that if she went through with this, he'd never see her again.

He sensed her surprise, and an instant later she relaxed in his embrace. "I have to."

"You don't," he insisted, squeezing her tighter to him. His instincts demanded that he not let her go, that he should do whatever it took to keep her safe here with him. Except he knew that was impossible, just as he knew that if he pushed this too far she'd never forgive him.

"I *do*," she countered. "And if you'd drop the alpha male protective routine for two seconds, you'd see that."

He would never apologize for wanting to keep her

safe. Ever. Even if he knew it was crazy to ask her to stand down for this one. "It's too risky with him."

She turned in his embrace, stared up at him with that pissed off black gaze. "I know what I'm doing. I'm good at what I do."

"I *know* that," he answered, frustration pulsing through him. "It's him I don't trust." Not as far as he could pick Bautista up and fucking throw him. And he didn't trust Georgia much more than that either.

"I'll have Rycroft with me. And Bautista is not only emotionally invested in Georgia, he needs us to help him bring her in safely. He's no threat to me."

He stared at her for a taut moment. "He will be if killing you gets him what he wants."

She shook her head, lips pressed into a thin line of frustration. "You haven't read the psych evals on him. He's not a monster."

Could've fooled Matt. He knew what the asshole had done to his victims. He'd also watched his men shoot the bastard twice, then one of the guys pound the shit out of him afterward, and still Bautista had somehow pulled through.

"I don't need to read them to know he's unhinged and unpredictable. He's a walking time bomb and I don't want you anywhere near him, let alone risking your life by working with him on an op like this." Yeah, he knew he sounded like a possessive asshole right now, but he couldn't help it.

Her eyes chilled, but this time there was something else there besides anger. Disappointment. And the sight of it made him feel like someone had just kicked him in the stomach. "I can handle it." She broke eye contact and gave a sharp push to his shoulder.

Matt refused to let her go.

He took hold of her face, forced her to meet his gaze. She didn't understand. She was insulted because she thought he doubted her ability as an operator. That wasn't it. Not at all.

He felt frantic inside, on the verge of losing it. "Do you know what it would do to me if anything happened to you?" he demanded in a rough voice. "Do you know what it's like to lose someone you can't live without? Because I do."

At that her expression softened and the anger faded from her eyes.

He shook her once gently, desperate to get through to her. "I can't go through that again, Briar. Not with you. It would fucking kill me." When he'd lost Lisa he'd been shattered, mentally and emotionally. He couldn't go through it a second time. Wouldn't, and everything in him told him he risked just that if Briar went on this op.

He swallowed as his throat closed up, old fears and the pain he thought he'd buried rushing to the surface, stabbing at him like red-hot needles.

Her gaze softened. She shook her head and reached up to cup his cheeks, her eyes searching his. "You're not going to lose me. Promise."

The fear clawed relentlessly at his insides, tearing him wide open. Her mind was made up. She was going to walk out that door and go on this op no matter what he said, no matter what the risk, or the cost.

"I couldn't take it," he rasped out, feeling like his heart was being shredded all over again.

Those dark eyes stared into his, full of new understanding...and a love that made his heart pound. Then, without a word, she went up on tiptoe and covered his mouth with hers.

The feel of her mouth on his tripped some primal switch in his brain.

Just that fast all the fear and dread transformed into lust. He wanted to own her, strip her naked and drive deep inside her right that instant, leave his mark on her so that when she walked out that door, she'd feel him for days afterward and be reminded every moment they were apart why she needed to come home alive.

Seizing her hips, Matt lifted her and whirled them around, then backed her up against the wall beside the door, their mouths still fused. Briar whimpered into his mouth and met every desperate stroke of his tongue, rubbing her body against him. The animal inside him took over.

Seams tore as they fought to peel shirts and pants away, then he ripped off her panties and grabbed the cheeks of her ass, hoisting her up against him once more. She wound her strong legs around his waist and ground against his rigid cock while he continued with the punishing kiss, his entire body aching with the need to plunge into her slick heat. Her taut, bare breasts rubbed against his chest as he devoured her mouth, her wet folds sliding up and down his abdomen, the feel of her making him insane.

With a low growl he spun them again and stalked out into the bedroom to lay her across the foot of their king-size bed. Briar welcomed his weight with an encouraging moan and hooked her ankles around his thighs, giving her better leverage to rub her open sex against him.

Frantic now, desperate to join them in the most intimate way possible, he released her mouth and blazed a path of hungry, nipping kisses down her chin, over the side of her neck, lower to her breasts. The pert brown nipples waiting for him were already hard and he couldn't wait a moment longer to taste them.

He dragged his tongue across one, then raked his teeth across it, reveling in the way her fingers bit into his scalp, urging him closer, begging for more. There was nothing gentle in the way he handled her, the hunger inside him too great. Her desperate cries rang throughout the room as he sucked and nipped.

"Matt, now," she begged, her voice hoarse with desire as she tried to drag him up and impale herself on his rigid length. "I'm so ready."

Releasing her swollen nipple, he seized handfuls of her hair and fisted his hands tight as he brought his mouth down on hers. He drove his tongue deep into her mouth, an unspoken claim at the exact same moment he entered her, burying himself to the hilt in her sweet warmth.

Briar jerked slightly then let out a keening cry that spurred him on even more, writhing in his possessive grip. He didn't wait, didn't give her time to adjust to the intrusion. Instead he held her down and took her with hard, rough strokes, the desperate sounds of pleasure she made ratcheting his need higher.

Ecstasy swamped him, building hot and fast as he pumped, his tongue tangled with hers, fists clenched in her silky hair. She was fucking his and no one was taking her from him. He was going to own her the same way she owned him, body and soul. He wanted her to remember this every moment she was away from him: the way he felt inside of and against her, the way he tasted.

Her muscles strained as she rolled her hips, rubbing her clit against his body and meeting each forceful thrust. He swallowed her plaintive moan, pulled one hand from her hair to slide an arm beneath her hips and lock her to him, adding pressure and friction where she needed it most.

Sweat rolled down his spine but the hunger kept driving him, each agonizing thrust taking them both closer to the edge. He caught the hitch in her breath, felt her tremble and open her legs wider, her inner muscles milking him.

You're mine, he told her with every plunge of his hips, every demanding stroke of his tongue.

A second later Briar tore her mouth free and twisted her head aside, an expression of erotic ecstasy etched into her face.

The sight destroyed what little was left of his control. *He'd* made her feel that good. And she trusted him enough to let go completely, make herself vulnerable to him, still loved him even though he already knew he'd lost the battle to keep her sidelined on this op.

Her core contracted around his cock, and her wild moans of release pushed him over the edge. He plunged over it with a loud groan, his body shuddering with every wrenching pulse as the orgasm slammed into him.

When it finally faded he eased down to cover her, his face resting in the hollow of her throat. But the best part was the way she held him close, her arms and legs wrapped around him, one hand stroking the back of his hair.

Matt pressed closer and squeezed his eyes shut, breathing in her scent. The frantic edge was gone, leaving only a stark bleakness behind. He couldn't protect her this time. Couldn't be there to keep her safe, and it was tearing him up.

"I love you," she murmured.

Pushing out a sigh, he raised his head and stared down at her. Her dark eyes were solemn, full of resignation. "I love you too." More than anything.

And because of that, it didn't matter what he felt or what he wanted. He had no choice but to accept her decision to go through with this. Accept that her job and career required her to take risks he couldn't protect her from.

Even if he fucking hated it.

Forcing that thought aside, he lowered his head to kiss her tenderly, his lips lingering on hers. He didn't know how to shelve the worry and his protectiveness when it came to her work, but he had to find a way. If they were going to stay together and make this work, then he couldn't ask her not to go on ops. God knew relationships were hard enough, but their jobs made it a hundred times more difficult and he couldn't let his fears tear them apart.

"I do trust you out there," he murmured against her mouth. "And fuck, I'm sorry I..." He pressed his face against her hair, took a deep breath, pulling in her enticing scent. "I know you'd never ask me not to be who I am. I shouldn't have done it to you."

"You're right, on both counts," she answered, her voice drowsy with satisfaction. Her fingers kneaded the tense muscles at the nape of his neck. "So let's put that behind us and move on now, okay?"

He nodded against her hair, glad that she wasn't still angry and that she'd forgiven him. God he wished he could go with her now though, be there to help and guard her until this was over.

But that was impossible. He was commander for both HRT teams, and they'd all been damn busy lately. The way the world was going, they'd be busy for the foreseeable future.

"How long do we have left?" he murmured a few minutes later.

She glanced over at the clock on the nightstand, then back at him. "Not long." He heard the regret in her voice, knew she hated the thought of leaving him too. That soothed the rawness inside him a little, but not much.

He slid his fingers into her hair, stroked his thumbs over her cheekbones. She was so beautiful and strong. This woman was his whole world. "Then let's not waste any of it," he murmured, and covered her mouth with his again.

Chapter Three

The target still hadn't come out of the hotel yet and Georgia was starting to get antsy.

She'd been waiting here, stretched out across the back seat of the stolen car and hidden from view, for nearly two hours now. Staying put much longer wasn't possible. And that wasn't her only problem at the moment.

Something was wrong with her.

She'd first noticed the nausea about an hour ago but it was progressively getting worse, along with the other symptoms. She was wearing a heavy coat and huddled under a thick blanket to hide her and her weapon from anyone walking past, and yet she was freezing. It seemed she grew colder with each passing minute.

Keeping watch on the front doors through her scope, she locked her jaw to keep her teeth from chattering as another wave of cold swept through her, wracking her body with shivers. She was getting worried. Her mouth and throat were dry and she was having dizzy spells. Her head pounded and her stomach churned.

She tried to think what it might be. Food poisoning?

Doubtful. All she'd eaten today was a protein bar, some fruit she'd brought with her, and a coffee from a drive thru.

She swallowed again as another wave of nausea hit her, this one stronger than all the others. Sweat broke out on her forehead and across her upper lip. Giving her head a little shake in the hopes of clearing it, she put her eye back to the scope. But this time she saw two sets of doors at the front entrance, and four guards instead of two.

Blinking to clear her vision, she struggled to focus on the target before her. It didn't help. And the fatigue that had begun to creep through her system was making it all too tempting to put her head down and sleep right here.

She bit down hard on the inside of her cheek, used the sharp pain to snap her out of the dangerous pull to sleep, a trick she'd been taught long ago by one of her instructors. Her muscles cramped with the effort of lying still for so long but she grimly held her position.

Rossland would be coming out those doors anytime now, and when he did, he was *hers*. But she couldn't afford to blow her chance and get either killed or arrested in the process.

More minutes ticked past. Guests trickled out of the doors in small groups, none of them containing Rossland or his guards. There was a possibility he'd left around back, but she didn't think so. The rear exit was too closed-off, too tight, the perfect place for an ambush. No, his security would want to take him straight out the front, thinking safety lay in numbers.

Her stomach suddenly twisted hard and there was no fighting this one. She gagged, turned her head and emptied what little had been in her stomach all over the right rear foot well.

Gasping and shaking, she wiped her mouth with the back of her wrist. She'd carried out missions before while ill, but this was different. Considering the people hunting her and their skillsets, she was pretty sure they'd poisoned her somehow. But with what? When?

Her mind churned as she reviewed her movements over the past thirty-odd hours. She'd been so sure that no one had been able to follow her.

No one had tailed her on the way to and from her surveillance op this morning, and no one had followed her to the motel later on. All her anti-trespassing devices had been undisturbed as far as she could tell, so no one had opened the door after she—

She sucked in a sharp breath as the answer hit her.

The doorknob.

Someone must have either seen her enter the motel room last night or leave it this morning. They'd waited until she'd left, or maybe they'd been waiting for her to return, and when she hadn't, they'd put something on the doorknob. When she'd touched it, she'd absorbed the toxin into her skin.

It was the only explanation she could think of. Because if they'd known where she was, a shot to the head would have been more efficient and far less risky.

So what the hell had they poisoned her with, she wondered frantically. Janaia and Frank had both been killed with hydrogen cyanide, had suffocated in a matter of minutes after contact. Georgia wasn't having trouble breathing, even though her heart was beating way too fast at the moment.

The fingers of her left hand clamped around the stock of the rifle. She might be able to tough it out through the nausea and vomiting, but the double vision made it impossible to get a clear shot off and there were too many innocents around for her to risk it.

Shit. She'd been determined to get Rossland tonight but now she had no choice but to pack it in for today, get out of here before the hunters found her, then find a safe place to lie low and see about medical treatment, if it wasn't already too late.

The logical side of her told her she hadn't absorbed a fatal dose of whatever it was, as the onset had been too slow. Could still mean she was in big trouble though, and she needed to hole up now before she became any more vulnerable.

Covering her weapon, she climbed to her hands and knees and dry heaved as another bout of nausea gripped her. When it faded she barely had the strength to crawl into the driver's seat.

Her hands were clumsy as she twisted the key in the ignition and began to steer out of the parking lot. She squinted to minimize the double vision, prayed she didn't hit anything or anyone as she lurched onto the road. Last thing she needed right now was to get in an accident or be pulled over by the cops.

A wave of fatigue made her eyelids droop as she came to a stoplight. This time she bit down on the inside of her cheek hard enough to draw blood. Her heart hammered as she waited for the light to change and the cars in front of her to move.

Come on, come on, she urged them impatiently.

Finally the light turned green. She stepped on the gas, risked one last glance in her rearview at the bright lights of the hotel behind her. Dammit. Time was ticking. She still had two men left to kill before the hunters caught up to her.

And they would catch her eventually, it was inevitable.

When they came for her at last, she'd do everything in her power to take them out first.

****

Seated in the backseat of the SUV, Bautista glanced over at Rycroft as he slid into the front passenger seat and shut the door.

"Rossland's still at the benefit," the NSA agent said to him and Briar. "Just got off the phone with his security people. They're on alert but there's been no suspicious activity and the hotel security is currently reviewing CCTV footage of the building and parking lot. Nothing's surfaced so far."

"So maybe he's not one of her marks," Briar said from behind the wheel.

Rycroft grunted. "I'm betting he is. Head to the hotel. They're waiting for us."

Briar started the engine and drove away from NSA headquarters, the massive complex that had been his prison for the past five weeks. Nobody talked on the way over, except for Rycroft, who was on his phone constantly. Bautista was glad he didn't have to talk to anyone; he was tense enough as it was without having to engage with his new "teammates".

For one, he was still suspicious as to what Rycroft's end game really was. The agent had told him he wanted to recruit Georgia for the agency, but Bautista wasn't stupid. There had to be more to it than that, especially if the NSA was desperate enough to bring *him* into the fold.

As far as Briar went, he didn't have a good enough handle on her yet to know what he thought of her. If she'd truly been friends with Georgia though, then her inclusion on this mission was a bonus and could only help them.

First thing they had to do was find Georgia, and from what he already knew, that wasn't going to be easy. Even though the NSA had leaked his survival to certain sources, it would take a while for word to spread. She might not even hear about it before they caught up to her.

For now, it was just the three of them involved with the op, along with some higher ups and analysts hand-picked by Rycroft at the NSA. They could call in backup at any time. Keeping the team small made it less of a risk that Georgia would spot them and get scared off.

At the swanky hotel they went directly into the security center, where the head of the department was waiting for them. Bautista stayed close to the exit with his back to the wall. Being locked in a room with strangers was something he'd never be comfortable with again, but standing here without a weapon made him feel completely naked.

Rycroft wouldn't arm him, though the agent had to know Bautista could disarm any number of people in the room if he chose to. For right now though, he was going to play by their rules. Until he saw a reason not to.

Rycroft and Briar stood at a desk before him, watching security footage on a series of monitors. Bautista took it all in, automatically scanned through the recorded crowd filing past the cameras to see if he could spot Georgia. If she'd even come here.

Three or four women on screen caught his attention, but when he moved forward to take a closer look, he saw they didn't have the right build and didn't move like Georgia did. She had an innate confidence, a kind of swagger that was impossible to miss.

Even if she disguised her normal gait, he was sure he'd be able to spot her. During their brief, albeit intense physical relationship, he'd committed every detail about her body to memory.

"Anything?" Rycroft asked. Both Bautista and Briar shook their heads. "Let's take a look outside," he said to the head of security, who pulled up footage from the cameras outside and scattered throughout the parking lot.

On the one screen still showing footage of the event in the main ballroom, Bautista got his first good look at David Rossland. The former CIA officer-turned-politician looked to be in his early fifties, with a muscular build, short graying hair and light brown skin.

He was onstage giving a speech to the audience,

dressed in a tux, his imposing image and bearing broadcasting that he'd been former military. Bautista bet he'd been much more than that, but again, he was on a need-to-know basis and the NSA didn't think he needed to be informed about whoever Rossland really was.

Rossland had been high up on the list of probabilities for Georgia's targets though, and that alone made Bautista want to know more about him. Bautista stared at the man as he spoke to the crowd, his arrogance evident even without hearing what he was saying.

If Georgia wanted him dead, he reasoned, then there had to be good motive. She didn't strike him as the frivolous sort, wouldn't risk her life unless going after him was worth it. What had he done to her? Rycroft and Briar hadn't told him why Rossland was on their list, but he could guess.

Revenge.

That was a concept Bautista was intimately familiar with. So if Georgia wanted Rossland dead, it meant he'd either hurt or wronged her in some unforgivable way.

His eyes shot back to the screen showing the speech and his hands curled into fists beneath his crossed arms. If Rossland had hurt her, Bautista would make sure he paid.

****

Nico checked himself in the staff bathroom mirror one last time, smoothing a hand over the tie he'd tucked beneath the overlapped lapels of his black suit jacket. The two Glocks he'd brought were hidden beneath it in his custom-fitted shoulder holsters. His other gear was stashed in a hiding spot behind the hotel, ready if needed.

If he got an opportunity to carry out this hit tonight, he'd take it.

Satisfied that his disguise and fake hotel ID were

perfect, he exited the bathroom and headed down the hall toward the security room. There was a high percentage chance that his target would be here tonight. Somewhere. He didn't know who she was after or why, and he didn't care.

His job was to kill her, the sooner the better.

She not only knew things that if turned over to the wrong hands could threaten his entire organization, but she might also be out to assassinate one or more of its members. He had to take her out before she could do either. And so far, Georgia Randall had proved she wasn't an easy mark.

For almost four months now he'd been trying to track her, with no real success. Twice he'd gotten close, but she'd always slipped out of his reach before he could act. Reviewing the hotel's security footage might give him the break he needed to help locate her. Because she'd been annoyingly elusive up to now.

Guests and other staff members barely paid any attention to him as he strode down the wide, brightly lit hallway, the soles of his polished dress shoes sinking into the thick carpet. This place was fancier than anything he'd ever set foot in before, aside from an abandoned palace in Kabul back when Nico had been in the Army. But after receiving a dishonorable discharge eighteen months ago, he'd found a better and far more lucrative job where he could put his military skill set to use.

Man, Melissa would love this place. Their wedding was only four months away. After this job he'd have enough money to put them up in a place like this on their honeymoon to the Maldives as well as the lavish wedding she'd been dreaming about since she was nine. She didn't know about the side jobs he took on and that's the way he wanted it to stay.

This one was way bigger than all the rest. He'd told her he had to go out of town for business, which wasn't a lie. The payday made all the risks worthwhile.

He turned sideways to avoid bumping into a well-dressed couple heading toward the ballroom where the benefit was being held, scanning the people he passed on the small chance that Georgia might appear before him. She was good with disguises though; better than anyone he'd come up against before. The challenge of it was exciting.

He studied each female face carefully, but didn't spot her. Not that he was surprised.

The door to the security room was fifty feet up the hall, to his left. It opened as he approached and three people exited, two men and a woman. He stared at her in startled recognition.

Briar Jones, who'd once been in the same program as his target.

Tearing his gaze off her for a moment, he looked at the men. The first man was older, middle-aged, and the younger one—

Nico stopped dead, quickly moved back against the wall and pretended to be looking at the guests at the other end of the hallway, his heart rate kicking up. He couldn't believe what he'd just seen.

When a large group of people moved between him and the security room he risked a glance back to confirm his suspicions. And sucked in a swift breath as the truth slammed home.

Holy *shit*. Bautista.

And the legendary enforcer was not only alive, he was with that other female operative and whoever the older guy was.

A warning buzz started up in the pit of his stomach. This changed everything. And it was an added complication he wasn't equipped to deal with right now.

He didn't dare pull out his phone to take a picture. It would look too suspicious and if Bautista saw him…

Nico turned and headed back the way he'd come with long strides. Not too hurried, because that would get him noticed and he didn't want any more attention on him than he was currently getting. He rushed to the bathroom, grabbed the change of clothes he'd left stowed in a locker, then headed straight out to his vehicle on the south side of the hotel.

Trying to locate Georgia would have to wait. His boss would want to hear about this new development.

When he was safely on the road a block from the hotel, Nico called him on a secure cell phone.

Diego picked up with a brusque, "Yes."

"I've got some new intel."

"Just a second." Nico heard the high-pitched chatter of teenage girls in the background. "Got a birthday sleepover situation going on here. Gimme a minute to get to my office."

Nico knew from personal experience that Diego's office was soundproofed, and that he swept it for listening devices three times a day. That constant state of vigilance and paranoia had saved his life more than a few times.

Footsteps echoed in the background, then a door shut. "Okay, let's hear it."

"Bautista's alive," Nico said without preamble.

A shocked silence crackled across the line for a few heartbeats. "What?" he croaked out. "That's not possible."

"I just saw him leaving the hotel security room, along with Briar Jones and some other guy I didn't recognize."

"It can't be. You must be mistaken."

He barely withheld a snort. "I'm not mistaken. I know what I saw."

"I would have been told."

"Well I guess someone forgot to send you the memo."

He could practically hear the wheels in Diego's head

turning as he awaited a response. "Send me a picture. I want to see him myself."

The insistence didn't surprise Nico. "Sure." All he needed to do was to go back into the security room and access the security camera footage. He could be in and out in under ten minutes. "What do you want me to do after that? I know the girl was your first priority, but now—"

"Get me that picture," he commanded. "If it's him I want you to find out who else he's with, and why, whether he's working for anyone." A pause. "If he's with Jones then he has to be going after the target."

Nico nodded. "Yeah, that's what I thought too." The intel he'd been given said that Bautista and Georgia had been lovers for a short while, up until the day Bautista had been killed. Or, as it seemed now, just badly injured. Things must not have ended well between them if Bautista was after her now.

"So you still want me to go after her?" A part of Nico almost felt sorry for her. He would make it a clean kill. A single bullet through the heart, maybe the head. Quick. Almost instantaneous, barely any time for pain to register. Unlike most of the kills his former mentor had done.

Bautista was a known sadist. As the notorious *el Santo* he had enjoyed inflicting the worst kind of pain on his victims, usually carving his trademark halo into their flesh before they died. If he got to the target first, she'd beg for death a hundred times over before he finally finished her off.

Diego grunted. "He'll find her before you do. I'd tell you to just follow him and make it easier on yourself, but we both know how futile that would be."

Nico set his jaw at the slight, even as he acknowledged that the man was likely right. Bautista was the best in the business. No one had ever caught him, not until the day the FBI's HRT had taken him down. "Just tell me who you want me to follow so I can get moving,"

BETRAYED

he muttered, out of patience. They were wasting time.

"Her," came the immediate reply. "Then wait until he shows up."

Nico frowned, confused. "So you don't want me to take her out?"

A tense pause followed, then a heavy sigh, full of regret. "Take them both out. I want all loose ends tied up as soon as possible." He hung up.

Whoa. That was one order he hadn't expected.

Nico absorbed the news as he set his phone down in his lap and took a right at the next corner, heading back toward the hotel. He'd send Diego the image he'd asked for, do a little digging then try to pick up Georgia's trail and follow her.

Diego might not have much faith in him being able to find Bautista, yet he'd just ordered Nico to kill him. The toughest assignment he'd ever been given, and he was going to have to be at the top of his game to pull it off.

But the truth was, even though Bautista was a nearly impossible target, Nico had a better shot at finding him than anyone.

Once upon a time, Bautista had taught him everything he knew about how to hunt and kill a target.

39

Chapter Four

S till in the security room, Bautista's gaze fell on the folder lying open on the desk, the picture of Georgia's face staring back at him. *Where are you?* he wondered. He just hoped she was still okay.

"Here's another view of the parking lot," the security manager said.

Bautista moved to stand beside Briar and turned his attention to the new footage, focused on the people coming and going at or near the front entrance. He and the others had already looked at the layout of the hotel before coming here.

The back and side entrances were too enclosed for Rossland's security team to risk taking him out that way. They'd have to use the front. So if Bautista had been setting up for a shot, he'd do it from one of the far corners of the front parking lot.

"Can you get a better view of the far northeast corner?" Rycroft asked, mirroring Bautista's thoughts.

"Sure."

The camera angle switched. On screen cars entered and exited the parking lot through the closest access point, located in the north end. Mostly new vehicles, many of them pricey ones like Lexus, BMW a few Teslas.

He only saw a handful of older models, but all the vehicles were all too far away from the cameras for him to get a decent look at the drivers' faces and he didn't see movement in any of the parked ones.

He was becoming convinced this was a complete waste of time, when Rycroft took another call and his head snapped up, his gaze locking on Briar and Bautista. "Go on," he said to the caller. "Did you get a plate number?" A moment later he snapped his fingers to get the head of security's attention and pointed at the camera showing the far northeast angle. Oh yeah, he definitely had something. "Zoom in there."

Sensing his urgency, Bautista leaned in closer to better see the screen. "What are we looking for?"

"Late nineties model silver Chrysler, four door," he answered, already scanning for it, phone held to his ear. "Go back to fifteen minutes before the start of the event and play up 'til now."

The man did as he said, playing the recording at double the speed.

There was no car matching the description for the first ten minutes. Then at the fifteen-minute mark, Bautista saw it. "There," he said, touching a fingertip to the screen where the car matching the description pulled into the lot.

The head of security paused, then slowed the footage and hit *play*. All of them watched as the car turned right into the lot and quickly drove out of view.

"Back it up," Rycroft ordered. "Can you get a close-up shot of the driver?"

But the angle was wrong, the image too blurry to make out anything more than what appeared to be a female silhouette in the driver's seat. Bautista's heart beat a little faster as he looked at Rycroft. "What have you got?"

Rycroft straightened and motioned for them to follow him out the door. In the hallway he spoke as they hurried for the parking lot. "Same car was reported stolen over an hour ago. Cops found it a few blocks from here, back door left wide open. Apparently there was some evidence left inside."

Was it Georgia? Bautista jumped into the back of the SUV as Briar fired it up and headed to the scene. Three police cars were already there.

At the side of the quiet access road he spotted the silver Chrysler parked at a haphazard angle on the shoulder, its left rear passenger door wide open. Whoever had taken it had left in a helluva hurry.

He got out and followed the others over to the cops, waited while Rycroft showed his ID and gained access to the vehicle.

"We're just waiting for the forensics guys to get here," one of the cops was saying to him.

"They're not going to find any prints," Rycroft said to him, using his sleeve to open the driver's side door and take a look inside, and spoke to Briar. "See if you can find anything else we can use."

Bautista followed her over while the cops gathered around. As soon as he got near the rear door, he caught the sour smell of vomit.

A glance inside showed someone had thrown up in the back, on the floor. Whoever it was had also left a heavy blanket crumpled up on the backseat so there would definitely be plenty of DNA left behind for them to analyze.

He glanced up, shared a long look with Briar and knew from the grim set of her mouth that she didn't like the feel of this any better than he did.

Rycroft was on the phone to someone named Zahra back at NSA headquarters. "Check CCTV footage from the surrounding area. See if you can get a decent shot of the driver's face."

The chances of them getting footage of her leaving the car were as low as finding her prints anywhere inside that vehicle. And there was still a large chance it wasn't her at all.

Bautista dragged his attention away from him and glanced to the backseat again for a moment before turning to scan the surrounding area. The shops and businesses here were mostly industrial, and spaced far apart. There were any number of places the driver could have disappeared to.

The thought that it might be Georgia filled him with a mixture of hope and frustration. They'd been so close to her, and now the opportunity was likely lost.

The forensics people arrived. Rycroft's phone rang a few minutes later. Bautista watched as he talked, saw the moment his face brightened. Bautista knew what the agent was going to say before he opened his mouth.

"It's her," Rycroft said, his tone one of complete confidence.

The news hit him like a jolt of electricity. Bautista spun about and searched around them again, a sense of urgency humming through him.

Georgia was seriously ill. It was the only explanation for why she'd left the car like this, in plain view of anyone who came across it, and without scrubbing it of any evidence first. Leaving evidence behind was sloppy, way too amateurish for someone like her.

Which meant she had to be in bad shape.

"Fan out and take a look around," Rycroft said to him and Briar, his posture tense. "If she's that sick she couldn't have gone far. Bautista, you're with me."

He tightened his jaw in resentment of the command. "You've already got a tracker on me."

The tiny electronic capsule was smaller than a grain

of rice and currently embedded somewhere under the skin. All so the NSA could keep tabs on his every move. If he tried to breach the contract and disappear, they'd be able to track him until he carved it out of his own flesh, and even then the residual isotope could give off a signal for their satellites to follow.

"I don't need a damn babysitter," he snapped. "And I can cover more ground on my own." Georgia was in serious trouble. She was out there somewhere, and she was damn sick. Maybe even dying. She needed help right *now*.

"It's not up for discussion," the agent answered tersely, and walked past him without another glance.

Bautista shoved back the bitterness rising inside him and followed in silence. His gut already told him they wouldn't find her. Not here, anyway. Not tonight and probably not for a few days at least—if they got lucky and caught a lead.

Unless she was unconscious or dead.

He dismissed the possibility outright. The thought of finding her body now, after all this time they'd been apart, while knowing there was a chance she still had feelings for him, was unthinkable. He refused to accept it.

No. If she was still functional she'd have stolen another vehicle by now, be on her way out of town. She was weak. Would want to go to ground. But where?

And what if she's sprawled on the floor in one of those buildings across the road right now?

"Dammit," he muttered under his breath and followed Rycroft across the street toward a group of warehouses.

The countdown was on, and it was shorter than he'd ever imagined. They had to find and stop Georgia before she got herself killed trying to take out the targets on her hit list.

Once they did, if he found out what they'd shared

was real, he'd move heaven and earth to get her to safety.

If it had been real, then he was going to make her his.

****

Georgia wiped the sweat from her face with an unsteady hand and strained to see the curving mountain road through the glare of her headlights reflecting off the wet pavement and the rain currently lashing against the windshield.

The wipers swished back and forth in a blur of movement on their fastest setting, and still they didn't clear away the drops fast enough. She shook as another chill snaked through her despite the heater being cranked up to high, the clammy sweat trapped against her skin making her feel cold all over.

She slowed to take a sharp curve in the road, ignoring the impatient blare of a horn from the driver behind her. It was all she could do to stay upright and concentrate on steering right now.

The moment the road straightened out the truck that had been stuck behind her pulled out and passed her with another long blast of its horn. Georgia shuddered as another wave of cold swept through her, kept both hands locked around the wheel.

She'd crossed the state line into North Carolina hours ago, after changing cars and having to stop and be sick several times. Her stomach was long since empty but didn't seem to care or notice.

By now it was clear that whoever had poisoned her hadn't intended to kill her. Yet. Had they just intended to weaken her, so they could move in and take her alive?

In her current state she couldn't focus properly, knew she'd been sloppy back in D.C. The cops would have long since found the first car she'd ditched.

Whoever was after her might have seen it, may have

been able to pick up the trail and follow her. She'd switched cars three more times over the past eight hours but it might not be enough.

It has to be enough, she thought fiercely. She refused to be caught when she'd been so close to killing one of her remaining targets. He needed to die for what he'd done.

The road turned into a series of switchbacks as it climbed higher into the mountains, the constant swerving of the car making the nausea worse. God, her head was pounding and fatigue was making the rest of her numb.

Her hiding place wasn't too much farther now. All she had to do was ditch the car and get there, lock the place down tight before crashing for a few hours.

But she didn't have the strength to walk far, so she'd have to risk leaving the vehicle closer to her hideout than she wanted. She needed fluids, meds, and she needed sleep.

If her body could just recover from whatever this was, then she could plan her next move and get back into action. Though she hated to lose any time, there was no way she was capable of carrying out a hit right now, much less locate her target and plan an op.

When the sign welcoming her to Bryson City finally came into view an hour before dawn, she could have wept from relief. On the far side of the historic district she turned down a mountain road that led out of town. A mile out, when she was certain the road was empty, she ditched the car in an abandoned farmer's field and began hauling out her stuff.

To the east the sky was beginning to lighten behind the trees. The rain was freezing against her hot skin, her muscles shaking from the effort of carrying the guitar case and duffel. Her boots left prints in the muddy dirt road but she didn't dare stray into the woods bordering either side of it.

She was too weak right now to climb over branches and rocks, too far gone to worry about anyone tracking her footprints. Best she could hope for was the heavy rain would help wash them away over the next several hours.

Georgia set her jaw and stumbled onward. She hated the weakness, the helplessness.

She'd spent her entire life learning to be self-sufficient, had vowed never to make herself vulnerable to another person ever again. Yet she was more vulnerable than she'd been since that awful day when she was nine. With each wobbly step she knew that whoever was hunting her was drawing ever closer.

Her teeth chattered, every muscle and joint aching as she doggedly forced one foot in front of the other. *Not much farther, just a little more*, she ordered herself. *You can do this. You* have *to do this.*

Amazing, the endurance the human body was capable of when faced with a life or death situation. Because that's what this was. If she dropped down into the mud and slept like every part of her body ached to right now, she would die.

Maybe not in the next few hours, but soon. The hunters would come, even here, where she'd retreated to buy herself time. Eventually, they would find her. Before that happened she needed to get stronger and prepare to defend herself.

The will to survive drove her onward, step by painful step.

By the time the tiny cabin set near the creek appeared through the trees at last, her hair was plastered to her skull and her clothes soaked through. She was numb from the neck down, pushed beyond her limits.

Dropping her things onto the wooden porch, she stumbled a few dozen yards away to the rock at the foot of the oak tree where she'd hidden the keys. She gagged once, leaned forward to brace herself on her hands, the ends of her wet hair dragging through the mud as her stomach heaved. There was nothing to come up, not even bile.

When it faded she began to dig. Her numb fingers scraped through the layer of fallen leaves and through the mud until they hit metal. She unearthed the small box and removed the keys, then replaced everything and shoved to her feet, weaving for a second until she found her balance.

Exhaustion pulled at her like a lead weight, making every movement slow, her eyelids heavy. The cabin looked old and decrepit but it held more than a few state-of-the-art surprises, and it had the supplies she needed.

Taking a cursory look around at the anti-tampering devices she'd set into place near the front door, didn't see anything off, and disarmed them. Her hand shook as she at last shoved the key into the lock and opened the door with a creak. A faintly musty rush of air tinged with the scent of old wood hit her.

She hauled her bags inside, locked the door and set the alarm, then pulled off her muddy boots and wove toward the back room. Her wet clothes hit the old floorboards with a slap as she peeled each item off and dumped them on the floor on the way to the bedroom.

Through the open doorway, there was just enough light coming through from the front of the cabin to reveal the neatly-made bed waiting for her, covered with a thick down comforter. After stopping in the adjoining bathroom to take something for the fever and pain, she stumbled to the bed.

Naked and shivering violently, she pulled back the covers and slid inside, wincing at the chill of the sheets against her sore skin. Within moments of being huddled beneath the covers her body began to warm the bedding, bringing with it a surge of relief.

Before the heavy wave of sleep could drag her under she remembered to grab the monitor for the surveillance system from the bedside table and switched it on. She didn't even remember her head hitting the pillow.

A sharp beep brought her awake sometime later.

Rain pattered against the walls and roof. Disoriented, feeling bruised all over, she blinked into the darkness, then remembered where she was and what the beeping meant. The alarm.

Someone had breached the perimeter.

Her stomach rebelled with a hard twist when she rolled over to grab the monitor and sat up. The display showed a single heat signature moving around about a quarter mile to the north, near the road. It was too big to be an animal.

As she watched, the monitor beeped again. Seconds later three more signatures appeared on screen, two to the west, one to the northwest.

Cold spread through her gut.

They're here.

A spike of adrenaline shot through her, erasing the chill. But it didn't erase the sharp edge of fear it brought with it.

Now, at her weakest and most vulnerable, she was going to have to fight for her life.

Ignoring the tremors that shook her she rushed for her duffel and quickly pulled on dry clothes, then unlocked the guitar case and took out her sniper rifle.

Armed and ready, she laced on her boots and headed for the door, prepared to meet her fate. Whoever had come here thought they could get the drop on her while she was debilitated, but they were wrong.

She would take them out first or die trying.

Chapter Five

*Y*ou *have to get out of the cabin and hunt your enemies down before they find you first.*

Shivering with fever, Georgia pushed aside the antique trunk set against the wall to reveal the secret trapdoor beneath it. This, along with the cache of weapons and supplies she'd hidden in here and the cabin's secluded location were why she'd risked everything to make it here yesterday.

The old hinges groaned as she pulled the trapdoor open. A rush of damp, earthy-smelling air wafted out. Inside the cellar beneath it was pitch dark. So dark that even with the night vision goggles she'd grabbed they wouldn't help her to see once she climbed down and closed the trapdoor above her.

Moving fast, she slung her rifle across her back, climbed onto the short ladder that led into the old root cellar, then shut the wooden door above her head. Unable to see anything, she navigated her way to the access tunnel by memory. The supplies she'd wrapped in waterproof tarps lay undisturbed where she'd left them.

Seventeen paces ahead, she raised her hands, felt

along the rough stone wall until she found the opening and crawled through it. Some old prospector must have dug the tunnel back in the 1800s.

She crouched to avoid hitting her head on the ceiling and hurried through the thirty-yard-long tunnel. At the far end, another trapdoor was set into the rock roof. Her muscles strained as she pushed at it. It had been more than five years since she'd last used it.

Inch by inch, it began to lift. By the time she got it open enough to boost herself through it, exhaustion was already pulling at her again. She shook her head, forced herself to focus. Staying low, she ran through the woods on unsteady feet.

The rain slapped at her face, her goggles protecting her eyes and allowing her to see the uneven terrain in the increasing darkness. The remote monitor she held still showed four heat signatures drawing nearer. She didn't know who they were, but how the hell had they found her so quickly? The sun had just gone down, which meant she'd been asleep for a damn long time.

It felt like she hadn't slept at all.

Her boot slipped on a slick tree root. She shot out one hand to grasp an overhead branch and stop the fall, silently cursing herself. One misstep now could mean her death.

Escape and evasion weren't options for her now. It didn't matter how they'd found her. These were skilled hunters after her; she was too ill, too weak at the moment. She'd never be able to outrun them. And staying put inside the cabin would have been signing her own death warrant.

Never, she vowed grimly as she headed up the long slope that led away from the creek bed. The single target was still isolated from the others.

Had to be the sniper with the kill team. She needed to circle around behind him, use her insider knowledge of the area and the terrain to get in position and take him out before the others realized what was happening and rush to his aid. The customized silencer would help conceal her first kill, and that was crucial to help buy her enough time to sneak up on the other targets.

Her only chance was to use the element of surprise and keep the survivors divided, take them out individually so they couldn't attack together.

She shivered as she climbed a group of boulders buried into the muddy hillside, every muscle and joint aching in protest. Her pulse was a dull, heavy beat in her ears, drowning out the sound of the rain and the distant rush of the creek. She kept mostly to the rocks, doing everything in her power to avoid leaving an obvious trail for them to follow.

Squinting against the dizziness assaulting her, she paused to check the monitor once more. The single target was still moving away from the others, heading toward her cabin. Big mistake.

Jaw set, she angled to the right and veered across the property, heading for the slight rise that sat on the hill above the cabin. The climb cost her. She gasped for breath. Halfway up her leg muscles began to tremble with fatigue.

Gritting her teeth, she forced her feet one step at a time up the hill. When she reached the spot she was panting, almost swaying on her feet.

It was a relief to lie down and stretch out on her stomach, but the exhaustion was so heavy, dragging her down into mud. She shook her head violently to clear it, forced her eyes to stay open.

The feel of her rifle in her hands was comforting. She gathered sticks, branches, leaves and foliage then began covering herself with them. There was no time to do more but this would hopefully conceal her position enough to keep her alive until she'd neutralized the threat.

A trickle of mud poured down the rocks to her left, scattering small stones and other debris with it.

She stared at it through the goggles, heart tripping in alarm. The sudden motion in the otherwise still landscape would draw the eye of anyone in the area looking for her. It could give her away.

She didn't dare move, huddled beneath the hastily-constructed camouflage. A glance at the monitor showed the target should be coming into view any moment now. Poised with her eye to the scope, she waited for her prey to wander into her crosshairs. Any second now.

She slowed her breathing, ignored the physical discomfort of lying freezing on the muddy forest floor, watching. *Step into my office, asshole.*

But Mother Nature had other ideas.

Seconds later the trickle beside her turned into a small mudslide, slithering its way down toward the creek bed. Rocks and other debris began to tumble down the incline as it gained power, the sound carrying louder with every heartbeat.

Shit, she mentally cursed, and began backing up as fast as she dared, away from the noise that would draw attention.

Each careful shift of her body put her at risk. Whoever was out here would have night vision equipment too. Maybe even access to drones, though the terrain and weather would surely impede their effectiveness.

Regardless, she couldn't stay here. She had no choice but to get to her hands and knees and crawl up the hill before her location was compromised.

Even sick as she was, her training took over, stopping her from obeying the instinctive reaction to get up and flee. Slowly, careful not to disturb the brush around her, she inched backward up the incline.

The angle was bad, making each movement awkward. Already weak from the fever, the muscles in her arms and legs shook with the effort. Her heart careened in her chest as her right hand slipped.

She threw out the left one blindly to catch herself and stop from sliding headfirst down the hill. The heel of it shoved against a sharp stone wedged into the mud, dislodging it.

A sickening burst of fear broke over her.

Frozen in place, Georgia watched in slow motion as the rock tumbled down the hill. It bounced and gained momentum, taking chunks of mud with it, each thud like a hammer blow against her pulsing eardrums.

She might as well have been lit up by a spotlight.

Shouldering her rifle, she pushed to her feet and ran up the hill, needing to get out of there immediately. She'd barely gone three steps when a hot, sharp pain lanced through her right hip.

She stopped short, an angry cry ripping from her lips. Stunned, she glanced down to see something sticking out of the side of her hip. Automatically she reached down and yanked it out, stared numbly at the dart in her hand.

Mother*fucker*.

Throwing it aside into the mud, desperate to escape before whatever the shooter had hit her with took effect, she put on a burst of speed and ran toward a trail that she knew ran close to the road.

She made it less than thirty yards before the drugs took hold. The world seemed to tilt sideways and no amount of struggle against it helped.

Her legs began to give out. She flung out a hand to grab for a supporting branch, missed. Her knees hit the ground with a jarring thud, then her hands. Already she could feel the weakness stealing through her veins. Paralyzing her.

Her gaze strayed to the right near the top of the ridge, where the shot had come from. She thought she saw something moving off to the far left up there, at the edge of her peripheral vision.

No. *No*, she screamed silently. It couldn't end like this. She couldn't die like this.

Her heart beat a frantic, desperate rhythm against her ribs. But she couldn't move. Was already sinking under the pull of the drugs, her limbs too heavy to move.

She hit the forest floor facedown and lay there, unable to move. Her face was wet, and she knew it wasn't just the rain.

A string of images flashed through her mind, one after the other, at high speed. Of her earliest memories of her mother. Her Valkyrie-trained sisters who had once been like family to her. Of Frank.

And Miguel.

As the vision of his hard, handsome face swam through her mind, a sharp burst of grief detonated in her chest.

She'd never expected to care about him. Had never imagined there was so much decency and kindness inside him after all that he'd done. Yet in him, she'd seen her own chance at redemption. A fleeting dream shattered by a few well-placed bullets.

Maybe I'll see him again, she thought, a wild surge of fear mixed with hope rising inside her.

Even as she thought it she knew it would never happen. After the lives she'd taken in this life, she would never go to heaven, even if such a realm existed.

Her body was limp, her muscles lax. She knew she was dying. But there was no peace, no warmth or floating sensation she'd heard people talk about after having a near death experience. There was only a cold so intense it burned, the drugs searing her veins as they sped through her bloodstream.

The night vision goggles were still in place. Her disoriented gaze landed on a fallen leaf inches in front of her face, snagged and focused for a moment. The raindrops collected on its surface looked like tears.

The sky is crying for me because no one else will.

It was her last thought before the black wave of unconsciousness engulfed her.

****

What the hell?

Nico lifted his head from where he'd been staring through the scope of his rifle and scanned the area around him, just to be sure. Seeing nothing but branches and foliage in the green glow of his night optics device, he quickly looked back through the scope again.

He didn't have a clear view but Georgia was definitely down, and she wasn't moving. Shit. It was supposed to be his kill. He'd chosen this spot specifically, had planned everything out, all for nothing. When he'd talked to that old timer in the bar earlier, he'd thought it had been his lucky break.

The long-time resident had seen a woman matching Georgia's description heading down the deserted road last night. He'd told Nico about the old miner's cabin down by the creek, then Nico had found and followed the rain-washed tracks in the road.

He had no idea why she'd chosen to hole up here, but he didn't care. He'd been so sure the lead would give him the edge on her and whoever else was targeting her.

Who the fuck had shot her? The individual set of tracks he'd seen before had been fresh and well to the northeast. He'd been careful to move southwest, away from the road, to avoid any contact until he was able to identify who it was. And this shot had come from a spot that whoever had made those tracks could not have reached in time.

Which meant there was another threat out here for him to worry about.

He shifted his rifle an inch to the left, tried to get a better look at her. He'd seen her stumble into view through the screen of trees seconds ago, then she'd just collapsed. He knew several organizations had a vested interest in taking her out. Knew that at least two other assassins were lurking in these woods tonight.

Bautista.

The hair on the back of his neck stood up at the mere possibility. If it was Bautista, if he was that close without Nico being aware of it, then Nico needed to move. Fast.

Because if Bautista was aware of his presence, then it meant he was living on borrowed time. And if Bautista wasn't aware yet, chances are he soon would be.

Careful not to disturb the brush that had served as his camouflage, Nico picked up his rifle and eased back behind the sturdy tree trunk a few yards behind him. Nothing moved in the undergrowth around him, there was no sound except for the steady patter of rain and the distant rush of the creek below.

It didn't ease the dread coiling in his gut.

His thoughts flashed to Melissa, her hazel eyes glowing in the sunlight as she smiled up at him the morning he'd left for this job. She was his whole life, the only one who had ever given him a chance and not dismissed him as a fuckup. Well, her and his uncle. He'd taken this job to give them a better life, but that was before he'd found out it meant killing Bautista.

Don't think about it. He's just another target. Do your job.

Creeping back out of the bush, he paused to do another sweep with his rifle. He could just make out Georgia's legs sprawled out, in the gap between two tree trunks.

A quick look to both sides of her showed no movement. Whoever had shot her would be coming to confirm their kill though. Might be closing in on her now.

Nico didn't think he'd been spotted yet, and he planned to keep it that way. The rain would help conceal the few tracks he inadvertently left behind, but a skilled tracker would be able to follow him no matter what. His orders were to kill both Bautista and the woman. He might be able to carry out both hits tonight, if he was smart and a little bit lucky.

He clenched his jaw. Before Melissa he'd been reckless, would have taken stupid risks at a time like this. Not anymore. She'd changed him. Captured his whole heart and made him realize he had more to live for than just himself.

He had to be careful now, think this through instead of charging ahead. He'd left an ATV ditched in a hidden cache about three miles from here. He'd pull back for now, find a safe place to keep watch from and find out what the hell was going on. He needed a lot more intel before he could plan out his next move and act on it.

There were too many players involved in this mess for his liking right now, too many unknowns. He had to get the hell out of here now, before anyone spotted him.

Turning around, he hurried up the hill and melted into the protection of the forest.

Chapter Six

Georgia was down.

Bautista remained still and kept sight of her through his scope, while everything in him demanded that he run to her. A stupid move that could get them all killed. He blocked the impulse.

"Got movement to your two o'clock, about eighty yards out," Rycroft murmured through his earpiece. "Hold your position while we check it out."

Not bothering to reply Bautista remained stretched out on his belly, took a quick look around then locked his gaze on the woman lying prone on the wet ground. Despite his training, despite that until recently he'd made an obscene amount of money operating as a contract killer, it bothered him to leave her lying there like that in the rain when he knew she was already gravely ill. The cold and the wet wouldn't be good for her.

At least from his vantage point he could protect her, he told himself. His vigilance was ingrained from years of operating off grid with only his own wits to keep him alive.

If anyone besides Rycroft and Briar were moving

around out there and hoping to take a shot on Georgia, they would be shocked when he took them out instead. For the second or two it took for them to die, anyway.

As he waited, the minutes ticked past with agonizing slowness, each one ratcheting the pressure inside him higher. He'd done rescue before, back in his military days. But never in an op like this one, where he'd been personally involved with the victim they were trying to save.

Complex and tangled up as his feelings for Georgia might be, they were still there. Every second she lay there in front of him cost him, and the struggle to hold back was real.

He was more than willing to risk going to her before he got the all-clear from Rycroft. In fact, he was leaning toward ignoring the order altogether and going to her when the man's voice sounded in his earpiece again.

"Possible suspect sighted. I'm in pursuit. Briar's moving back toward you. You'll both take the target back to the cabin and wait for me there."

He knew some kind of response was expected so he muttered, "Affirm."

"You're clear," Briar reported to him a moment later. "I'll cover you from here."

He didn't know her well enough to know how good she was with a rifle but she must be pretty decent if Rycroft had allowed her this kind of operational latitude, and even though he didn't know exactly what her background was, he understood it meant she'd had decent training.

Anyway, Bautista didn't give a shit about any of that or even his own safety right now. All he cared about was getting to Georgia and taking her to the cabin so they could give her medical care and, when she was coherent, get some answers.

"Go," Briar said.

Slinging his rifle across his back, he broke from cover and ran in a crouch the few dozen yards separating them. When he reached her he dropped to his knees, realized his heart was pounding.

She was facedown, her head turned toward him, her pale face streaked with mud and her hair wet and matted. He gently removed the NVGs she was wearing.

The sight of her up close for the first time in so many weeks hit him like a roundhouse to the chest. Even ill and covered in mud, she was beautiful, and he found himself wishing she'd just open those big blue eyes and look at him, let him know she was okay.

Who are you, really? he wondered.

Reaching out a hand, he touched two fingers to the vulnerable spot beneath her ear. A sensitive place he'd licked and raked his teeth over during the one and only night they'd spent together.

A night he'd never forget as long as he lived.

Her skin was hot to the touch but relief slid through him when he felt her pulse. Slow but steady, and she was breathing okay, albeit shallowly.

He swept the wet tangle of hair off her forehead, leaning over her to shelter her from the rain. After checking her for further injuries and finding nothing, he bent and scooped her up into his arms.

She'd lost weight. That was his first thought as he stood and immediately began carrying her in the direction of the cabin she'd vacated less than an hour ago.

They'd been damn lucky to find her in time, catching sight of her as she'd darted through the forest and away from the cabin they'd been headed for. She was way thinner than she'd been back in June, having lost at least ten pounds. Life on the run had obviously taken its toll on her.

It made the deeply buried nurturing part of him want to take care of her even more.

Even though he tried to steel himself, the feel of her tucked against his chest, so still and fragile, filled him with raw protectiveness. She didn't stir as he made his way down the hill, keeping her cradled against his chest.

He could feel the unnatural heat rising from her body through her wet clothing. The tranq he'd darted her with had been strong enough to bring her down, but now he worried that the dosage might have been too high given how ill she was.

"Still clear. Coming up on your six o'clock," Briar murmured.

Without answering or looking over his shoulder for her, he headed straight for the cabin, staying alert for any hint of movement or that telltale tingle at the base of his spine that would alert him to danger.

Thankfully there was nothing. He stepped up onto the front porch, waited while Briar did a sweep of the structure and then moved to the front door.

She examined it for a moment, then began disabling the countermeasures Georgia must have left on it to keep trespassers away. Seeing them was yet another stark reminder that the woman he held was a different person than the one he'd fallen for.

It was important he remembered that. The warm and kind-hearted "accountant" who had volunteered at his *abuela's* care facility twice a week for those three months he'd gotten to know her was a hardened assassin. It was still hard to believe. He'd thought he'd been so careful, thought he'd done a thorough background check.

Not so much.

Briar disabled the last one and opened the door, allowing him to sweep past her. As she shut the door behind them Bautista took a look around. The cabin was old but appeared well kept and tidy.

Without him having to ask, Briar immediately did a sweep of the other two rooms before moving about checking to ensure that all the windows were covered. "Clear," she said and flipped on a lamp in the back room, illuminating a rumpled bed.

Bautista carried Georgia in and lay her down on top of the covers then pulled off his night optics device and tossed it onto the bedside table. "She's burning up," he told Briar.

"I'll get some towels."

He took off her dirty coat and reached for the hem of her damp sweater, then stopped. It seemed wrong somehow, to strip her like this when she was defenseless, especially after they'd slept together.

He mentally shook himself. *Screw it.*

Working fast he pulled off her sweater, boots, socks and peeled her wet jeans off her legs. Every inch of creamy white skin he revealed reminded him of how she'd felt in his arms that night last summer, of how she'd touched him, held him, the feel of her mouth beneath his as her hips rose to meet every thrust…

He brutally squashed those thoughts and focused on getting her warm and dry. When she was left with only her bra and panties on he pulled the covers over her.

Briar appeared at the other side of the bed with a handful of towels. Without waiting for her to do it he took one and began drying Georgia's hair.

Her skin was pale except for the bright red fever spots burning in her cheeks, and there was a bluish tinge to the skin under her eyes. Her pulse was rapid, her breathing shallow.

"We need to start an IV," he said. His gut told him she wasn't suffering from the flu. Had she been poisoned?

They'd move her to somewhere more secure, an NSA safe house maybe, just as soon as the threat outside was neutralized and they could get their SUV down that single road that led to the cabin—a dangerous place to travel when there were potential snipers waiting in the woods.

Briar nodded and went to retrieve her rucksack she'd left inside the door. "Here," she said, handing him the med kit. "I found an open bottle of ibuprofen tablets on the bathroom counter. She might have taken some earlier."

"If she did, they didn't do much for her." He ripped open the IV kit, took out the supplies and grasped her left forearm in his hand.

His gaze snagged on the healed wound there, where a bullet had torn through. It looked like she'd had surgery to repair the bone. Her hands and feet were ice cold, and the rest of her was too damn hot. They needed to get fluids into her then wait for the tranquilizer to wear off so they could find out what had made her so sick.

Pulling the rubber tourniquet tight around her forearm, he positioned the long needle and slid it into her vein, inserted the catheter and taped it into place, then started the drip. "Gimme a fresh pair of socks."

Briar dug into her pack and handed him one. She said nothing while he pulled the covers back and slid the socks onto Georgia's feet then began to rub them between his hands to warm them, but the way she stared at him was starting to get on his nerves.

He shot her a hard look, didn't stop the brisk movement of his hands over Georgia's left foot. "What?"

Briar shook her head. "It's just…strange, watching you with her."

"Why's that," he muttered, looking back down.

"Because I wasn't a hundred percent certain until just now, but I can see you really do care."

He stopped, his entire body stilling for a moment. He resented her trying to analyze him, hated the feeling of vulnerability he felt at that moment.

Straightening, Bautista pulled the covers over her legs once more, the cynical part of him taking over.

He'd fallen for the woman he'd known as Julia. The

woman lying on the bed was a total stranger to him, and he wasn't even sure he'd find any of Julia in her at all once she woke. He needed to remember that.

The thought made a hard ball of dread form in the pit of his stomach. By signing that contract he'd essentially locked himself into a life of servitude to the NSA, on the off chance that he could find and reconnect with the woman he'd lost.

He knew it was insane to have taken such a huge risk. What would he do if it turned out this was all for nothing?

It's still better than rotting in prison. If she didn't want him, he could still run. Or at least try to, provided he could find that damn tracking device.

"Stay with her while I go help Rycroft track down whoever else is out there," he muttered, turning on his heel and striding from the bed.

"I'll go if you want to stay with her."

At her quiet words Bautista looked back at her over his shoulder. His gaze unerringly slid to Georgia, so still and pale in that bed.

Part of him wanted to take the opportunity Briar had offered him, driven by some deep-seated need to take care of Georgia. His heart didn't care what her name was. It only saw the woman who'd managed to capture it.

Which was insane, and he'd better lock his old feelings for her down for good until he saw how this situation played out. Bad enough that he'd signed his life over to the government and had to work with his "teammates" on this mission. It was a hundred times worse to have them watching his every reaction to Georgia, scrutinizing them. A total invasion of privacy he couldn't afford to let them capitalize on.

Except they'd already capitalized on it, hadn't they? It's why he was even here in the first place.

When she woke up, he had to have his game face firmly in place.

"No. You stay. She'll be more comfortable finding you here when she wakes up." It also gave him a reprieve, temporary though it was.

For a moment Briar looked like she might argue, but then nodded. "I'll alert you guys if she wakes up before you get back."

Bautista turned for the door and grabbed his weapon, already back in operational mode. He was far better at killing than he was at nurturing anyway.

Go do what you're good at and stop trying to be something you're not.

He'd find out soon enough whether his forced resurrection was worth it.

****

Someone was moving around nearby.

Heart hammering, Georgia struggled to pry her heavy eyelids apart. What was wrong with her? Everything hurt and her stomach rolled.

Her body wouldn't obey her when she tried to move and her limbs felt like they weighed a ton. A dull throb beat at her skull and the cold was still there, wracking her with convulsive shivers.

Slowly it all came back to her. Her escape through the tunnel, the run through the woods.

She'd been shot with a dart. Must have been a tranquilizer rather than something lethal, otherwise she wouldn't have woken up at all. But why? Who had done it? Did they plan to torture her before killing her?

A terrible sense of helplessness stole over her, quickly replaced by sheer resolve. She would never surrender. It wasn't in her hardwiring.

Finally she managed to peel her eyelids open a fraction of an inch, wincing as the light hit her eyes. Her cabin, she realized. She was in her bed. How had she gotten here? She couldn't remember.

A chill swept through her, this time having nothing to do with the fever. There was so much she didn't remember, didn't know.

Summoning her strength, she forced her head to turn so that she could see the threat. Someone was just outside the bedroom door. A female, if Georgia assessed the build right.

Her weapons. She needed her weapons.

Move, dammit, she ordered herself, refusing to give into the sluggishness pervading her. She needed to keep sharp, get control of her body so she could defend herself.

Her heart rate was elevated. Good. The faster her heart pumped, the more adrenaline her adrenal glands released, the faster it could counteract whatever drugs she'd been hit with. If there was only one person in the cabin with her, she might still be able to take them out and escape.

As silently as she could she rolled to her side. It seemed to take forever. And when she moved her arm she realized there was an IV tube plugged into the back of it.

Alarm jumped inside her. Her gaze shot to the bag hanging from the old brass headboard. It read Ringer's solution but it might be fake. They could be drugging her still, keeping her helpless.

Fuck. Them.

Her fingers had just closed around the insertion site in the back of her forearm when a female voice from the doorway stopped her cold.

"You're finally awake. Good."

Georgia squinted as the woman came into view, trying to bring the blurry shape into focus. She sucked in a sharp breath when she recognized Briar standing there. For a moment she was too stunned to speak, just stared.

"What are you doing here?" she finally rasped out, her throat dry and tight.

"Rescuing you."

She mentally snorted. "You're here to bring me in." The words were loaded with accusation.

Briar acknowledged the charge with a small shrug, those dark eyes locked on her. "However you want to look at it."

Pain and betrayal ripped through her. There were only two Valkyries she'd bonded with during the program: Briar and Trinity. They'd been like sisters, protecting each other throughout the long, harsh training period. They'd shared a room together, shared secrets and hopes and dreams together. And now one of them had turned on her. That cut deep.

"Who are you working for?" Last she'd heard, there were rumors that Briar had been recruited by one of the intelligence agencies. But no confirmation about which one.

"The good guys."

Yeah. Right. There were no good guys. Briar was here to bring her in, probably for some government agency, to try to stop her from carrying out her vendetta.

That wasn't happening.

Georgia cast another frantic look around, but didn't detect anyone else in the cabin with them. She reached for the IV needle again.

"Leave it. You're dehydrated and fighting off some kind of infection."

Georgia ignored her, began ripping at the tape holding the needle in place.

Quick footsteps sounded on the weathered floorboards, then Briar's hand locked around her fingers and pried them free. "I said, *leave* it. If you don't, I'll cuff you."

Georgia gritted her teeth and tried to pull free but couldn't. She suppressed a growl, frustrated at how weak she was, and met Briar's hard stare with one of her own.

"You need to let me go," she ground out, her survival instinct pushing her to flee. "You don't understand, you're in danger here. There are others coming. I don't have much time."

"The rest of my team is taking care of the 'others' right now. You don't need to worry."

She let out a bitter laugh, fighting the wooziness that wouldn't go away. "You have no idea what's happening." She needed to get free and go after her two remaining targets. They had to die for what they'd done, and she'd make sure they did, no matter what.

"Oh, I think I've got a pretty good idea, actually. And either the CIA or one of Fuentes's former goons is out there in the forest right now. So until I get the all clear from my team leader, we're not going anywhere."

Before Georgia could respond, Briar reached up and tapped her left ear. An earpiece, she realized. "She's awake."

Georgia tensed at the words. "Who are you talking to?" she demanded, heart beating even faster now.

"My team."

The cryptic words ignited a rush of anger. She gathered herself, ready to spring and fight Briar for her freedom if that's what it took. Weak or not, she'd damn well go down fighting.

Footsteps echoed outside on the wooden front porch. Georgia froze, her gaze shooting past Briar and back again. Another person in the cabin meant it would be nearly impossible for her to escape through the tunnel. "Who is it? Who's coming?"

"Someone I hope you'll be happy to see," Briar replied.

What? Georgia shook her head, fought to hold back the anger clawing deep in her chest. She couldn't believe Briar was in on this. "Why are you doing this?"

That black gaze was unflinching. "Because I care

about you and I don't want you to die."

The front door opened before either of them could get another word out. Quiet footfalls tread across the floorboards, but the person stopped outside the doorway, in the darkness outside the edge of the glowing circle cast by the bedside lamp.

Her pulse thudded in her ears in the sudden silence. She was aware of Briar watching her, registered the subtle but silent worry coming from the former Valkyrie.

Georgia didn't dare tear her eyes off the doorway, determined to face this new threat. Heart in her throat she waited for a long moment, the tension coiling tighter and tighter in her stomach.

Gaze riveted on the rectangle of darkness outlined by the doorframe, she stared in stunned silence as a familiar figure materialized out of the shadows and stepped into the light.

A ghost.

Chapter Seven

Bautista stood unmoving in the doorway, aware of how hard his heart was thudding against his ribs. Those piercing, sky blue eyes seemed to bore right through him, full of shock.

And there was something else there too, something that looked a lot like wounded accusation. As if she couldn't believe he'd purposely let her think he'd been dead all this time.

That single look floored him, and confirmed she'd never received the intel the NSA had leaked to certain sources about him being alive. His gut said that glimpse of emotion he'd just seen had been real, and he didn't know what to do with that.

"What... You can't..." She trailed off, staring at him in disbelief. "I saw you die." She shook her head. "You can't be him." She flashed a panicked look at Briar, clearly convinced they were playing some kind of trick on her.

"It's me," he said softly, steeling himself against being sucked in by the wide-eyed routine. Sick or not, she'd already proven what a skillful actress she was.

Her gaze swung back to him and held, wary now. Confused. "I saw you die," she whispered, and the naked pain in her voice stabbed him at the same time as it fueled the unstoppable tide of hope rising inside his heart.

She already duped you once, the cynical voice in his head reminded him.

"I almost did." Maintaining eye contact, he reached up and pulled the neckline of his sweater down to reveal the puckered scar at the top of his chest.

The bullet had smashed right through his body and exited out his upper back. Surgeons had operated four times to repair his damaged lung alone, not to mention all the others to deal with the bullet that had hit him in the back beneath the armpit and the one in his lower abdomen.

"It was close," he murmured.

Staring at the irrefutable evidence before her, she swallowed, and when she lifted her gaze to his once more he caught a flash of vulnerability he'd never expected to see. He squashed the answering flood of tenderness it brought.

Dammit. Even though his game face was firmly in place, even though he'd sworn to keep his emotional distance until he knew all the missing information he wanted from her, he could already feel his guard slipping.

Which meant he was in big trouble. Because if he found out she'd been honest with him as far as their relationship had gone, he was fucking screwed.

Then she narrowed her eyes at him. "Wait. Did you dart me?"

"Yes." And he didn't feel the slightest bit guilty about it now that she'd come out of the anesthetic. Not if it might have saved her life.

"What did you tranq me with?"

"Ketamine." She had to still be dizzy and nauseated from it.

Her jaw worked once, then she bit out, "How much?"

"Enough to make sure you were down and give us enough time to get you to shelter. The effects should wear off completely within another ten minutes." He hoped. He'd never tranqed any of his targets before. A single shot through the heart or head had always been called for in his previous assignments.

She glared up at him. "Like I wasn't feeling sick enough already."

"When did you first get sick?" Briar asked. "Do you know what it is?"

Giving him one last glare, Georgia finally shifted her attention to her. "Poison, two days ago. I think someone must have covered the doorknob of my motel room back in D.C. with some sort of toxin, but I can't be sure. The symptoms came on suddenly, a few hours after I touched it."

Briar nodded. "What are they?"

"Fever. Nausea. Vomiting. Stomach pain. Body aches." She aimed another accusing look at him. "A little like the side-effects of ketamine."

Bautista didn't look away as he ran through a list of possibilities. Could be any number of toxins, none of them good. They needed to get a blood panel and urinalysis done, make sure there was no permanent organ damage or anything like that.

"Whoever did it was either inept or hoping to make you just sick enough to slow you down so they could capture you," he said.

At that she lost some of her hostile edge. "I know."

"Who's after you?" He had some theories and he was sure Rycroft and Briar had some of their own, but since they'd told him basically sweet fuck all about anything, he was forced to make his own deductions.

She lifted a golden brown eyebrow. "Other than you guys?"

"Yes."

"I don't know."

"But you have a good idea."

She shrugged. "Does it matter?"

It mattered to him, and he had to be damn careful not to let her know it. He wanted confirmation of who she was after, what she knew or had that would make people want to silence her forever, and what would prompt Rycroft to take on this op personally. It had to be something big.

He needed to know what she was up against. What they were up against. Because there was no way in hell he was stepping aside and letting her fight this fight on her own. Not after the unguarded shock and relief he'd seen in her eyes when she'd first seen him.

And that probably made him the dumbest son of a bitch on the planet, but it was what it was.

He would just have to accept the weakness and make sure he didn't give her the opportunity to hurt him again. The internal wound she'd inflicted with her deception hurt every bit as much as the bullet wounds that had nearly killed him. Not that he'd ever let her know it.

"And how the hell did you guys find me, anyway?" she asked.

"You messed up," he said simply, part of him enjoying the flash of outrage in those cool blue eyes. He realized she'd slipped up because she was sick and desperate, but facts were facts.

"You got tagged on a security camera at the gas station where you stole the third vehicle. An analyst connected it with the first stolen car and from there it was just a matter of following the breadcrumbs. We were already getting close when you reached Bryson City. There weren't many places you could go, and we got word of a local reporting an abandoned car in the woods. After that, it was easy." She hadn't covered her tracks very well. Little wonder the others had managed to locate the cabin as well.

Georgia didn't look too happy at the analysis. "Well there you go," she muttered with a pissed-off expression.

"Your fever's pretty high," Briar said. "We're going to get you looked at as soon as we can get to a safe house. But there's at least one other person still in the area right now and we're not sure of the threat level. We can't move until we get the all clear from our boss."

Georgia jerked her gaze to Briar, then back to him, her face full of incredulity. "Who's your boss?"

"Alex Rycroft," he answered. If she was or had been a government asset, then she'd know who the major players in the intelligence world were and would recognize the name.

She frowned. "From the NSA? *That's* who you're both working for now?" Her tone was scathing, as if she thought they'd sold themselves out. And she was right about him at least, because he certainly had.

For her.

"It's a long story," he said. And one he would share only after he got some answers of his own.

But now wasn't the time for that private conversation—if Briar and Rycroft would even allow it. Right now they had to treat Georgia's symptoms, neutralize any remaining threats in the immediate vicinity before they could get her out of there.

"When's the last time you ate? Are you hungry? Thirsty?" he asked.

She sighed and leaned back against the brass headboard, looking exhausted all of a sudden. "Thirsty, but I'm not sure anything will stay down."

"The IV will help, and we've got some meds that might help with the nausea." God, there were so many critical things he was dying to ask her, and yet he was reduced to this banal conversation instead. He strode for the pack he'd left in the corner of the room, took out a bottle of water and two anti-nausea tablets.

Crossing over to the bed, he couldn't help but notice how stiff she was, how wary her expression. He didn't like her looking at him that way but understood exactly how she was feeling.

Because the uncertainty and mistrust went both ways.

He didn't like that either. Was dying for the moment he could begin to peel back the layers and discover who this woman truly was, find out what was real and what had been a lie.

"Here." Twisting off the cap, he handed it to her with the tablets.

She accepted them, swallowed the pills then divided a look between them. "Look. Unless Rycroft is here to arrest me because he's got charges pending, you can't hold me against my will. You both need to let me go. If either of you ever really cared for me at all, you'll let me out of here and not follow me."

It stung, the way she flung that out, considering she'd been the one to deceive him and not the other way around. He'd hidden things from her, true, but he hadn't outright lied to her. Hadn't purposely tried to deceive her.

"Not gonna happen," answered Briar, who was watching her with a closed expression.

Georgia's already pale gaze turned ice cold. "There are at least two professional assets after me that I know of. Maybe more."

She nodded. "We know. Rycroft is out there right now tracking one of them."

"Why do you even care? This isn't your fight."

Briar stalked forward now, stopping at the side of the bed. Eyes narrowed, she tugged down the side of her black cargo pants to expose a small tattoo on her left hip.

The same one Georgia had on her left hip, he realized with a start.

He'd glimpsed it for only a second when he'd stripped that dress off her the night he'd picked her up for their one and only date. Instead of going to dinner as planned they'd spent the entire night in her bed, feasting on each other in the darkness. He hadn't had the chance to see her tat in the light. What did it signify?

"Because no matter what else has happened, *this* still means something to me," Briar snapped before jerking her waistband up again. "We took an oath. All of us. And you, Trin and I were closer than blood sisters. We vowed to always be faithful to one another, to never leave one of us behind. That's why I'm here and it's why I'm risking my life to help you. Deal with it."

But there had to be more to it than that, Bautista thought, at least for Rycroft. Way more.

A bitter laugh escaped Georgia. "I don't deserve your loyalty. For godsake, I tried to kill you last year."

Bautista's eyes shot to Briar in surprise, but she didn't deny it. Well well, wasn't that interesting.

Watching her face off with Briar, Bautista was even more intrigued about this mysterious woman who'd managed to tangle him up inside. He shouldn't be thinking about getting her naked again but an idea was already forming in his mind.

Georgia wouldn't be easy to crack. The best way for him to find out what he wanted might be to have her naked and at his mercy.

Georgia's heart was pounding, making the throb in her skull ten times worse. The pills she'd taken and the mouthful of water were rolling precariously around her stomach. God dammit, she *hated* this. Detested being weak and helpless, trapped.

She was acutely aware of Miguel watching her in silence at the other side of the bed and didn't know what to think, what to feel. She was so confused. Seeing him had left her reeling, tearing open wounds that had only recently begun to close. She couldn't believe he was alive, that she hadn't found out. That he hadn't told her before now.

Not that he'd have been able to find you, she reminded herself.

He had to know about her past by now, had to know that she'd lied to him before. He wouldn't trust her now, would never believe she'd been falling for him back in Miami. Since then, for some reason her feelings for him had only deepened. Now that she knew he was alive, she didn't know what to do with them.

The bitter irony didn't escape her. He was alive, but any chance of rekindling their relationship was long dead now. A sharp arrow of grief embedded in her heart at the realization.

Pushing the thoughts from her mind for now, she focused on Briar as the taut silence stretched between them. She couldn't believe this was all happening.

Briar gave a small shrug. "You were following orders. And I'm over it. But that doesn't change how things stand right now because you're not going anywhere."

Georgia's cheeks were flushed from fever, her body on fire with it. Her nostrils flared, anger tightening her features as she glared up at Briar. She had no right to interfere. None. Not anymore. "It's my life! My choice."

Briar shook her head. "I won't sit back and watch you get killed because you're bent on revenge. I won't do it."

Revenge? That was too simple. What she burned for was the chance to mete out the kind of justice the government that had created her would never sanction. Even having Miguel standing before her alive and well didn't change that.

Those murderous traitors had killed Frank, and she was going to see to it they paid dearly for it. "I never asked you to," Georgia answered coldly.

Briar didn't even blink. "Too bad. I'm not walking away from this. From you."

Georgia glared up at her, aware that her breathing had turned rapid, shallow. The surge of anger threatened to steal her breath.

Her Valkyrie sister and former lover were setting her up.

Anguish twisted inside her. It hurt, this betrayal. Way more than she'd expected, proving she wasn't dead inside after all, as she'd wrongly assumed all this time.

She thought of the night she'd been taken away from the training facility. They'd come to take her away without any warning in the middle of the night, pulling her from her bed and ordering Trinity and Briar to stay put.

She still remembered the look in Briar's eyes. Utter devastation. Grief. The trainers had decided the three of them were too close, that their bond was disrupting the cadres efforts to turn them into killing machines. And so they'd taken steps to shatter that bond.

Georgia would never admit it to anyone, but that first night in her new facility she'd buried her face in her pillow and cried herself to sleep, afraid and alone without her sisters. But the next morning she'd woken up and realized that part of her life was over. Forever. She'd moved on because she'd had no choice.

Georgia pulled in a calming breath. She might not know why Briar and Miguel were doing this, but she had her suspicions. All the intelligence and law enforcement agencies interested in her case must at least suspect that she'd been the one to kill Garcia in Miami this past June. They just didn't have enough hard evidence to pin it on her. She'd made absolutely sure of that.

Even if they tried to charge her with it, they wouldn't want to admit that she was an assassin trained by the U.S. government. Without forensic evidence and a reason to arraign/prosecute her publicly, they'd have no choice but to let her go. Because no DA in their right mind would ever take the case on without substantial evidence in place, not when they'd risk looking stupid and it might harm their career.

Right now she had the power in this equation and intended to capitalize on it. The freaking U.S. government and its broken justice system could suck on that for a while and see how they liked it.

Swallowing, she forced herself to meet the eyes of the man who'd managed to steal beneath every defense she'd put around her jaded and cynical heart. Just the sight of him sent twin shots of warmth and trepidation through her. What he must think of her now that he knew the truth. "And what about you? Why are you here?"

Dark as black coffee those eyes stared back at her, unreadable as his expression. She knew she deserved the mistrust, but she regretted it nonetheless. Back in Miami she'd been playing a role to get close to him, had never expected to fall for him.

Now that he was standing before her, she didn't know what to believe about his motives, whether she could trust him. And she was the farthest thing from naïve. There had to be something in it for him. Especially for a man like him.

"They offered me a deal," he said, his deep voice stroking over her like a caress. "I took it."

So that was it. He'd likely received a reduced sentence in turn for his cooperation. She didn't begrudge him that. Not after everything he'd been through.

She raised her chin, looked from him to Briar. "Have you got a warrant? Because I won't turn myself in." *I'm going to finish what I started.* She had the evidence she found at Frank's house after she found his body, and it was more than enough to indict the men involved in the plot to kill him.

But she would only give that up once they were dead. By *her* hand.

"We're not here to arrest you," Briar said quietly. "And we're not charging you with anything."

"So why all this?" She gestured to the both of them, the IV. They either wanted or needed something big from her. Maybe not them personally, but the NSA did. "Why go to the trouble of basically kidnapping me?"

"You'll just have to trust us."

She withheld a humorless laugh. The woman was impossible to read, though Georgia shouldn't have been surprised. During their training, displaying emotion had been met with severe consequences from the trainers. Starvation. Beatings. Even solitary confinement.

It was only after dropping off grid that Georgia had finally been free to express the anger that drove her. Everything else, she hid carefully behind an icy mask.

Except for those times she'd spent with Miguel in Miami, she admitted to herself. Those had the most genuine human interactions she could ever recall having, apart from the relationship she used to have with her Valkyrie sisters. But that was all over now.

A sudden beeping wrenched her gaze to the bag Miguel had pulled the water from. She recognized the sound immediately. The portable monitor for her security system. He must have picked it up after he'd tranqed her.

Miguel turned toward the bag but Georgia wasn't waiting. She already knew what it meant.

Instantly she reached for the IV site, began pulling the catheter free from her vein as she spoke. "Someone's breached the security perimeter," she told the others, applying pressure to the open IV site as she forced herself to her feet beside the bed.

Briar threw out a hand to steady her as she wobbled slightly, and tapped her earpiece. "Could be Rycroft. Where are you?" she asked a moment later. A pause, then she met Georgia's gaze. "He's one-point-three klicks northwest of here."

Cold air washed over Georgia's fevered skin, but Briar's words sent a chill skittering up her spine. She was acutely aware of her near nakedness as she stood there, of the way Miguel's stare was locked on her, magnetic and forceful. "Whoever that is on the monitor is less than four hundred yards away and closing."

Miguel reached out and wrapped a hand around her upper arm, pulling her after him. "We're getting you out of here, *now*."

****

Nico crept away from where he'd hidden his ATV this last time and headed southeast on foot, back toward the area where he'd seen Georgia. It was after twenty-three-hundred hours now, more than an hour since she'd been shot.

The rain was still steady, helping reduce visibility and covering his tracks somewhat. In the time since leaving the site where Georgia had fallen he hadn't seen a single vehicle on the road leading to the cabin, nor had he heard the sound of another motor moving along the forest trails.

He edged as close as he dared to the spot where she'd fallen. He still wasn't sure she was dead. And if Bautista had been the one to shoot her, it was possible he'd only shot her with a tranq dart or something.

At first he'd assumed Bautista was working with the NSA to kill her, but now he suspected it might be more complicated than that. His former mentor had a strong aversion to killing women. Luckily Nico wasn't as fussy about what targets he was willing to take out.

Hidden as well as he could be from any prying eyes in the area, unless they had a thermal imaging device, Nico looked through his binos, unsurprised to see that her body was gone. Whoever had shot her must have taken her.

But where? Carrying her on foot in this terrain and weather would be slow and cumbersome, and the shooter had to know they weren't alone out here.

Bautista would certainly know, so he'd either be in evasion mode or seek-and-destroy mode. The hunting cabin was the only shelter Nico had seen for miles around in any direction. He might have gone there, maybe left Georgia with the guy he now knew was Alex Rycroft, or Jones before heading back out on the hunt.

The idea of his former mentor prowling these same woods, looking for him, was both thrilling and worrisome. Ever since he'd seen Bautista in that hotel, he'd known they were on a collision course.

Anticipation flowed hot through his veins. Sometime soon he'd finally have the chance to take him out, prove once and for all that he was the better sniper. A chance he'd been waiting for for years, though he'd never expected it would come from killing him.

Except his gut told him there was still someone else out here, waiting. Watching.

Moving with caution he slipped from one concealed position to the next, never staying put more than a few minutes at a time. He'd been ordered to kill both Georgia and Bautista. Whether or not she was already dead didn't matter to him.

He had a feeling that once he found one of them, he'd find the other. All he had to do was get DNA from both bodies before he disposed of them, and Diego would pay him not only his usual sum, but a hefty bonus as well. He and Melissa would live a life of luxury, at least for a little while.

A few hundred yards down the slope, he found a natural hide site made out of an outcropping of stone. Sliding into it, he lay on his belly, wedged back deep in the crevice for maximum camouflage and peered out at the darkened forest through his high-powered scope.

It was a tight fit and a jagged part of the stone dug into his belly but he didn't move. Snipers were trained relentlessly to ignore physical discomfort during an op.

Motionless, he surveyed the area. And his patience paid off.

Minutes later a slight movement through the screen of trees to his eight 'o clock caught his attention. A man, his crouched silhouette mostly hidden behind a thick tree trunk.

Bautista? Or someone else? Likely headed for the cabin.

Nico pushed the unwanted rush of excitement from his mind. He waited in position, perfectly still, his heart rate calm, breathing slow and steady as he watched this new threat.

From this position he couldn't get a decent shot off but he would be able to watch the person easily enough, maybe ID him. He'd stay right here and watch how things unfolded, move in to make the kill if necessary.

This hunter was either part of Nico's prey, or he was about to lead him right to them.

Chapter Eight

———◦————

"We need to make sure we're not seen," Briar said as Georgia exited the bedroom. "And we have to get you out of here without contact with anyone else."

"Why?" she asked, already heading for the tunnel entrance.

"Because this mission is off the books, technically speaking."

More questions piled up in her mind but now wasn't the time to ask them. "This way. There's a tunnel we can use."

"A tunnel?"

"Yes." It would give them a better tactical advantage than exiting the cabin through a door or window.

Dressed in dry clothes and boots, Georgia pulled on her waterproof jacket and hurried as fast as she could on unsteady legs to the trapdoor with Briar and Miguel right behind her.

Even with only one confirmed threat out there, they'd both made it clear that staying and fighting wasn't an option. Their priority was to get her out of the area and hidden in a safe house for immediate medical attention.

"In here," she said, bending to pull it open.

Miguel took it from her and she didn't protest. Right now her illness and the lingering effects of the tranquilizer put her at a distinct disadvantage, as far as escaping or staging a counterattack went. Without the others to help her, she would have been nearly helpless.

But even with backup, staying barricaded in the cabin with an attacker closing in was stupid when they didn't know what kind of threat they were facing. The one individual out there right now could simply be the point man of a hunter/killer team, and might be armed with anything, even an RPG. They could regroup in the tunnel, come up with a plan and then use the secret exit to buy them time and give them the element of surprise.

"Once we've got you secured, we'll handle whoever's out there," Briar told her.

Georgia steadied herself with a hand on the wall before going to her knees beside the opening. "There's a short ladder that drops into the cellar. You'll have to duck down, the ceiling's low."

She went first, dropping down into the blackness. Her knees buckled on impact, sending her tumbling to the rough ground. She shook it off, scrambled into a crouch. As she moved away from the ladder two more light thumps sounded behind her, then a louder one as the trap door closed above them.

Turning on the tactical flashlight she held, she aimed it at the corner of the cellar. For a moment the sway of the beam increased her dizziness. She blinked to clear her vision, the rush of adrenaline through her veins helping to dispel her symptoms.

"I've got weapons, ammo and other supplies in here," she said, unwrapping one of the bundles to expose a box of grenades. "Help yourselves."

Miguel crouched down beside her and rummaged through the bundles, taking a couple grenades and some ammo, stuffing them into his pockets. "Where does the tunnel lead?"

"A trapdoor on the far end that opens into the forest. It's just far enough away from the cabin to give us a head start."

"So that's how you got out before."

"Yes." She glanced back at Briar, who was shoving an extra pistol into the back of her waistband, then checked the monitor she'd brought. "This still shows only one target moving out there. Just over three hundred yards out now."

"Rycroft hasn't seen anything yet. He's going to move in to cover us from above," Briar said.

Georgia aimed the beam of the flashlight down the tunnel so the others could see their path, and how tight the tunnel was. "At the other end I'll check to—"

A firm hand on her shoulder stopped her midsentence. Even through her sweater and jacket the pressure of Miguel's touch tingled all the way down her arm to her fingertips.

He'd been like that in bed, she remembered. Powerful, commanding. And shockingly, meltingly sensual.

She'd never been the same since, mentally or emotionally.

Forcing the disturbing thought away, she half turned to look up at him. His already hard features were even more pronounced in the shadows cast by the glow of the flashlight.

He withdrew his hand, but the unwanted tingles didn't disappear completely. "You're not well enough to take point on this. If we leave this tunnel I go first, then you, then Briar. I'll check things out first and we'll go from there."

Her immediate instinct was to argue, but she clamped her jaw shut.

He was right. In her condition she was a liability to the others. Going out the exit first would put them all at even greater risk. The darkness wouldn't shield them if the shooter had thermal imaging—he would most certainly have night vision—and leaving the safety of the tunnel was risky.

No matter how much it chafed, she had to submit to someone else's authority this time. It surprised her that Briar didn't protest, until she realized that Briar was likely allowing him to take the lead so that she could keep a close eye on her.

Georgia set her jaw. They were right to be suspicious of her motives. Unless they had something to offer her that would change her mind, she planned to give them the slip the first chance she got.

"I think I've already proven that I'm not in any shape to try and take off alone. No need to waste resources by keeping an eagle eye on me."

"I'm more worried about you keeling over at the moment, to be honest," Briar replied, and nodded at Miguel. "Let's go."

Georgia switched off the flashlight, plunging them all into inky blackness so that the high-powered beam wouldn't seep through the cracks in the trapdoors and give them away.

A big hand caught hers, squeezed, then that deep, dark voice spoke close to her. "Hold onto me."

The words punched through her, triggering a vivid memory of the two of them, naked in her bedroom at the place she'd rented in Miami. His weight pressed her down into the mattress, his wicked hands moving all over her body in the darkness, the thick length of his cock buried inside her and his low voice a silken rasp in her ear, urging her higher.

Hold onto me, angel.

She had, for dear life, while he'd taken her to a place

of pure rapture.

She'd never experienced anything like it, that kind of total surrender to a man. He'd given her no choice and she hadn't wanted one. Because even then she'd known that one night was all they'd have together.

Just once, she'd wanted to experience what it felt like to let go completely. He'd not only given her that freedom, he'd shown her such vivid, aching pleasure that it had cracked her icy-cold core wide open and left her struggling to keep her emotions contained.

Banishing the memory, she reached out and placed her hand on top of his right shoulder. Through his jacket she could feel the raw, undiluted power of him humming beneath her palm.

The weight he'd lost during his recovery had acted like a crucible of sorts, rendering him down into a pure, concentrated version of his former self. If the pull she'd felt toward him had been magnetic before, now it was damn near irresistible.

And if she could recognize that when she was this sick and weak, then he was also a threat she couldn't afford to risk again.

With her hand on him she followed in the darkness, stepping carefully on the uneven floor of the tunnel. It helped steady her. She was still a little woozy from the tranquilizer, and her earlier run through the woods had sapped her pitiful energy reserves.

Having Miguel and Briar with her felt strange after operating on her own these past months. Strange…and yet oddly comforting.

The muscles in Miguel's shoulder tensed beneath her hand a split second before he stopped beneath the trapdoor. They were all silent, straining to hear in the darkness. "Stay put," he whispered after a minute.

Georgia didn't know if he'd aimed that at her, Briar, or both, but remained silent as he cautiously cracked the trapdoor open a fraction of an inch. A welcome rush of fresh, damp air flooded into the musty tunnel.

Outside it was nearly as dark as where they stood. Unmoving behind Miguel, she shifted her rifle in her hands while he took stock of the situation using night vision binos.

A few minutes later he shut the door silently above him and spoke in a whisper. "I caught a slight movement about a hundred yards from the cabin. Only one heat signature. I need a good ten seconds' lead-time to make it to a decent hide site up the hill. Once I get in position I'm gonna toss a couple grenades between him and the cabin, make him freeze where he is and hopefully go to ground. After I move in to take him out from above, I'll alert Briar via our comms. You guys stay in here until either Rycroft or I give the all clear."

Without thinking, Georgia grabbed hold of his arm. Why was he doing this? Putting himself at risk for her sake? "Don't. Let Rycroft get into position and take the other shooter out himself."

"There's not enough time," he answered.

"He's right. There are probably others nearby," Briar said. "We need to get out of here, get you to a safe house. The sooner that shooter's out of action, the sooner we can move and make our way out of here."

Miguel gently pulled his arm free. "Stay with Briar."

Georgia bit back more protests, stood there feeling useless and helpless as Miguel eased the trapdoor open once again. Moments later he boosted himself up and through the opening, then silently closed the door behind him, enveloping her and Briar in a smothering silence.

The quiet pressed in on her from all sides. She wasn't claustrophobic but the soundless black space was oppressive nonetheless. And then there was the unsettling sensation of dread gathering inside her. Fear for Miguel.

He was out there all alone facing at least one trained

shooter, maybe more who were hidden out of sight. To have found him again after all this time and then to have to stand by and watch him risk his life to protect her while she did nothing made it feel like a hot coal burned beneath her sternum.

She'd already had his death on her conscience. She didn't want to relive that a second time.

"He'll be okay," Briar murmured, correctly guessing the direction of her thoughts, much to Georgia's irritation.

Was she so transparent? Briar had known her well once. Georgia had to make sure she kept her feelings hidden for the remainder of this "mission of mercy" as they seemed to want her to believe it was.

Her fingers tightened around her weapon. She didn't answer, all her attention riveted on the area above her where the trapdoor was, ready to explode through it in a second's notice if he needed backup.

****

With the cold rain falling on him Bautista paused behind a stand of oaks and stood stock still, barely breathing as he waited to see if his target had noticed him. He'd darted across the small open space to this spot as fast as he could, his boots barely making any sound on the dense carpet of mud and leaves that littered the forest floor. It was possible he'd just exposed himself to an enemy bullet.

But as the minutes crept past there were no shots and no sound of movement to his left, only the patter of the rain and the sigh of the wind in the half-naked branches above and around him. Rycroft, acting as his lookout, remained silent.

Time for the diversion.

He eyed the distance to the cabin, mentally calculated the range then picked a spot partway between it and his target. Reaching into his pocket with slow, careful movements, he pulled out two grenades, palmed them both.

Making sure there was nothing blocking his trajectory, he seized his chance. Taking a step to his right, he pulled the pin from the first grenade and hurled it as hard as he could toward the spot he'd chosen. A few seconds later he lobbed the next.

Dual explosions burst through the night, moments apart.

Hunkered down behind a large boulder, Bautista watched the area where he'd seen the movement. Sure enough, a branch swayed slightly. The shooter had either hit the ground or was moving away from the explosions.

Time to make his move.

Bautista's blood pumped swift and hot through his veins, but he remained ice calm inside as he set out after his prey. He slipped from tree to tree without making a sound, stealth and the hunt second nature to him. He might be a bit slower now than he had been a few months ago, but he hadn't lost his edge. He was still at the top of his game.

At a lip below the ridgeline, he finally had a good visual of his target. The man was lying facedown in the brush, unmoving, eye to the scope of his rifle.

With fluid, practiced movements, Bautista stretched out behind a log and propped the barrel of his weapon on top of it. Through the scope the view was even better.

He lined up the crosshairs on the man's back. Normally he'd take him out without hesitating but the rules of engagement were different now. It was Rycroft's call as to whether he wanted this man dead or taken alive.

He clicked his earpiece to alert Rycroft that he was in position and had the target in his sights.

"Green light," came the instant reply.

Without missing a beat, Bautista squeezed the

trigger. The silencer deadened most of the report. He hit the target dead between the shoulder blades, severing his spinal cord and slicing through his heart.

"Target down." He did a quick sweep of the area and waited to see if anyone else materialized. "Moving in for a closer look," he whispered. Rifle to his shoulder, he covered the distance to the body with swift strides, staying alert for any other signs of movement.

"You're still clear," Rycroft told him.

The other sniper lay facedown on the ground, stretched out over his weapon. His eyes were half open, blood spilling out of his nose and partially open mouth from the bullet that had torn through his body, imploding his lung and ripping through his heart.

Checking the man's pulse, Bautista was unsurprised that there wasn't one. "He's dead." A relief, since he'd been way too close to the cabin, and Georgia, for Bautista's comfort.

Rycroft's voice came through the earpiece, a mere whisper of sound. "I'm sixty meters to your five o'clock."

"Roger that," he whispered back, automatically turning to scan his surroundings and provide cover for Rycroft.

A few moments later Rycroft materialized out of the bushes and hunkered down next to the body. He pulled out a device from his pocket and took digital images of the man's fingerprints, then got on his phone while Bautista provided overwatch. "Zahra. Run these prints right away through every system we have, and let me know if you get a hit."

He put the phone and device away, stood and took a cautious look around before tapping his earpiece to contact Briar. "We've got more company out here," he murmured. "One more shooter for sure, maybe others, I couldn't be sure from the tracks. We need to get the target to the vehicle immediately," he finished, his tone urgent.

"Copy that," Briar answered. "Moving out of the tunnel exit now."

Bautista turned and ran for the secret tunnel exit. The sooner they got Georgia out of here, the better.

Chapter Nine

Georgia's head snapped up when it began to droop for the third time in the back of the SUV. After Miguel had taken out the other shooter, they'd moved her to the vehicle they'd left in a farmer's shed when they'd first arrived.

It humiliated her that she hadn't been able to keep up on her own. There was nothing she hated more than being helpless. A few minutes into the trek Miguel had put her across his shoulders and carried her the rest of the way, just to keep the pace.

"You should sleep," he said to her now, seated beside her in the backseat.

She shook her head stubbornly. They'd helped her, yes, but technically they were still holding her against her will and she didn't like it. First chance she got, she was making a break for it.

No matter how exhausted she was, no matter that she had history and some level of trust for the three of them, she knew it wasn't smart to let her guard down. And until they were honest with her about what they wanted from her, she wasn't telling them anything.

"How much longer until we reach the safe house?" she asked.

"Couple hours," Rycroft answered from behind the wheel as he drove along the nearly deserted mountain road. He hadn't said a word about where they were headed and she was too tired to fight with him about it.

She knew it would be useless anyway. The man had been former SF and was one of the toughest interrogators she'd ever met.

She'd found that out firsthand when he'd taken her into custody last December. She'd been lucky he'd let her go in exchange for the intel she'd shared back then, rather than charging her and locking her up.

She should have known then that he wasn't done with her yet.

Now that she was warm, dry and safe—well, relatively speaking, anyway—all she wanted to do was collapse into a heap and rest. But a couple hours more? She wasn't sure she could force herself to stay awake that long.

God, she was tired. And sore. At least her stomach was feeling a little better now. She was almost hungry. Maybe she could eat something, then sleep a bit.

"Here," Miguel murmured, and reached into a bag behind him to pull out a protein bar. "Can you eat a little?"

She eyed it, then met his gaze, felt the impact of it deep inside her. Even now she had to fight the invisible pull drawing her to him.

She'd slept with this man. Laid herself bare to him for those few hours in a way she'd never done with anyone else.

At some point they'd have to have a long overdue conversation about what had happened. She dreaded it as much as she needed it. She was insanely curious why he'd come on this job, and what sort of deal he'd taken.

"Maybe." Murmuring a thank you, she accepted it

and took a small nibble. Her stomach growled, desperate for food. She hoped it stayed down.

Someone's cell phone went off. Rycroft immediately pulled his out and answered. "Yeah, okay," he said after a moment, and his tone was so dark that Georgia looked at him in the rearview mirror. His expression was full-on pissed. "Keep digging and don't alert anyone else. I'll handle this myself."

"What?" Briar asked him when he hung up.

"Zahra got a hit on our shooter." He paused a second. "His ID was buried deep, she needed to use all the tricks that come with her top secret security clearance and then call in a few favors to find out who he was. Apparently he was a CIA asset. Went off grid about a year ago and this is the first time he's turned up since."

Georgia frowned. "Any idea who he's working for?"

Rycroft met her gaze in the mirror. "I'm betting he's still on The Company's payroll."

The words only confirmed her own suspicions, but a chill snaked up her spine anyway. She turned her gaze out the window and watched the darkened landscape pass by in a blur. Soon her eyelids began to droop and her head began to loll.

Her head snapped up at a rustling sound and a second later a rolled up jacket appeared before her. "Here. Use this."

She hesitated a moment, then took it. "Thanks," she murmured, and tucked it beneath her head to rest against the doorframe.

The scents of leather and the uniquely masculine spice that was Miguel filled her nose, instantly transporting her back to that night they'd spent together, but also reminding her of the first time she'd seen him smile. Really smile. At the nursing home.

Georgia had been puttering around his grandmother's room, dusting her picture frames and watering her plants. She couldn't even remember what she'd been talking to him about but when she'd looked over her shoulder at him, she'd found him smiling at her. It had startled her so much she'd just stared at him, holding her breath at the beauty of it, a current of warmth curling deep in her belly.

That was the first time she'd seen the man behind the mask, and right then she'd known that *el Santo* wasn't a monster at all.

Georgia had never gotten over him. Having him this close with a mountain of questions and mistrust between them was torture.

It went against everything ingrained in her to sleep in an uncertain situation like this. She let herself drift, not surrendering to the lure of the deep sleep her body craved, but allowing a light doze. Only to wake what felt like seconds later when the SUV took the sharp curve in the mountain road.

Miguel reached across the seat to undo her seatbelt and grab the jacket. He set it in his lap then wrapped a hand around her right shoulder and pulled. "Lie down. Sleep a while." His tone was commanding, a little gruff and she could tell he was annoyed at her stubbornness.

They weren't out to hurt her, she realized that. And she still trusted him deep down, even though it was crazy given their history. Sleep was what she needed most right now. It would give her a chance to recharge, hopefully let her body flush the last of the poison from her system, and get her energy back.

And the truth was, she wanted to be close to him. She'd missed him terribly. This gave her the perfect excuse to steal a little more time with him.

Pushing away from the door, she curled up on her side and laid her head in his lap on top of the jacket, allowed her eyes to close and this time, let go. Just as she was about to slide under, she thought she felt the gentle sweep of a hand over her hair.

Sometime later she woke when the vehicle slowed to turn a corner. She sat up, took a groggy look around and fought to clear the fog from her brain. They were in a residential neighborhood, with neat rows of two-story houses with tidy, manicured lawns and gardens. Suburbia at its finest.

Rycroft turned left at the next street and drove to the end of a quiet cul-de-sac, pulling into the driveway of the last house on the right. Immediately the garage door opened and he drove inside, parked next to a gray SUV.

"Had a friend of mine check everything out for us," Rycroft said by way of explanation. Before he'd even shut off the engine the door leading into the house opened and a man stepped through it.

He was tall, over six feet, and built, with short reddish-blond hair. The black T-shirt he wore stretched over wide shoulders and chest ripped with muscle and revealed the full sleeves of tats that ran the length of both arms.

Rycroft got out and shook hands with him. Both of them were grinning, seemed at ease together. When he gestured for the others to get out, Georgia slid out of the back and stood off to the side as Rycroft made the introductions.

"This is Gage Wallace," he said. "He's with Titanium Security."

Georgia had heard of the company. Founded by a former SEAL, they now provided security contractors for various ops around the world, but specialized in the Middle East.

"We've worked together in the past and I sometimes call him up when I need a favor."

"You know I love doing you favors. Only excitement I get these days." Wallace acknowledged each of them with a nod, his bright blue eyes sharp. "Everything's ready. Claire's just stocking the upstairs bathrooms." He gave a small smile that softened his face completely. "She's got the place set up like a hotel now, complete with hand towels, facecloths and little travel soaps."

The door opened again and a blonde appeared there. She smiled at them and turned a glare at Wallace. "I heard that. Only excitement you get these days? So being married to me is boring now?"

"No, never boring," he answered, scooping her up in one big arm and giving her a squeeze. "Just miss the action of the old days sometimes, that's all."

"I know you do." She turned her gaze on Rycroft, gave him a grin as she shook a warning finger. "But he's officially retired, so don't be thinking you can bring him back into anything. Including whatever this is," she finished, indicating the rest of them with a wave of her hand.

Wallace chuckled. "She's a little protective of me," he said, sounding amused.

"Well someone has to be. I swear your guardian angel must be a raving alcoholic."

He grinned down at her. "Well you can relax now. I'm out of the game." His gaze slid to Rycroft. "Officially speaking. Unless something really important comes up." He raised his eyebrows questioningly, and though Georgia didn't know him, she could tell he was hopeful.

"Wouldn't dream of asking you to get back into the game," Rycroft answered in a tone that was clearly sardonic. "Claire, meet Briar, Miguel and Georgia. Everyone, this is Claire, Gage's keeper."

The blonde smiled at them all. "Hi. Well come on inside and get settled in. I thought you guys might be hungry so I put a lasagna in the oven when we got here. Should be ready in another hour or so, and there's some salad and other stuff in the fridge."

Georgia followed Briar inside the house, acutely

aware of Miguel right behind her. The moment they entered the kitchen the scents of basil and roasted tomatoes filled the air. Her stomach growled and her mouth watered.

Rycroft must have heard it because he looked back at her, his expression calm. "Go on upstairs and sleep awhile longer. I'll see about getting a doctor to—"

"I don't need a doctor."

He gave her a dubious look.

"I don't. I'm already way better than I was. At least, before the tranq dart," she added with a pointed look at Miguel.

"Sorry. Already called one and he's on his way. I want him to look you over, take some blood samples so we can verify what's wrong with you. If it's poison and we can find out which kind it is, we might be able to get a better idea of who did it."

Okay, that part was actually pretty smart. "Fine."

His phone rang. He picked up, listened. "Perfect timing, we just got in. We'll be expecting you." Rycroft ended the call. "That was the doc. He'll be here in a few minutes."

Georgia plunked herself down in a chair at the table, took the meds Briar passed her and waited for the doctor. The mid-fortyish man came in, checked her vitals, drew some blood and promised to get the results back to them as soon as they came back from the lab.

"You need fluids and rest," he told her. "Clear fluids, no dairy and nothing solid for a day or two."

When he left Rycroft nodded toward the stairs. "Go up and get some more sleep. We'll get you something light to eat after you wake up, if you're up to it. After that, we've got some things to talk about."

The warning tone sent a frisson of foreboding through her. Glancing at Gage and Claire, who were watching her with open curiosity, she turned and headed for the stairs. Footsteps behind her made her swing around. Briar was ten feet behind her.

"What are you doing?" she demanded.

"Following you to your room."

Oh, for— "I guess you plan on watching me sleep, too, to make sure I don't try to escape?"

She shrugged. "I know you too well. And it'll be just like old times. We can stay up all night talking the way we used to."

Yeah, Briar did know her too well, and right now that pissed Georgia off. "You're the ones who kidnapped me, so don't expect me to tell you anything."

She paused and looked back at Rycroft, still standing in the kitchen with the others. He stared right back, completely unapologetic. She could feel the added weight of Miguel's stare, pressing on her.

"Fine," she muttered, and continued up the stairs.

But a part of her wished that if she had to have a babysitter to keep watch inside the bedroom, that it could be Miguel instead. And she was all too aware that whenever she left her room, her reprieve would be over.

Fortunately she wouldn't have to endure their company—and questions—much longer. As soon as she was well enough, she was getting out of here and finishing her mission.

Alone.

****

The bedroom door opened just as Bautista raised a hand to knock. He stepped back as Briar came forward, his gaze automatically sliding behind her to Georgia. She must have just taken a shower, because her golden brown hair was damp around her shoulders. Her cheeks were still flushed. Even sick she was striking.

"Feeling any better?" he asked as Briar edged past

him into the hallway. Georgia had been asleep for a long time, almost twelve hours.

She nodded, her blue eyes clearer than he'd seen them since they found her. "Much."

Wanting to judge for himself, he reached out and placed a palm on her forehead. She froze at his touch, her expression closing completely. He lowered his hand. "You're still warm."

"I'm okay. Way better than I was. A good night's sleep and I'll be almost back to normal."

He hoped so. God, she was beautiful.

Standing here alone with her, the urge to step into the room, shut the door behind him and find out everything he wanted to know was almost overwhelming. It was killing him not to know, but Rycroft was waiting downstairs with questions of his own, and since he was the boss, his questions took precedence. He'd just have to wait until tonight.

She broke eye contact for a second then looked at him again. "Is there any dinner left?"

He blinked. She and Briar must not have spoken at all after she woke up. "From last night?"

She frowned. "What? What time is it?" She swung around to look behind her, probably checking for a clock on the nightstand.

"You slept almost twelve hours. But I put on some chicken noodle soup for you a bit ago, in case you were hungry."

She stared at him a moment, as though she couldn't imagine why he'd do such a thing. The truth was, he didn't want to examine his reasons too closely.

He'd been going stir-crazy, prowling the house waiting for her to come downstairs. And she'd been too long without food, so she'd need something bland like broth to settle her stomach. Rycroft had watched him in amusement but hadn't said anything and Bautista didn't care what he thought. His only concern right now was Georgia.

"Thank you," she murmured.

He shrugged. "It's from a package, but it's what my *abuelita* always gave me when I was sick. She swore it cured everything."

At the mention of his grandmother, a sharp current of tension flowed between them.

He watched Georgia's face closely for reaction, her body language. How had she ever found out about his grandmother in the first place?

It was the only thing he could think of that would explain how she'd managed to track him down at all. After that, she'd used the guise of volunteering at his grandmother's facility as an excuse to get close to him.

And he'd fallen for the charade completely.

Georgia lowered her gaze, but not before he swore he caught a flash of guilt on her face. Probably wishful thinking. He had no idea if she had enough of a conscience left to feel guilt at all. Of course, people could say the same about him.

But they'd be wrong.

"How is she?" she asked.

"The same." In a vegetative state being kept alive by machines in her care home in Miami, same as she had for the past twenty-two years. Her big heart simply refused to quit. "They let me talk to her after I signed the contract."

It had been one of his conditions. She couldn't respond, of course, but he knew she could hear and understand him. Over the years he'd made it a point to visit her regularly and whenever he did her heart rate had calmed and leveled out. He owed her everything.

"You're very loyal to her. She's lucky to have you." The hint of bitterness in her tone told him she hadn't experienced that kind of loyalty in her life. At least not often.

"I was luckier to have her, believe me." She'd stepped up and taken him in, shown him what true unconditional love was when he'd needed it most. And then he'd lost her to a senseless act of violence that had caved his entire world in again, and changed him forever.

Although he suspected that Georgia knew far more about that story and the rest of his background than he had previously realized. If she'd been good enough to figure out who his grandmother was and where she was kept in order to get close to him, then she'd no doubt know all about his early life. He hated being at that kind of disadvantage.

"Better come down and eat," he said gruffly, turning so she could pass him and head down the stairs first.

She stepped past him, giving him another whiff of that clean, feminine scent that threatened to tangle up his brain. "Are the Wallaces still here?"

"No, they left last night, about an hour after you went upstairs."

Gage was working on something for Rycroft right now pertaining to this job, and Claire was on call if Rycroft needed anything from her. Apparently Gage was former SF and a good operator, and his wife had been an NSA analyst working for Rycroft up until the op that had injured her husband and pushed him into early retirement.

Georgia descended the stairs easily, moving at a brisk pace, showing none of her earlier unsteadiness. Bautista couldn't help but stare at the way her tight, shapely ass moved in the jeans she'd changed into.

Tearing his eyes off her rear end, he went to the stove and ladled some soup into a bowl for her.

"You look better," Rycroft commented as Georgia headed for the table.

"Feeling better," she answered, her tone giving nothing away, even though she was still running a slight fever and likely felt like shit.

Chairs scraped on the hardwood floor behind Bautista. When he turned around he saw that Georgia was seated on the far side of the table across from Briar and Rycroft. She was watching them warily, her expression closed as though she was bracing for an interrogation.

Bautista almost felt sorry for her. But this conversation was long overdue and with other hunters out there looking for her they couldn't wait any longer. Their "team", such as it was, needed answers.

Her blue eyes flashed up to his when he brought the soup over, and she forced a small smile. "Thanks."

"Welcome." He took the seat at the head of the table, ignoring his instinct to sit next to her.

The immediate reaction to protect her annoyed him. He wasn't her ally. Wasn't her friend. Wasn't her *anything*, and he had to remember that.

Avoiding eye contact with them all, Georgia picked up her spoon and began stirring it through the soup. The quiet clink of the metal against the bowl in the silent room began to grate on Bautista's nerves.

Bautista shot Rycroft a sharp look, noticed Briar was looking at him too. *We going to do this, or what?*

Cool as ever, Rycroft leaned forward and rested his forearms on the table, watching Georgia. "So the doc called with the lab results."

She looked up at him. "And?"

"Botulism."

Hell. It made Bautista furious to think of someone trying to kill her that way. Far more humane to put a bullet through her heart than to let her suffer and die such a slow, painful death.

Unless that's what they'd wanted.

"Oh," was all she said. "That explains a lot."

"Yeah, but it doesn't give us a way to track whoever it was, because it's so common." Rycroft cocked his head, regarding her. "Wasn't easy to find you. Took my people weeks to get a decent lead on you. I was impressed you stayed off the radar for so long, and I don't impress easily."

She didn't answer, just kept stirring the soup while the steam curled from its surface in wisps.

Rycroft finally cut through the bullshit. "You might not believe it yet, but we really are here to help you. But we can't do that unless you tell us what we need to know."

Georgia looked up then, nailing him with a cold stare that told Bautista just how much she resented being put in this situation. Right now she was cornered and powerless. And he couldn't blame her for hating it. "You can ask whatever you want, but it doesn't mean I'm going to tell you a damn thing."

Chapter Ten

———————

Georgia held that steel gray stare and refused to be the first to look away no matter how thick the tension in the room grew.

The corner of Rycroft's mouth tipped upward, sending a fresh rush of anger through her. He found her amusing, did he? "We're on the same side here," he said quietly.

She didn't respond to that. There was nothing she could say that wouldn't make things worse and she had no intention of digging the hole she was in any deeper.

At the moment she was acutely aware of the three pairs of eyes fixed on her. Bad enough that he was basically interrogating her. It was unbearable that Briar and Miguel were witnessing her humiliation.

"We want the same things," Rycroft continued in a tone that was so reasonable-sounding it set her teeth on edge. "I don't know exactly who you were after, but I've got a pretty good idea. And I've also got a pretty good idea why you're targeting them."

Folding her arms, she gave him a cold smile. "Enlighten me."

"The people you're after, you know something about

them. Something big, and they want you dead before you can expose them. That's where we come in. To keep you alive," he clarified, glancing to the others and back to her.

Georgia's heart beat faster despite her every effort to remain calm, the chaotic mix of emotions churning inside her becoming harder and harder to contain. In the ultra-secret Valkyrie Program the trainers had begun breaking her down and reprogramming her when she was nothing more than a kid.

They'd purged her of her impulsivity and penchant for emotional outbursts. Now that she'd begun to allow her emotions to seep back to the surface, they were building inside her with the explosive force of a bomb.

The increasing lack of control frightened her.

Something in her expression must have given her away because Rycroft leaned forward, the sense of urgency radiating from him palpable. "Who is it?" He waited a beat. "Jamie Rossland?"

Just the mention of the name tested the limits of her control. *Don't react. Don't give him anything else. You've screwed up enough already.*

Rycroft watched her the way a hungry eagle eyed a juicy salmon. "That shooter Bautista took care of for us in the forest last night? No longer with The Company, yet after some magic, my people were able to ping a series of phone calls between him and Rossland, dating back to just after the incident with Bautista in Miami. I'm thinking that's a very interesting coincidence."

It was no surprise to her that Rossland would dispatch a hitter to kill her before she could leak the evidence she had against him. And the NSA must have worked for weeks to trace those calls back to them, because Rossland and the hitter must have used either encrypted or burner phones for those conversations.

She set her jaw, forced herself to take a slow, calming breath before responding. Rycroft was acting like he knew about the evidence she had. "You can't keep me here against my will."

He acknowledged her point with a dip of his head. "True. That's why I'm hoping you'll *want* to stay and help us."

She mentally laughed at the idea but then he continued, his posture and expression radiating earnestness. "If there are dirty CIA officers and politicians out there with blood on their hands, I want to take them down. Tell me who it is and give me what you've got on them, and I'll make sure they go down. I might even let you help us do it."

She frowned at the last bit. "What do you mean?"

"You're every bit as good as she is." He nodded at Briar before meeting her gaze again. "I need motivated people with your skill set on my team. Everything I know about you says you're what I'm looking for. The NSA needs more people like you."

She flicked a questioning glance at Briar, then stared at him in disbelief. "You want to recruit me?" It instantly upped her suspicion level. Why her? He knew damn well she'd killed Garcia back in Miami, maybe he suspected her of other hits as well, only he couldn't prove any of it. He already had two highly skilled contract killers on this team. Did he really need a third?

He nodded, a spark of wry humor warming his eyes. "Big time."

"It's one of the reasons we started looking for you in the first place," Briar added. "I identified you off video footage taken in Miami and alerted Alex. After putting the pieces together it wasn't too hard to figure out what you were doing, or why you disappeared. That upped the timeline for finding you, but we still didn't have a strong enough message to get your attention."

She shot a meaningful look at Miguel before turning her attention back to Georgia. "So when we discovered he'd come out of the medically-induced coma, much to everyone's surprise by the way, we recruited him too."

To sweeten the deal, she meant. Make the offer so irresistible that Georgia would abandon her private vendetta and sign on to be part of their team.

She didn't dare look at Miguel right now, knowing she'd never be able to mask her emotions completely. Did he think she'd merely manipulated and used him in Miami? He must. She would, in his shoes.

Worse would be if he assumed *everything* they'd done together was all for show. Because taking him to her bed had been anything but fake, and she'd done it for the purely selfish reason that she simply couldn't walk away from him.

Stop thinking about it. You have more important things to worry about right now.

No one said anything as she absorbed the new details. She had to admit Rycroft's offer was damn tempting. Too tempting.

Living off the grid was exhausting. Having professional assassins on her tail made it even more so.

Teaming up with Rycroft and the others would be a huge relief in so many ways. She knew he was basically a good guy, a straight shooter, and that Briar would never work for anyone she didn't respect. But joining with them would mean Georgia wouldn't be able to kill her targets when they found them.

Unless…she could use this to her advantage.

Let Rycroft and the others help her get close enough to her targets that she could take them out. At least one of them, anyway.

"Just think about it," Rycroft said, taking her by surprise when he pushed to his feet.

Georgia blinked. That was it? Interrogation over? She'd expected him to continue pushing, force her into a tighter and tighter corner until she had no choice but to capitulate.

"We've likely got one more day here before we have to move. Take some time to rest and mull things over. Talk with the other two about it if you want." He paused, his gray eyes searching hers, his stare penetrating. "Like I said, we're all on the same team here. Whoever's behind Janaia and Frank's murders, I want them to pay."

She wanted that too, but by different means. Rycroft wanted them to face justice and serve jail time for what they'd done. She wanted them *dead*. Big difference. But Rycroft had resources she didn't, and he could prove highly useful to her goal.

Stretching his arms over his head, he let out a huge yawn. "I'm beat. Gonna go crash for a bit, because I'm getting old. You guys catch up, I'll see you in the morning." He headed for the stairs.

Georgia watched him go, still suspicious, her brain working overtime.

"Your soup's gone cold."

She jerked her gaze to Miguel, found herself falling into those dark eyes for a moment. "Oh. No, it's fine." She'd completely forgotten about it. Picking up her spoon, she took a mouthful of the soup, suddenly famished.

"You're gonna need more fluids than that," Briar said, getting up and crossing to the fridge. She came back with a bottled sports drink and set it down in front of her.

"Thanks." It was weird, having others make a fuss over her after she'd been alone so long. But she kind of liked it, in a way.

She ate a few more spoonfuls of soup, aware of the lingering strain between the three of them. Out of nowhere a memory surfaced, of back when they were in the Valkyrie program. After receiving yet another punishment Georgia had been locked in a cell, so hungry she felt sick. She'd lost her temper during a training session and as punishment she'd been put into solitary confinement for a day without any food.

A key scraped and squeaked in the windowless cell door. Georgia sat up, tensed as she waited to see who had come for her. It was dinnertime; no one should be at the barracks except for the guard posted outside her door.

But when the door opened, Briar and Trinity stood in the opening. "Hey," Briar murmured, giving her a cocky smile as she sauntered inside.

Georgia pushed to her feet, shooting a wary glance out into the dim hallway. "What are you guys doing here?" she demanded in a whisper. "You'll get a day of solitary as well if they catch you here."

"The guard never saw us coming and Briar disabled all the security cameras in here," Trinity answered, walking over to hand her a brown paper lunch bag. Her lips curved in a sharp smile. "They're not the only ones who know a few tricks."

With a hesitant smile, Georgia took the bag. It was heavier than it looked. Opening it, she found two sandwiches, some fruit and bottles of water. She looked up at her friends, felt an unexpected lump in her throat. "Thank you," she said, her voice catching.

Briar reached out and squeezed her shoulders. "The cadre are assholes and their methods of breaking us are medieval. We didn't think you should starve just because they're assholes."

Georgia laughed, precariously close to tears. No one had ever looked out for her like this. Before meeting Trinity and Briar, no one had ever cared. "They are assholes."

"Yep. And misogynistic assholes to boot," Trinity added. She scrutinized Georgia for a long moment. "You gonna be okay in here for another nine hours?"

I will now. *"Yeah."*

Briar glanced behind them out into the hallway.

113

"We'd better get going. The sleeping agent we slipped into his coffee is weak, it won't last long."

Georgia gave them a wide smile. "I love you guys."

Briar winked. "We know. See you when you get out."

They left and locked the cell door behind them, but Georgia didn't feel alone anymore. Not when she knew she had friends like Briar and Trinity to have her back.

Georgia blinked and pulled herself out of the past, got to the issue at hand. "Rycroft's offer, it's legit?" she finally asked Briar.

Briar nodded. "One hundred percent. I'm happy with my position at the agency. I still get to do the things I loved most about my previous work, only now it's all legal. He's a good boss, never asks you to do something he wouldn't do himself. The hours are way better than what I was pulling on my own, and I travel less. I consider both those things big perks now," she added with a contented smile. "I like being close to home these days."

"You still with DeLuca then?" The commander of the FBI's Hostage Rescue Team. The ones who had nearly killed Miguel.

"Yes. Couldn't be happier. I'm a lucky girl."

Georgia smiled back, glad for her. She'd never envisioned any of them falling in love and having a normal relationship, but it seemed Briar had done just that. "That's good to hear." Gathering her nerve, she turned her head to look at Miguel. "And what about you? Are you happy you signed on with the agency?"

"That remains to be seen," he answered, his dark eyes delving into hers. It was so damn hard to read him. He was the ultimate expert in poker faces. Even back when they'd been together in Miami, she'd always known he was keeping things from her. It had surprised her that he'd tried to warn her at all.

I'm not the man you think I am, he'd told her.

But the reality was, she'd known exactly who and

what he was. And that still hadn't been enough to make her keep her emotional distance.

She glanced away, nerves coiling tight in the pit of her belly. Rycroft and Briar had known he'd be her weak point. She had to be careful not to prove them right.

Briar cleared her throat and pushed her chair back, the legs scraping over the floor. "I'm gonna leave you two alone for a while. I'm sure you've got a lot to talk about and would rather do it without a fifth wheel hanging around."

Startled, Georgia stared helplessly after her as Briar jogged up the stairs, abandoning her to her fate. It felt like she took all the oxygen in the room with her.

In the oppressive quiet that followed she focused back on her soup, barely tasting it at all with Miguel's silent stare making her want to squirm in her seat.

But he was patient. And shrewd. He waited until she'd nearly drained the bowl before speaking. "Rycroft really would do it," he began. "Grant you a clean record in exchange for you signing up."

It seemed unreal, given all the things she'd done, the lives she'd taken in the name of duty. All except Garcia, whose murder of course hadn't been sanctioned by the government. She'd done the world a favor by killing that piece of shit for poisoning Frank. "Is that what he did for you?"

Miguel nodded. In this lighting she noticed there were shadows beneath his deep-set eyes, whether from exhaustion or because he hadn't fully recovered from his injuries, she wasn't sure. And it…bothered her to think of him tired and in pain, especially after everything he'd already been through. He hadn't had an easy life, especially as a child.

She had to resist the urge to reach out and trail her fingers across his bristled cheek. "How long do you have to work for him?"

His lips quirked. "I think until death, basically."

That's what she'd figured. "So why did you sign it?"

He shrugged those broad shoulders, lean with muscle. "Better than rotting away inside a jail cell for the rest of my life. After I was shot I wasn't expecting to ever wake up again, so when I did that was one hell of a shock. And the job has certain perks I wouldn't have enjoyed otherwise." A beat passed as he watched her. "I got to see you again."

Georgia stared at him, aware of the way her heart rattled against her ribs. "That's why you did it? To see me?" It was stupid, to hope that was the case after everything she'd done, but she couldn't help it. During those months in Miami when she'd got to know him, he'd slipped beneath her skin without her being able to prevent it.

"No." A muscle twitched at the side of his jaw and he folded his arms across his chest, the move making her aware of his size, the sheer power of him.

Even with twenty pounds less muscle on him and legally having turned from the dark side, the man still radiated danger. He was still deadly. A predator to his core.

His eyes chilled as he spoke again. "I'm here because I want answers."

Chapter Eleven

Bautista was done with waiting.

Georgia was sitting right in front of him, they were alone with at least the illusion of what little privacy they were going to get for the duration of this mission, and she wasn't going anywhere until he got the information he wanted.

He didn't expect her to just spill her guts, however, and she didn't disappoint, giving him the same frosty look she had Rycroft earlier. Then she grabbed her bowl and made to stand, as if she planned to leave.

Not happening.

He flashed out a hand and grabbed her forearm, squeezed with just enough pressure to freeze her in place. "Sit. Down." His voice was quiet, but held the sting of a whip.

She jerked her arm from his grasp and lowered herself into her chair, thunking the bowl down on the table hard enough to rattle the spoon around. She tossed her hair over one shoulder, squared her shoulders and shot him a hostile glare. "Fine. Let's do this."

Bet your sweet ass we will. "Who are you?"

She scoffed. "If you're on this mission, then you

know exactly who I am."

"No, I don't. I know your name, that you used to be some kind of government assassin and that you were trained with Briar. I know you suddenly appeared at my *abuelita's* care facility out of the blue one day and posed as a volunteer there. For months. And the whole time you were doing it to get close to me."

The worst part was, he'd actually fallen for it and let her in.

He narrowed his eyes at her, fighting the anger snapping through him. "So who the hell are you?" It felt good to finally ask it.

She gave him a sarcastic look. "I'm supposed to believe you haven't already memorized everything in whatever file on me they gave to you by now?"

He shook his head, increasingly frustrated by this entire situation. He didn't like being off-center like this, working under parameters he was unfamiliar with. It unsettled him. "It was made crystal clear to me from day one that I operate on this team on a need-to-know basis, and so far they haven't told me shit."

A frown creased her brow, as though she was trying to figure out whether to believe him about that or not.

He sighed, decided to try a different question. "How did you find me?"

"You messed up," she said, flinging his earlier line to her back in his face.

"Yeah?" He had to work to keep from grinding his back teeth together. "How's that?" Because he'd been damn careful during his time as Perez's enforcer. No one should have been able to figure out his identity, much less find him. He'd changed his name from Miguel Salvador to Miguel Bautista, and in the criminal underworld he'd gone by the moniker *el Santo*.

"The short answer? You didn't cover your tracks well enough. Even the legendary and terrifying '*el Santo*' had to have a real name."

"*El Santo* is dead," he growled.

"Maybe so. But there were plenty of rumors going around about you back then. So I started pulling on threads I'd heard about relating to your background, beginning with your grandmother. I figured out you settled her in the care home under a fake name, but given her injuries and the story of the attack, after a lot of digging I managed to verify that it was her. Once I knew that, I went to Miami and began volunteering at the care home. My gut said it was only a matter of time until you showed up, given how close you were to her. And I was right." She shrugged. "Wasn't rocket science."

It was damn hard not to react to that explanation, and the little verbal barb at the end. "Who told you?" he growled.

He'd paid an obscene amount of money to put her in that home because she'd not only get the best care there, but because it was renowned for its privacy and the staff's discretion. He hated seeing her lying there like that in her bed, limbs all twisted from the brain damage, being fed by a tube. But he couldn't stay away. He loved her and owed it to her to visit whenever he could.

Dammit, he'd made absolutely certain that the staff didn't know who he was, using a fake ID on all the paperwork, and he'd been careful not to ever talk about the cowardly attack that had resulted in such horrific brain trauma that it had left her brain dead.

A terrible case of being in the wrong place at the wrong time.

He'd purposely left his lunch behind that day in grade school because he'd planned to skip class to avoid the bullies that kept tormenting him and made his life a living hell. Not realizing his intentions, she'd raced home to get it for him. She'd walked in to find two neighborhood thugs robbing her house and when she'd confronted them they'd split her skull open with a baseball bat and left her for dead.

In a way, it was his fault. Not really, he knew that on an intellectual level, but he still blamed himself. His grandmother had given him the only loving home he'd ever known, taking him in without question or hesitation when her only daughter had died of a drug overdose, leaving him an orphan. Before that, he hadn't known what unconditional love looked like. Felt like. Hadn't known what it meant to have a safe, clean place to lay his head down every night and go to bed with a full stomach.

And she'd paid dearly for her decision to take him in.

He still remembered the horror of finding her that day. Lying on the floor with the back of her head caved in, eyes partially open. All the blood. He'd screamed and screamed, raced in a panic to the neighbor's house to get help.

But he'd made certain those fuckers responsible for her suffering paid dearly, he thought as he curled his hands into fists. Because of the opportunity and intel Perez had given him, they'd become *el Santo's* first victims. The first of many. He would always owe his former boss for that.

Now he was faced with the unwelcome knowledge that all his efforts at secrecy since then hadn't been good enough. But who had verified his *abuela's* tragic story to Georgia?

Then it hit him and his mouth twisted into a sneer of disdain. "The doctors. One of them must have either talked about her story, or leaked her records." Either way, it was unacceptable.

Another shrug. "It wasn't one thing or one person in particular. More like I got bits and pieces of info from various sources and put it all together on my own. When I began volunteering I broke into the security area and first saw you that way. You matched the description of what *el Santo* supposedly looked like, and you were the right age.

"You never visited in a regular pattern though, so I knew I had to sit back and wait for you to show again. I still wasn't a hundred percent sure you were *el Santo*, but the moment I saw you in person, I knew you were an operator from the way you moved. I did more research, looking at your travel patterns. I'm not the most patient hitter out there, but I managed to wait it out, and in this case it paid off."

That all made sense but it also scared the shit out of him, to realize how vulnerable and transparent he'd been, when the whole time he'd thought he was untouchable. And he had a whole new level of respect for just how fucking smart she was. How patient and formidable a foe she'd make.

He shook his head slowly, impressed in spite of himself. This young, gorgeous woman sitting in front of him had managed to do the impossible—figure out his identity when no one else ever had, and then proceed to sneak past his defenses.

So, are you ever going to ask me out? She'd flung the verbal challenge at him, and he'd taken the bait.

Talk about a swift kick in the ego.

"Why did you target me?" he asked. "I didn't kill your former handler."

Her eyes narrowed on him. "Frank wasn't just my *handler*. He was the closest thing to a father I'd ever known." She drew in a deep breath, seemed to work at calming herself before continuing. "I needed to find Villa."

Bautista tensed at the mention of the other Fuentes cartel enforcer. The one he'd hunted and killed for Perez.

"He was involved with Frank's murder, maybe even the one who'd planted the cyanide, and I couldn't track him down on my own. Then I heard through the grapevine that Perez wanted Villa 'dealt with'. So, you being Perez's right hand man and all, I knew you'd be the one going after him."

And she'd been right.

He remembered the exact conversation he'd had with Perez, when his boss had ordered him to "put Villa down" like the rabid animal he was. After weeks of investigating various leads—weeks when he'd become more and more attached to the pretty volunteer who it turned out was actually using him—Bautista had finally gotten insider knowledge that Villa was planning to do a hit in Key West on that fateful day back in June.

He'd driven down there the morning after he'd spent the entire night tangled with Georgia in her bed.

Ignoring the thousand other questions about the more personal aspects of his so-called "relationship" with her, he focused on the Villa op. "That morning, you followed me to Key West." It was the only way things could have unfolded the way they had.

"Yes."

He didn't know how she'd managed it without him noticing, but she had. Unreal. "You knew I was going there for Villa."

"Yes."

It was incredible. That she'd been able to slip past his defenses in the first place, and in the second, that she'd been able to follow him to Key West without him ever being the wiser. How had he been so blind? So oblivious?

"And then what?"

She frowned. "What do you mean?"

"I'd tracked Villa to Clancy's house." The dirty cartel money launderer Villa had been sent to kill. "Then what happened?" He wanted to know if she'd been close enough to have actually seen any of it.

"Marisol and the rest of her legal team showed up at

the target house. Villa took out Clancy and most of her team. He would have killed her too, if you hadn't been there. I saw you rescue her and followed you back to Miami."

"How did you see me?" he demanded. He'd only made the last second, knee-jerk decision to save Marisol because he knew her. They'd grown up in the same neighborhood. She was a nice person, not to mention innocent. He hadn't been able to stomach standing by and watching her die when he could prevent it.

That fateful decision had almost cost him his life.

Georgia maintained eye contact with him, unflinching in the face of his growing anger. He admired that.

Grown men who had considered themselves hardened killers had been known to weep and piss themselves when he showed up to confront them, long before he'd ever pulled out one of his blades and gotten to work on them. But not Georgia. She held her ground, undaunted.

"I was hidden in the front garden of the lot across the street. I had plenty of concealment and you were too busy saving Marisol to notice me," she said.

True. "And then you followed me to the marina in Miami," he finished.

She conceded that with a nod. "I knew Villa was close by, and I knew the FBI thought you were to blame for killing Clancy and the others. Only Marisol and I knew the truth and since I couldn't go to them to clear your name, I went onboard the boat you'd left her on and asked her to do it." She faltered for a second, looked down at her hands. "And then everything went to hell."

Yeah, it had, and he bore the scars to prove it.

"Why did you care about clearing my name?" he asked, heart rate picking up.

"Because. It wasn't fair for you to take the fall for

someone else's actions."

She was lying, holding something else back, he could see it in her eyes. It made him wonder. Had she wanted to help him because she had feelings for him?

He dragged in a breath, trying to make sense of it all. "But you helped them. My grandmother. Marisol. You helped them both when you didn't have to."

She'd tended to his grandmother with such gentleness, and she'd protected Marisol when Villa had attacked at the marina. He just couldn't accept that it had all been fake, that she'd done it to fool him. Didn't *want* to believe it.

He wanted to believe there was something of Julia alive in her still.

Her pale blue eyes flashed up to his, surprise and a little confusion in their depths. "They were innocent."

"But if I was one of your targets, hurting my grandmother would have been a good way to hurt me. You had the means and the opportunity."

Her expression transformed into one of disgust. "They were never my targets. They hadn't done anything wrong and didn't deserve to suffer. So I did what I could to help them. I may be a hitter, but I'm not some pathological killer. I still know right from wrong, no matter what you think of me or what I've done."

So that part of Julia was real at least. And he and she were far more alike than she realized.

"Then what about me? I was a risk to you after all was said and done, if I ever suspected what you were up to. You're a pro. I was a loose end you should have eliminated once I led you to Villa, for your own safety. So why didn't you kill me when you had the chance?" Logically, it didn't make sense to him.

The question hung between them like a bomb waiting to detonate.

Suddenly Georgia lurched from her chair, blurting

"None of your business," as she darted around the table.

Bautista exploded out of his chair and cut off her retreat to the stairs, bodily blocking her way. She stopped dead a few feet from him, her face turning even paler except for the bright pink fever spots in her cheeks.

"None of my business?" he repeated, his tone low, as dangerous as he felt in that moment. The beast he kept so carefully caged was rattling the bars, ready to break free. It wanted to devour her.

She raised her chin, stared right back at him with such defiance that part of him couldn't help but be impressed. "That's right. Now get out of my way. I'm done talking."

I don't think so, angel.

She'd protected his grandmother and Marisol. She'd tried to clear his name.

A woman like her wouldn't do all that unless she cared about him. A lot.

He stalked toward her, a pulse of savage satisfaction hitting him when she backed up, kept going until her hips hit the table.

He stopped inches away from her. Close enough to breathe in her tempting scent, for him to see the way her pupils dilated, and knew it wasn't from fear. Not if the way she curled her fingers around the edge of the table was any indication, as though she was afraid she might be tempted to touch him otherwise, and the way the pulse in her throat fluttered hard and fast.

She still wanted him. He knew she did, no matter how hard she tried to hide it. He just wasn't sure if there was anything more to it than simple chemistry.

His need to find out was hijacking his common sense in a way that could prove dangerous.

"Why?" he pressed, needing an answer. An honest answer. "Why didn't you try to kill me?" She'd been so far off his radar in terms of seeing her as a threat, she might even have managed it. Another sobering realization.

She was breathing fast now, her breasts rising and falling in a rapid rhythm that might have distracted him at any other time. He could see the outline of her nipples beaded against her shirt. Aroused, confused, and fighting both like hell.

It made his blood run even hotter. The beast inside him roared, demanding to be let loose.

He didn't dare set it free, because once he put his mouth on her, he knew he wouldn't be able to stop.

Her eyes searched his, full of irritation and something else he couldn't define. "Because I couldn't, okay? Is that what you wanted to hear?"

Shaking his head, he stopped fighting the need to touch her and took her face between his hands. Her cheeks were warm, too warm, but her skin was so damn soft and despite everything he wanted to kiss her, take care of her.

All the lies she'd told him and herself didn't matter right now. He wanted to see her let her guard down for him. Wanted to pull her close and hold her tight, tell her everything would be okay because he would *make* it okay, if only she'd open up and trust him.

Georgia froze at his touch and drew in a shaky breath, her gaze filling with unease.

He didn't let go. Couldn't. This was too important. He still woke at night with her scent in his nose, still heard her voice echoing in his ears as she cried out his name, and still felt the shape of her body imprinted in his skin.

He couldn't go on like this, the not knowing was killing him. Apparently the universe wasn't done jerking him around yet though because as it turned out, living without her was a thousand times harder than dying for her.

"What about the rest?" There was no way she could misunderstand what he meant. That night he'd spent in her bed was permanently burned into his mind. "Was that all a lie too? Part of your cover?"

A flash of anger obliterated that trace of vulnerability in her eyes. "You lied to me too."

He shook his head. He'd even tried to tell her what kind of man he was. "No I didn't. Not ever. I withheld certain things for safety reasons, but I never outright lied to you about who I was or tried to manipulate you." But she'd done exactly that to him.

She swallowed but didn't deny it, her body stiff. Because she knew he was right.

He gave her a tiny shake, kept his hold firm but gentle, careful not to hurt her. God dammit, he was aching inside, felt like his chest might explode. "Was it all a lie, angel?"

She closed her eyes at the endearment, the word he'd whispered to her that night while he'd caressed and kissed every inch of her body. "Let me go," she whispered.

I wish the hell I could, but I can't.

He leaned down to rest his forehead against hers. She flinched but didn't fight him, and now he could feel the fine tremors wracking her slender frame. So afraid to come clean, to admit she'd felt something for him.

"Just tell me," he whispered back, insistent. "Give me that much."

Her eyes opened. He raised his head enough for her to focus on him, waited as she searched his gaze. The torment there speared him.

"Why? What does it matter now?" she asked, her voice a mere wisp of a sound.

"Because it does," he answered. Her response meant *everything*, and it was the reason he was standing here in this kitchen with her now.

It was the main reason he'd put his signature on that damn contract and signed his life away to the NSA. For this one answer and the prayer that there might still be a chance… "It matters to me."

A few taut seconds passed before she answered. "You already know the answer."

Not good enough. He wanted to shake her for real, force the truth out of her. His grip on the sides of her face tightened a fraction. "*Say* it."

"*No*," she cried.

Before he could figure out whether she'd just answered his question or if she'd merely put an end to the conversation, she wrenched her head free, shoved both hands against his chest hard enough to knock him back a half step and scrambled past him.

Facing him warily at the bottom of the stairs, she shook her head, and the unexpected sheen of tears in her eyes hit him in the stomach like a sledgehammer. "Like I said, I'm done talking. Now just stay the hell away from me." With that final command she turned and raced up the stairs.

Alone in the kitchen with his heart in his throat, he closed his eyes and took his first deep breath since she'd come out of her bedroom.

She cared. Or at least, she had.

And it fucking terrified her.

Bautista knew exactly how she felt. Because they had unfinished business that needed to be dealt with.

And there was no way in hell he could ever stay away from her now.

Chapter Twelve

Nico jerked awake when his phone rang, disoriented for a moment until he realized his head was resting against the window. Grabbing the phone from the passenger seat, he winced as he sat up to answer it, surprised to find that it was morning already.

Sleeping in two-hour snatches in the front seat of his rental car for the past two days wasn't the most comfortable thing, but he'd needed to be able to move at any moment. Disappointment filled him when he saw it wasn't Melissa calling. She should have his burner phone number on her phone's display. He missed her like hell.

"Yeah," he answered.

"Anything?" Diego asked, his tone uncharacteristically tense.

He sighed. All the leads he'd followed had been dead ends. He'd searched for any sign of Georgia and Bautista and so far come up empty. "No, not a damn thing. I'm going to try one more time and then I'm heading to Maryland. She's not in any of the hospitals I checked in the area. They've probably taken her to headquarters at Fort Meade by now."

"I don't think so. And I just got a tip that seems like it would be worth following up on."

Nico rubbed the spot where his neck and left shoulder met, stretched the tight muscle there. "I'm listening."

"I got a call from one of my sources, who's been following up on her banking information. Apparently there's a safety deposit box listed under an alias she's used at a bank in Asheville. My contact called to check it out, said he was a fed investigating a case pertaining to her. They wouldn't give him anything concrete over the phone. My contact's trying to trace some phone numbers right now to see if we can locate Rycroft but I'm not holding my breath waiting for anything to come of it."

Yeah, trying to trace an NSA encrypted phone was a waste of fucking time, so he wasn't even sure why they were bothering. "Which bank?"

His boss named a well-known bank and a location that wasn't far from where Nico was. "It's not that far away from Bryson City. My bet is she's got whatever evidence she gathered hidden in that safety deposit box. A hard drive, documents, who knows."

"Why here, in the middle of nowhere?"

"Because it's not on the beaten path. I think she went to hide out at that cabin because it was off grid and close to the bank. I think she was going to retrieve the deposit box as soon as she was well enough. My gut says she was going to leak the evidence to either the feds or the media, stir up a public shit storm, hoping to put a spotlight on us in the hopes that it would make it easier to target us."

If she did, they were screwed, because the only safe place to hide would be out of the country. Not easy to do when every intelligence agency in the country was looking for you.

Nico glanced at his watch. "How long ago did your contact call the bank?"

"Three hours. A few minutes after opening."

If Rycroft's people knew about it, they had a big head start on them then. Nico could make it there in under an hour, well before noon. "I'll go check it out. Is your contact still monitoring this?"

"I'll make sure he keeps on top of it and updates us with any developments. Keep trying your other sources to find her in the meantime. Trace whatever you can and keep digging." A heavy pause. "I don't need to remind you how critical it is that you find her and Bautista and deal with them immediately. There's too much at stake here."

Including his future with Melissa. Everything he wanted in life hinged on him pulling off these hits. That was all the motivation he needed.

He was determined to take Bautista down one way or another, prove he was the best. He was sick and fucking tired of everyone seeing him as merely some kind of understudy to the fabled enforcer. At this point he was ready to move on with his life with the big payout at the end of all this.

"I know. I got this. They can't stay invisible forever. Sooner or later they'll resurface." And when they did, he'd strike.

Diego grunted. "Let's hope so. I'll be in touch."

Nico ended the call and started the ignition. The safe deposit box seemed an unlikely bet, but it might be the only chance of finding them now. He'd go there straight away and set up surveillance, make sure he didn't miss Georgia and Bautista if they showed up.

If they did, it would make his life easier. He'd be able to take both of them out in a single op.

****

Amazing, what a solid sleep and a little perspective

could do for a woman.

After what had happened in the kitchen with Miguel late yesterday afternoon, most people in her position might have holed up in their room for the rest of their stay at the safe house.

Georgia might be antisocial and socially awkward in a lot of ways, but she wasn't a coward.

First thing the next morning she marched down the stairs to the kitchen and made herself toast and coffee while Rycroft and Miguel both watched her from the table where they were going over what looked like maps. Briar was still upstairs getting some much needed sleep, since the three of them kept taking shifts to make sure Georgia didn't attempt some kind of escape.

"How are you feeling?" Rycroft asked, a mug of coffee in hand as he stood next to the table. The light coming through the blinds behind him made all the silver streaks stand out in his brown hair.

"Good." Her fever was gone, she only hurt where she was bruised instead of all over, and she was ravenous for food. All good signs. She was definitely on the mend and would make her escape soon, the first instant any of them relaxed their guard.

Putting her back to both of them, trying and failing to ignore the weight of Miguel's stare, she bit into her toast and stared out the small window over the sink that overlooked the backyard. Every cell in her body was aware of his exact position in the room, and that he was still watching her.

And her body definitely remembered the heat in his eyes when he'd cornered her last night. Worse, she'd liked it way too much for her own comfort.

The sun was up but it was hidden behind a thick wall of dark gray clouds. Over the back fence she could see a ball being tossed around. So strange, to be in an NSA safe house in the middle of a neighborhood like this one.

The neighbors had no idea that she was a wanted woman who basically had a bull's eye painted on her chest, or that she posed a threat to them just by being here because of the people hunting her. Miguel might have killed the CIA assassin back at the cabin, but she knew without a doubt there would be others coming.

If they could find her. Another reason why she intended to be on the move shortly. She didn't want Miguel or Briar in danger because of her.

"We'll be leaving tonight," Rycroft added. "Soon as it gets dark."

"To where?" she asked without turning around.

"You tell me."

At that, she lowered the slice of toast she'd been munching on and turned to face him. He was watching her calmly, his posture relaxed. "You want me to tell you where to go?"

He smirked at the edge in her voice. "No, because I'm pretty sure you'd just tell me to go to hell and leave it at that. What I want to know is where you've stashed the evidence."

She raised an eyebrow, kept her expression impassive. "Who said I had any evidence to stash?" She did, of course; she just wondered how the hell he knew about it.

He shrugged, took a sip of coffee. "Call it…intuition."

Then it hit her. She narrowed her eyes. "Trinity."

Had to be. There was no other explanation because no one else knew about the flash drive except her fellow Valkyrie. Georgia had made two copies. One was in a safe deposit box near the cabin where she'd hidden out. The other was in a different bank in Connecticut.

He didn't deny it. "Briar finally got hold of her last night and updated her about you. I guess she was worried you were dead. During their conversation, the topic came up and she mentioned you had evidence against certain people. So. Where is it?"

In her peripheral she could see Miguel watching her, arms folded across his powerful chest. She didn't dare look at him. "Sure she didn't tell you that part too?"

Rycroft's lips curved upward. "Maybe I want to see how honest you're willing to be with me."

The bastard already knew where the evidence was, she could tell. It infuriated her. She'd hidden the flash drive under an alias, in a bank outside of Asheville to distance herself and everyone else from it, until she had reason to retrieve it. A reason she'd gotten when the hunters had closed in on her.

If he knew the location, then it didn't make sense why he was even asking her about it. "I guess you've got a warrant for it already then? Or there's one in the works?"

"I could go that route," he agreed. "But I'd prefer it if you shared it with me on your own. As a show of faith." He paused a moment. "Did you think over what I said last night?"

She had, but mostly she'd thought about the things Miguel had said. And the things he'd made her feel. Frightening, long-buried things she was finding nearly impossible to fight. She was already weakening where he was concerned; she had to get the hell away from him. "Yes."

"And?"

"And it's a nice offer, but you'll understand why I'm going to pass." Especially now that Miguel was involved. She couldn't work with him, be this close to him for any length of time and maintain her façade of indifference. Every time he looked at her, her heart squeezed. It was torture. For both of them, she was pretty sure.

"You could," Rycroft insisted. "Accepting my offer just makes this whole thing easier on all of us."

But the two men she'd been planning to kill would live. That wasn't acceptable.

Last night as she'd laid staring at the ceiling in the darkness with Briar stretched out next to her, she'd almost convinced herself to agree to Rycroft's terms and use the team to help her get close to her targets so she could kill them. But this morning she knew that was impossible. Not when she ached so badly to recapture what she'd had with Miguel for that short time in Miami.

"Leave her alone," Miguel muttered from his seat. "She gave you her answer."

Rycroft flicked him a sideways glance, his expression closed.

Footsteps on the stairs made her glance over her shoulder in time to see Briar appear at the bottom. "Morning. Did I miss anything exciting?" The former Valkyrie headed for the coffee pot, bleary-eyed.

Georgia was glad she wasn't the only one suffering from lack of sleep. "Yeah, I found out you and Trinity have been talking behind my back."

Briar stopped and turned to face her with an almost hurt expression on her face. "She called *me*. I've been trying to reach her for the past week to see if she knew anything that might help us find you, and last night she finally called."

Georgia shook her head, getting angry all over again. "I can't believe she told you about the flash drive." Secrets told between them were supposed to be sacred.

"It's a flash drive?" Rycroft said, his gaze sharp. "What's on it?"

She threw him a dark look. He wasn't stupid. If he hadn't known that already after Briar spoke to Trinity, he likely would already have guessed it for himself. "Enough to bury the men responsible for Janaia and Frank's murders."

"Then why not give it to me so I can make sure that

happens?"

Because I don't trust you.

She knew firsthand how corrupt government agents—*agencies*, for that matter—could be. She trusted Briar to some degree, Miguel the most in this scenario, but still not enough to give up control to any of them. "I can make it happen all on my own."

Her way. *Her* timeline. And once she leaked the evidence, once the story broke on national media, she'd be ready.

She'd already be in place, give her targets just enough time to absorb the news that they were wanted traitors before she put a bullet through their blackened hearts. She'd planned to take them out first and then leak the evidence, but now it had to be the other way around.

That's the way she wanted it, and that's the way it was going to happen.

"Georgia," Briar began, but Georgia cut her off with a hard look and even harder words.

"No. Whatever happened to loyalty? Huh? Didn't you just say to me the other night that our tats still mean something to you?"

"It does mean something to me. I *am* loyal." Her expression screamed frustration.

"You went straight to Rycroft after that phone call, instead of coming to me!" she accused.

"Because he's right," Briar answered matter-of-factly. "He can help make sure whoever is involved gets taken down. Only with him taking the lead, you won't go off and carry out two more hits that will either land you in prison for the rest of your life, or dead." She raised both eyebrows and stared right back, unapologetic.

Only if they can prove I did it, Georgia thought. And she certainly wouldn't make that easy for them to do.

Rycroft set his mug down on the counter and spoke to Miguel. "Your turn to watch her for a while. Briar and

I have things to discuss downstairs." With that he headed down the steps that led to the basement.

Mug of coffee in hand, Briar followed him, then stopped next to the doorway for a long moment and watched her with dark, eyes assessing. "Work with us on this. You can still get what you want and afterward you can get your life back. It's a win-win, for all of us."

When Georgia didn't respond, Briar shook her head and continued. "Aren't you tired? Tired of looking over your shoulder everywhere you go, wondering if every person you see is there to kill you?"

A hollowness opened up in her chest. It *was* exhausting. Not to mention lonely. And the thought of going back to that now that Miguel was here... Walking away from him was going to be hard. Maybe the hardest thing she'd ever done.

Briar pressed on. "Don't you wish you had a safe place to go home to every night? Someone to go home to?" She glanced over to Miguel and back, her meaning clear. "You forget, Georgia, I know you. Better than you seem to think, because until last December, I was living the same way you are, just existing from one job to the next. So I know you want more from this life than what you've gotten so far. It's time you set aside your need for revenge and started living again. It's not too late. Think about that."

The brutally honest words slammed into her heart like a hollow point round, shredding it. She swallowed as she watched Briar disappear down the stairs after Rycroft, stood there like an idiot at the sink, unable to move.

Could she really do that? Get her life back after everything that had happened, all she'd done?

It was dangerous to even want that. She was too damaged, too lost to ever have a real life again, let alone a relationship.

"She's right," Miguel said quietly after a minute.

She swung around to face him, immediately on the defensive. "About what?"

"All of it."

The way he watched her was unnerving, those dark eyes intense. It was as if he could see into her soul or something. "You lived the same kind of life as us," she flung back, meaning her and Briar. And Trinity. "If not for what happened in Miami, you would still be doing the same damn thing right now, so don't sit there and tell me you—"

"I was tired of it. I wanted out."

She blinked at that, shocked. "What?"

He nodded. "Villa was my last job. I called Perez on my way to Key West and told him so."

Right after leaving her bed.

He didn't say that, but he didn't have to, the heat and regret in his eyes said it for him. And it couldn't be coincidence that he'd made the call right after leaving her that morning.

Don't read anything into it. It doesn't mean anything.

But her heart wouldn't listen. The tiny bubble of hope inside her expanded, a painful pressure beneath her ribcage, squeezing her heart and lungs like an invisible fist.

She struggled to remain impassive. "And he was just going to let you walk away afterward? Just like that?" She found that hard to believe.

Perez was notoriously ruthless, and she still suspected he was somehow linked to Frank's murder, even though she couldn't prove it yet. The evidence on the others was solid. Emails she'd unencrypted with Trinity's help.

Recorded snatches of phone conversations. And the forensic evidence from Frank's house. She'd managed to get it all before the hitters could send in a cleanup crew.

"I wasn't giving him a choice," Miguel answered, his arrogant expression somehow only making him hotter. He had been the best in the business as far as hitters went, and he knew it. "But yeah. I think he would've let me go."

She couldn't believe it. There was no way he could have done the things he had, earned the reputation he had, and still be this naïve about Perez. "There's no way he would have let you go. Ever."

A muscle flexed in his jaw. "You don't know him."

"No, but I still don't see him letting you walk away after everything was said and done."

"I wasn't going to stay in Miami," he said, his tone full of sarcasm, "and I wasn't planning to stay in the States. I had a strategy put together and it would have worked if I hadn't run into a couple FBI bullets that day."

She hid a wince at the reminder. God, she'd never forget the terrible helplessness and grief she'd felt when he'd laid bleeding out in front of her.

The silence stretched out between them, each second making the guilt and yearning twist harder in her chest. She needed distance from him, space, and she needed it right *now*. "I'm gonna go take a shower," she muttered, and fled up the stairs.

She didn't risk stopping to grab anything on her way to the connecting bathroom because she knew Miguel would be only seconds behind her. Rycroft had ordered him to watch her, and he would.

The bedroom door didn't lock but the bathroom one did. She turned the lock and let out a slow breath, needing time to think. Alone.

Reaching into the tub, she pulled the shower curtain into place and turned on the faucet. When the water heated up, she hit the valve for the shower. Water rushed against the bottom of the tub in a soothing rhythm.

Turning to face the mirror, she stared at her reflection. She looked…haunted, and that's exactly how she felt.

Briar had been right about all of it.

She *was* lonely. She was tired of being on the run, of being alone. But what was the point of stopping now? The only man she'd ever fallen for was Miguel, and they would never work out.

Yeah, he still wanted her, might want to rip her clothes off and fuck her six ways from Sunday, but that didn't mean he wanted a relationship. And even if he did, that was impossible. Neither of them would ever be free now, whether she turned over the flash drive and went along with Rycroft's plan or not.

And she already knew it would slowly kill her to have him so close and have nothing more.

In the mirror, her expression hardened.

To hell with this. She had a job to do, one she'd sworn to finish, no matter what. If she stayed she had no bargaining power and Rycroft called the shots.

Maybe she wasn't at a hundred percent yet, but close enough. She had more than enough strength to escape and finish this on her own. But first, she needed to retrieve the flash drive in that safety deposit box in Asheville before Rycroft did.

Mind made up, she glanced toward the locked door. Miguel was probably out there in her room already. Rycroft and Briar were still down in the basement. If she was quiet enough, the noise of the shower might cover any sound she made getting out the window.

Her boots were set beside the vanity cabinet, along with the change of clothes Briar had given her. Lacing them up, she snagged the pistol on the counter and headed for the small, rectangular-shaped window set into the wall beside the toilet. It wasn't loaded, but she could get ammo later.

With careful motions she unlocked the window, slid it open and boosted herself upward, throwing her right leg out of it to balance herself over the thin frame. She scanned the side of the house and the backyard.

There was nothing to grab onto on the side of the house. The drop wasn't too bad, she could swing out and jump—

"Don't."

Her heart almost seized at the familiar voice behind her.

Whipping her head around, she found Miguel standing inside the bathroom doorway, a coldly furious expression on his face and his dark eyes burning a hole right through her.

Chapter Thirteen

Miguel took a menacing step forward. By reflex Georgia drew the pistol from the back of her pants and aimed it at his chest. Hopefully he wouldn't know it wasn't loaded.

He stopped, gave her a sardonic curl of his lips. "You gonna shoot me?"

She held the weapon steady. "Just stay back. Don't come any closer." Damn, her heart was pounding. "I'm leaving and you can't stop me."

"You know I can't let you go."

Because he was under direct orders to keep tabs on her from one of the NSA's top agents. If he disobeyed or tried to help her, he'd be thrown back in jail. "So I'm a hostage now?"

Ignoring the jab, he jerked his chin at the window opening. "From this height you could break something when you land. And even if you didn't, there are three of us here and one of you. You won't get far."

"Two, if I shoot you right now." Could he tell she was bluffing?

He took a step forward, lifted a mocking eyebrow.

"Then do it. But even if you managed to escape all of us, it's only a matter of time before you wind up dead. Given what and who you're up against, the odds aren't in your favor. You wouldn't last long out there alone now, and you know it."

Her lips pressed into a thin line of annoyance at the dare and his hard-hitting words. She was well aware of the odds she faced.

"Stop," she warned sharply, a tendril of panic winding around her chest. Her self-control was already shaky when it came to him. If he touched her, she was afraid he might shatter the rapidly crumbling wall between them.

He didn't stop. Just kept coming, one slow, deliberate step at a time, never looking away from her.

Georgia's heart sank even as it beat faster. The arrogant bastard might not know the weapon was unloaded, but he knew she couldn't pull the trigger regardless. He somehow knew she couldn't stomach the thought of hurting him.

Which meant she was trapped in this freaking window and there'd be no more chance of escape. After this, the entire team would keep a closer eye on her than ever. They would frame it in a way that they could insist she wasn't a hostage, but that's *exactly* what she was and it made her furious.

Paralyzed, she sat perched in the open window, not daring to move as he stopped directly in front of her. They stared at each other in the taut silence, until he reached up to grasp her wrist with one hand.

His long fingers curled around it, firm yet gentle, his touch shooting sparks of heat throughout her body. She barely stifled a gasp.

Staring into her eyes, he reached his other hand up to gently ease the weapon from her numb fingers and set it on the counter behind him. "Come here."

The low command in the deep timbre of his voice caused more heat to pool deep in her belly. There was nothing to do but allow him to help her down. She only half-resisted as he gripped her waist and pulled her back into the bathroom, placing her gently on her feet before him.

Too close. Way too close.

She leaned back, realized she had her spine pressed against the wall to avoid touching him. Because she was afraid if she did, she wouldn't be able to stop.

Without pause he reached up behind her to shut and lock the window. And when he looked down at her again, the mix of hunger and yearning in those dark eyes stole what little air remained in her lungs.

Desire pooled in her belly, thick and hot.

Lifting a hand, he brushed a lock of hair away from her temple with one finger, the light caress scattering goose bumps over her skin. He smelled so damn good and the urge to tangle her fingers in his hair and pull his mouth to hers was almost overwhelming.

Their chemistry was insane, had been right from the start, potent enough that part of her was considering ripping off his clothes just to feel that hard, lean body naked against her one more time.

All these months she'd thought he was dead. Now he was right in front of her, and it was clear he still wanted her. She'd lost so much in her life, been denied so many things, any sense of normal.

Except for that one night with him. The urge to take what he was offering was so acute she could barely breathe.

He placed both hands flat on the wall on either side of her head, caging her in with his big body. So close she could smell him, feel his warmth reaching out to her. Tormenting her with the promise of what he could do to her.

His gaze dipped to her mouth briefly before coming back to hers. "Was this part of it real?" he murmured, his smoky voice a seductive caress to her over-stimulated system.

She didn't pretend not to understand what he meant, all her senses heightened, the anticipation building higher with every heartbeat. Her eyes dropped to his mouth, the only hint of softness about him, set within the thick, dark stubble covering his lower face. Her lips tingled with the need to feel it on hers.

As though sensing her thoughts, Miguel leaned in closer, his chest and thighs barely brushing hers. She sucked in a sharp breath as another rush of heat tightened her nipples, made her breasts and the flesh between her thighs ache with the need to feel his hands and mouth on them.

"Was it?" His voice was a husky, seductive murmur. "Because it felt fucking real to me."

Yes, it was real, she wanted to blurt out. Only her ingrained sense of self-preservation kept her from saying it aloud. This was crazy. He was a weakness she couldn't afford.

He leaned in until only a breath of air separated their lips. Tension poured off him in tangible waves. She gazed into his eyes, felt herself get lost in those dark depths.

"It's never been like that for me before," he admitted. "Tell me that part wasn't a lie, at least."

It had been the most incredible night of her life. And she couldn't bear him thinking it was all a lie. But she didn't dare say it aloud.

Drowning under the weight of his gaze and the longing she heard in his voice, the last of her resistance crumbled. Dying for his kiss, unable to take it any longer, Georgia plunged her fingers into his hair and leaned up to cover his mouth with hers.

Instantly Miguel captured her head between his

hands and kissed her back, a low groan tearing from his throat.

It was like pouring accelerant on a fire.

A tidal wave of need swept through her, threatening to drown her and she didn't care. She couldn't think, could only feel. The only thing that mattered was now, this moment, being able to touch and taste him again, consequences be damned.

His tongue twined with hers, the kiss turning frantic. With a rough growl he turned them, walked her backward until her spine flattened against the wall beside the shower. A heartbeat later that hard, powerful body was pressed flush to hers.

Georgia moaned into his mouth and held on tight. She gripped his broad shoulders, fingers digging into the muscle there as she wrapped her legs around his waist. He grabbed her butt with one hand, holding her to him as he rubbed his confined erection right over the pulsing ache between her thighs.

He trailed hot kisses down her chin, over her jaw to the side of her neck. The rush of water beside them muted her gasps as his mouth hit every sensitive spot, the rasp of his stubble a rough counterpoint to the heated glide of his tongue.

It wasn't enough. She needed to feel him skin to skin.

Impatient, she grabbed the bottom of his T-shirt and pulled upward. He stopped kissing her long enough to reach down and peel it over his head, flinging it aside. She flattened her hands on the hard ridges of his pecs, her gaze immediately going to the puckered scars near the base of his throat.

With a distressed sound she pressed her lips to the marks, kept her hands tight to his chest so she could feel his heart thundering beneath her palms. So strong and steady, vital and alive when she'd been so sure she'd lost him forever.

She rubbed her cheek against his chest and closed her eyes, remembering those agonizing few minutes when she'd watched him fade away right in front of her on that boat.

Emotion crashed over her. "God," she whispered against his hot skin, fighting the rush of tears as she clung to him. It had gutted her to watch him die. For weeks afterward she'd walked around in a fog, feeling like someone had reached into her chest and ripped her heart out of her body.

A strong hand cradled her jaw, tipped her head up until she met his eyes. "Tell me it was real," he rasped out. "*Say* it."

There was no way she could deny him that. Not now. "It was real. I was more real with you than I've ever been with anyone," she admitted in a shaky whisper, and sought his mouth once more.

Relief and lust slammed into Bautista so hard it left him dizzy. He growled in triumph and took that sexy, swollen mouth again, desperate to get inside her, exploit this moment of weakness she'd just let him see.

She met every stroke of his tongue, each roll of his hips, her hands sliding over his naked torso with greedy intent. He wanted to claim her right here and now. To fucking *own* her.

He left the shower running, using the white noise to drown out any sounds they might make if either Briar or Rycroft came upstairs to check on them. Not that he gave a shit what either of them thought about him and Georgia. She was the sole reason for him taking this job and he was going to savor every moment of this.

But it wasn't enough to simply strip her the way he was dying to and plunge into her heat. The darkest part of him needed her stripped bare emotionally too, for her to be wide open and vulnerable like she had been the last time, desperate for release before he gave it to her.

And he would give it to her. As many times as she wanted before they were forced to leave the sanctuary of her bedroom and face the real world again.

But when they left it, he wanted to be absolutely sure they'd be facing the world together. He wouldn't accept anything less. Not with Georgia.

God, she made him so damn hot he could barely think. Easing back from her, he pushed her thighs from his hips, smothered her protest with another blistering kiss before peeling her shirt over her head and pulling her bra off. The soft mounds of her breasts spilled into his waiting hands, the taut pink centers begging to be sucked.

He was only too happy to oblige.

"I've dreamed about doing this again so many times," he said in a rough voice. One hand fisting in the back of her hair, he gripped her hip with the other and lowered his mouth to a straining nipple.

The instant he took it into his mouth her fingers clenched in his hair and she let out a ragged gasp, her spine bowing. Pushing her deeper into his mouth in a silent demand for more.

Her head fell back against the wall, her eyes drifting closed and an expression of rapture on her face. Fucking gorgeous, and all his. He was going to burn this moment into her mind, imprint himself in her skin so she'd never be free of him again, no matter what happened after this.

He wanted her to crave him with this same uncontrollable need she unleashed in him.

Sucking and teasing her other nipple, he reached between them and made short work of getting her pants undone and down her legs, taking her panties with them. She kicked them free of her feet and stood there completely naked in front of him.

For a second he thought his brain might melt. She was the hottest fucking thing he'd ever seen in his life, all lean, taut lines and creamy skin that was so damn soft, in direct contrast to her edginess.

Continuing to tease her nipples with his mouth, he smoothed one hand up her inner thigh. She shivered and widened her stance, sank her teeth into her lower lip as she watched him, waiting for him to touch the soft flesh between her thighs.

But he was enjoying himself too much to end their torment yet, no matter how badly his cock ached.

With slow, deliberate caresses he trailed his fingertips up her thigh, following the tendons on the inside and stopping just short of the tender folds he was dying to taste. He rubbed that smooth skin slowly, letting his fingers barely brush against the edge of her sex. She squirmed, made a mewling sound and pressed her hips toward him, still clutching his head to her breast.

Finally, he grazed that slick flesh, tormenting her with the promise of more, building the anticipation. God, she was so wet for him.

Her breathing was erratic now, tiny tremors shaking the muscles in her thighs and belly. Releasing her nipple, ignoring her groan of frustration, he pressed his lips to her stomach, added a little more pressure with his fingers.

"Miguel," she warned in a tight voice, tugging on his hair with a sharp movement. "You'd better damn well put out the fire you started or I swear to God I'll—" Her threat ended in a breathless gasp when he knelt before her, seized her hips in a firm grip and pressed his mouth to her tender core.

A soft, high-pitched cry left her lips as he opened his mouth and stroked his tongue along her folds, stopping directly over her clit. He let his own eyes close as he tasted her, teasing with soft flutters and licks.

Her fingers dug harder into his scalp, the prick of her nails making the hunger roar hotter. She was whimpering now, lost in her need, her hips moving in a ceaseless motion as she rubbed against his tongue.

He'd memorized everything about her response that night in Miami. What she liked, what she loved, what made her crazy.

He put it to good use now, driving her up to the peak but refusing to give her the release she was fighting for. Over and over he licked the taut bundle of nerves at the top of her sex, enjoying every cry he pulled out of her, every tremble in the muscles of her thighs and belly.

"God, please make me come," she gasped out. "I need it so bad."

Not until he was inside her. In Miami he'd taken her in the dark, his only regret from that night.

This time he wanted to see everything. He wanted them joined as intimately as possible, stare at her face while he made her come in broad daylight.

Surging to his feet, he fisted one hand in her hair as he took her mouth in a deep, urgent kiss and wrenched his pants open. His cock sprang free, hard and aching, desperate to plunge into her. Georgia grabbed his shoulders and wound a leg around his hip, her urgent cries drowned by the kiss.

With one hand cradling her ass he shifted her until the head of his cock lodged against her entrance. Then he broke the kiss, panting as he stared down into her face.

Her blue eyes were drugged with pleasure, with need. "Miguel," she groaned, arching into his hold.

You're fucking MINE, he thought in triumph.

Tightening his arm around her hips, he thrust upward, burying himself in her heat with one slow, inexorable stroke.

Her lips parted and her eyes squeezed shut at the feel of him inside her, a guttural cry of pleasure exploding from her. God, she was so tight, so hot around his cock. He sucked in a breath and locked his knees, ready to explode, fighting it.

She writhed in his hold, her movements tight, urgent. "Miguel," she pleaded, her voice rough, desperate. "Miguel, *now*."

Yes. *Now*.

Easing his hips back, he waited a beat before plunging deep once more, releasing her hair to slide his fingers between their bodies, finding and stroking the hard bud of her clit. The back of her head thumped against the wall, an expression of erotic torture spreading over her face.

Beautiful, angel. Miguel took her nice and slow, making her wait, forcing her to endure the ride as the pleasure spiraled higher and higher.

She was shaking now, her legs locked around him, hands digging into his shoulders with a frantic grip. When he couldn't stand it a second longer, when her desperate cries echoed in his ears, he took her hard and fast.

Georgia sobbed out his name and flexed backward, her lithe body forming a beautiful arch as the pleasure crested and burst.

Heart thundering against his ribs, he stared at her, drinking in every detail, relishing the moment as she surrendered to him, her core milking his cock. A groan ripped free of his chest.

He buried his face in the curve of her neck and thrust hard, roughly chasing after his own release. The muscles at the base of his spine tightened, a warning tingle spreading up from his balls and then he let himself go, exploding inside her.

He couldn't breathe, could only hold on, locked inside her as the orgasm hit. He was vaguely aware of saying her name, of her hands stroking over his bare shoulders and back, the warmth of her surrounding him.

When he finally found the strength to open his eyes and raise his head he found her watching him with a softness, a vulnerability in her gaze he'd never seen before. "So now what?" she whispered, running her fingers through his hair.

Catching her chin between his thumb and forefinger, he leaned in to capture her lips in a slow, lingering kiss. She sighed and melted for him, twining her arms around his neck.

He pulled back and lifted an eyebrow. "Any more questions?"

Searching his eyes, she gave him a tender smile that turned his heart inside out and shook her head. "Not at the moment, no."

"Good. Because you're all mine." He reached over to kill the shower switch. Without releasing her, he kicked his pants and underwear free then carried her out into the bedroom where he curled up in the big bed and held her tight in his arms.

Chapter Fourteen

"**G**ood morning, how may I help you?"

Nico gave the young female bank teller a polite smile. "I'd like to set up an account and open a safety deposit box, actually. A small one is fine. I just moved into town."

He leaned casually against the counter, one hand in the pocket of his dress slacks. He'd changed into business attire for the occasion, dark slacks and a white button-down shirt.

Professional but nondescript, completely forgettable. Which was exactly what he wanted.

"Of course, sir." She listed off the fees and the procedure and he agreed to the terms. "I'll get that all started for you. May I have two pieces of photo ID please? And here's the paperwork you'll need to fill out."

Nico handed over two pieces from a fake identity he'd made with a local address, and took the forms. He sat in the chair she indicated and began filling them out, sneaking little glances around while she worked on her computer.

He'd already noted the position of the security

cameras outside and inside the bank when he'd first entered. Not that he was worried about being caught on camera because his IDs were solid and he wasn't on any wanted lists.

Only because the feds hadn't been able to link him to any of his hits, he thought with a surge of pride.

Once the forms were filled out he handed them back, gave her a polite smile when he caught her watching him. He wasn't a bad looking guy but he didn't want her or anyone else in here to remember his face once he left.

She blushed a little and got back to work, verifying everything on his forms and checking his ID. "Very good, Mr. Allen. Do you have the item or items you'd like to put in the deposit box with you today?"

"Yes."

"Great. I'll just go get my manager to get everything set up for you. She'll take you back into the vault once it's all ready."

"Thank you." He passed the time waiting for the manager to process everything by scrolling through his phone. No new messages from his boss.

The bank was quiet, not surprising given how small this town was. He couldn't imagine it ever got too busy here so it should be easy enough to figure out if anyone had gained access to Georgia Randall's safety deposit box.

As long as his plan worked.

After a few minutes a middle-aged woman wearing glasses and a skirt suit emerged from an office in the back. "Mr. Allen." They shook hands and she gestured to the back. "Here's the key to your safety deposit box. If you'll come with me, I'll take you into the vault now."

Nico kept his eyes open for more cameras on the way to the vault, noting their position in case he had to break in after hours. The manager unlocked the vault and took him over to the safety deposit box area. Immediately he scanned the box numbers and found the one supposedly belonging to Georgia, at the top of the third row.

The manager opened the logbook, asked him to sign in and checked his signature to verify it. But his entry was the second one on a new page, someone having visited the vault an hour before him. Not Laura Johnson, the identity he'd been told to look for.

After pulling out his box, he followed the manager to a viewing area.

"Take your time," she said with a smile, and turned her back.

As expected, he didn't spot any cameras in here, which made sense for the bank's privacy policy. He used his new key and her master key to open the box.

As he dug into his pockets for the items he'd brought to put inside it—a replica antique pocket watch and other trinkets he'd picked up at a junk store before coming here—he coughed.

Two times. Four.

Sucking in a gasping breath, he faked a full-on coughing fit.

The manager turned back to him, an alarmed expression on her face. "Are you all right?"

He waved a hand at her, bent over with one hand on the desk as he pretended to wheeze through the bouts. "Sorry. Just getting…over a bad cold," he gasped.

She frowned in concern. "Can I get you some water?"

Bingo. He nodded. "Please."

The second she hurried out of there, he raced to the logbook and flipped it open. Still coughing to keep up the ruse, he scanned the last few pages, looking for any familiar names but didn't see any. He worked fast, knowing he only had moments.

Pretending to stifle the coughs, he listened. Footsteps on the carpeted hall outside the vault told him his time was up. Shutting the logbook, he rushed across the room and was back in position at the desk when the woman walked in with a cup of water.

He let out another few harsh coughs, gave her a pained smile as he reached for the cup. "Thanks," he whispered and gulped half of it.

"Tara mentioned that you've just moved here," she said, taking the cup back when he handed it to her. "The pharmacist at the local drug store is really good. Phil. You should go talk to him, because you don't sound too good."

"I'm okay." He wiped his face, expelled a shaky breath. "Thanks for the water. I'm all done here." He locked the box and left it for her.

Outside in his rental he immediately drove to a secluded area of town, changed and called Diego. "She hasn't accessed the box recently. At least not that I can tell."

Although that didn't mean much, since she likely used fake IDs all the time too. And he couldn't be sure whether that box was in fact the one she used. If Rycroft knew about it, he might have already sent someone in with a warrant and had the bank drill the original box open.

"Want me to get it?" She had to have other copies somewhere, but they didn't know where, so for now this was their best option.

"That would only solve part of the problem. No. If she's with Rycroft, then he'll know she's got evidence. If he doesn't know about the safety deposit box already, he will soon, either because she tells him or because his people will uncover it. Our best bet is for you to stay close and wait for them to come to you."

Still seemed like a long shot, but he had no other leads and he was being paid well to sit on his ass and wait. "Roger that. You still that sure she'll be with Bautista?"

A snort. "Yeah, I'm sure. Stay there. If they show, put them both down."

"I will."

Nico drove to a concealed spot across the street from the bank and settled in to wait. Waiting was boring as shit, but it might be his only chance to get his targets.

His rifle lay hidden in the floor of the backseat, cleaned and loaded and his hands itched to use it.

Patient. He had to be patient, take all emotion and excitement out of the equation. It was the only way he could kill his prey.

He imagined seeing that big deposit in his secret bank account. Imagined the clear, turquoise waters of the Maldives while he and Melissa lay on deck chairs at their private villa and stared out at the ocean, side by side. Imagined the love and joy in her eyes as he stripped her black bikini off her and covered her body with his own.

He blew out a breath, came back to the present. "Hurry up already," he muttered. Just one solid lead, and he'd finally hunt his targets down.

And this time, they would both die.

****

Because you're all mine.

The sheer possessiveness behind his words both shocked and thrilled Georgia. She knew she should be a whole lot more upset about being kept here against her will, but lying wrapped up in Miguel's arms right now after months of grieving his death, it was hard to care.

As was the fact that they hadn't used any protection. She was rigorous about getting her monthly birth control shot though.

"I still can't believe you're alive," she murmured. Those months she'd mourned his loss had been the darkest of her life.

"I thought what we just did in the bathroom was pretty solid proof of that, but if you want another demo,

I'd be happy to show you again right now." He nuzzled the side of her neck.

His teasing tone made her smile. "Wish we could." They'd stolen this time together but couldn't hide in here much longer.

She'd give anything to stay in here and make the rest of the world go away. With Miguel holding her like this she felt safe for the first time in…maybe ever. "But I'm sure the others are wondering what's going on up here."

He snorted softly. "I don't care what they think, but I'm pretty sure they already know." He pulled back, gave her a startled smile. "Wait. Are you blushing?"

"No." She hid her face against his chest.

A low chuckle rumbled beneath her cheek. "You totally are, you're blushing." He sounded amazed by that.

She poked him in the ribs. "So what if I am?"

"You're a professional assassin. How can you blush about other people knowing we just had sex?"

"Well I don't… I haven't had much experience in this area."

"Define 'area'."

She made a frustrated sound, fought the urge to wriggle away. "*This*," she said, snuggling in closer. He felt amazing, so warm and solid, and he truly cared about her. She felt protected. The whole thing was surreal. "And I don't spend a lot of time around other people, so I tend to be on the socially awkward side."

"One more thing we have in common," he said dryly. "But I have to ask you, because I've been dying to know. How much of Julia was actually you? Because back in Miami, socially awkward was the last thing I would ever have called you."

It was a good question, and one she'd wrestled with herself. "She's definitely part of me." The kinder, softer pieces of herself that she'd been taught long ago to hide from the rest of the world. "I guess…she's the person I wish I could have been, if I hadn't been recruited into the program. Warm. Kind. Passionate. Normal."

Free, she thought with a pang.

Georgia forced back the rush of emotion she felt at the word and concentrated on the present. Being with Miguel again was a gift she'd never expected to have again and she was determined to enjoy it to the fullest, not get caught up in thinking about what she couldn't have and that this couldn't last.

"I liked being her, even if it was only for a little while. I miss being those things sometimes."

"But you are those things," he murmured against her hair. "At least with me. And trust me, you're by far the sexiest, most passionate woman I've ever met."

"Just with you I'm those things," she clarified. "And maybe I'm normal to Briar and Trin, too." Because she trusted them. And because face it, none of them were *normal*.

Georgia held her breath, mentally cursing herself for being so stupid as to reveal that weakness to him.

But rather than exploit it, Miguel made a sound of understanding and kissed the top of her head. "I want you to be exactly who you are around me. And if it makes you feel any better, I let you see parts of me that no one else ever had."

She nodded, taking comfort in that. "I know. I wasn't expecting that."

"Me neither, believe me." His voice was wry. "You were damn good, slipping under my radar like that. And then you slipped under my skin." He stroked her hair.

He'd slipped far deeper than just beneath *her* skin. He'd buried himself in her heart.

They were quiet for a few moments, each of them lost in their own thoughts. It had to be strange for him, since she knew all about him and his background and he knew next to nothing about her, except for what she'd let him see in Miami.

"So what's the significance of the tattoo?" He trailed his fingers over the tat on her left hip. About the size of a silver dollar, it depicted a black crow with a sword held in its talons and *Valkyrja* written inside a stylized scroll beneath it.

Half-draped over him in the bed with one arm around his ribs and her cheek resting on the hard curve of his left pec, she never wanted to move again. "It's the mark of the Valkyries," she explained. "It means 'chooser of the slain' in Old Norse. Or something like that. We all got one when we graduated from the program. Like a symbol of solidarity or something." She'd liked being a Valkyrie, for the most part. The trainers had been careful to make them believe they were elite, that their status as one of the exclusive members of the program was something to be honored about. But it was a hard life, and a damn lonely one.

"How many of you were there?"

"No one knows for sure. The program was in a test phase when Briar, Trinity and I graduated. Lots of girls washed out and we never saw them again. As to the number who completed the program, only a few people know that." One of them being Rossland. "But I think there were around fourteen of us or so."

"How old were you when they recruited you?"

"Eleven." Not much older than he'd been when his grandmother had been viciously assaulted in her own home. She knew Miguel had been the one to find her like that. Her heart hurt thinking of the innocent little boy he'd been, all the pain he'd suffered.

His hand moved from her hip to her lower back, the weight of his palm against her skin warm, soothing. "What happened?"

She hated talking about her past. It wasn't a pretty story and she didn't want his pity. Still, she trusted him enough to tell him the truth. "I was dumped at an orphanage as a toddler. No one knew what happened to my parents but from what I found out, my mother was a hooker and a drug addict. Better that she gave me up."

He made a low sound that told her he was listening.

"I was put into the foster system when I was five. It…didn't go well. I had anger and trust issues. The short version is, I got bounced around from home to home until one day a woman showed up and took me to a special school at age eleven. I didn't realize then that it was a secret CIA program. I was assigned to Frank when I was fifteen." Seemed like another lifetime ago now, but it helped that Miguel would understand, being that he'd been through the foster system as well.

"You were close to him."

She nodded, a sharp pain lancing through her as the memories flooded in. "He was a good man. He never married or had children, so he treated me like I was his own daughter." It made her think of her first Christmas with him. He'd insisted she come and stay at his house, had the guest room all done up when she arrived. They'd decorated a tree together.

It almost made her teary now, thinking of it. Before that, the last time she could remember putting up a tree was at the orphanage. And in the morning, the stocking he'd hung for her on the fireplace was full and there had been presents for her under the tree. She'd felt bad that she hadn't gotten him anything but he'd just smiled and sipped his coffee, watching her open her gifts while carols played in the background.

"I would have done anything for him," she whispered, feeling the loss all over again. *But I couldn't save him.*

That soothing hand ran up her spine, back down again, bringing her back to the present. Hands capable of killing, of inflicting such pain that a man would tell him his darkest secrets and then beg him for death to end the suffering. And yet he'd only ever touched her and his grandmother with gentleness. "I'm sorry he's gone."

"Me too." She'd always miss him.

"How did he die?"

"Hydrogen cyanide poisoning." It killed her to think of him dying that way, suffocating, alone and panicked, clawing at his throat as he struggled for air. She'd found his body less than an hour after he'd died and she'd never forgive herself. "If I'd realized the threat an hour sooner, I might have been able to save him."

Miguel rolled her onto her side facing him and cradled the back of her head while he stared into her eyes. And she was not imagining the intent, hard light in his gaze. "Who did it?"

The buried anger in his voice surprised her. "People from the program who I'd trusted at one time," she answered simply. "I found out that they used enforcers within the Fuentes network for the hits so they could distance themselves from the murders, let the cartel pros do the dirty work for them."

And the men remaining on her list would die for that.

"That's why you took out Garcia, and why you wanted Villa. Because you found out Garcia ordered Villa to kill them," he finished.

There was no way she was going to actually admit to killing Garcia, but it was enough that he knew the truth. She broke eye contact, focused on the scars at the top of his chest where one of the bullets had hit him. "There was one more enforcer involved."

"Who?"

He wasn't going to like this. She took a deep breath before answering. "Someone connected to Perez."

She felt him stiffen against her. "I had nothing to do with it."

"I know. I meant someone else." She looked up in

time to see his eyebrows draw together.

"I was his chief enforcer. If Perez or anyone connected to him had been involved, I would have known. I swear I'm telling you the truth."

"I believe you," she soothed. "But I have evidence that shows Perez was using someone else for the job."

He looked so stunned by the news that she almost felt badly for telling him. "Who? And why? He barely ever used anyone besides me for jobs." he demanded, his urgency clear.

She shook her head. "You know I can't tell you that." Not yet, anyway.

Thankfully he didn't get angry at her refusal. "Why would former members of the program want two of their own handlers dead?"

"I'm not sure how much you know, but there was a former Valkyrie Project trainer involved with illegal arms deals. Will Balducci. Last December he sent me to kill Briar, saying she'd gone rogue."

The shock in his eyes was unmistakable.

She nodded. "Luckily I failed and Briar was able to prove to me that Balducci was not only a liar, but dirty. I tracked him down after that, was going to take him out but then Briar showed up with Rycroft and the FBI's HRT and I had to back down. He's rotting away in prison right now."

"I heard about it. He was high up in the CIA."

"Yes." She let out a breath. "Rycroft arrested me that night but let me go shortly thereafter because there wasn't enough evidence to hold me. Over the next few months I uncovered a trail of evidence that proved Balducci had hired Fuentes enforcers to kill Janaia—Briar's handler. I knew there had to be others involved so I called Frank immediately, was on my way to meet him and turn over the evidence when he was murdered."

She swallowed, remembering the pain she'd felt

upon finding his body lying on the floor. "I vowed then and there to find out who else was involved and expose them. Turns out the players involved wanted Janaia and Frank dead to cover up the Valkyrie program. But it wasn't just that. They wanted *everyone* involved with the Valkyrie Project eliminated, including me, Briar and Trinity because we knew about Balducci's back door arms deals in the Middle East."

Miguel shifted suddenly, rolling her to her back and bracing one arm over her, looming above her in the bed. "Don't run anymore. Let me help you. Let *us* help you. We'll get them. But we'll do it together."

She was so torn, could feel herself caving more with each second she spent with him. "I don't want to endanger any of you. They'll keep coming after me until one of them kills me."

"Then come away with me. We'll—" He stopped short.

"We'll what?"

He let out a harsh sigh. "I can't go with you. They implanted a tracking device on me somewhere. I don't know where it is. I've searched for it, but can't find it, so it has to be really small." He searched her eyes. "But I can still get you out of the country. I've got connections, people who owe me favors. You could leave and start over somewhere else where you won't be in danger once everyone involved is dealt with."

Her answer was immediate and adamant. "I'm not leaving you behind. No way." Too many emotions were bombarding her. Walking away from him now would break her.

She cupped his cheek in her hand, swallowed. He needed to know this part. "Do you know what it did to me that day, when I thought you died in front of me?" Her voice was rough. "It killed me. I was numb at first, just operating on autopilot. I barely remember what happened after that, how I got away from the feds and made it to a private surgeon to get my arm fixed." She paused when he took her left forearm and raised it to his lips to kiss the scars there.

Now that it was all flooding out of her, it was impossible to stop. "All I kept thinking was that it was my fault you'd died. If you hadn't been worried about saving me and Marisol, you never would have been shot. I put you in danger by interfering and freeing Marisol from that boat, and you paid for my mistake with your life."

"It wasn't your fault."

"Yes it was," she insisted angrily. "And God, that gutted me. I felt like I was walking around with a gaping hole in my chest, and the only thing that kept me going was the promise I'd made—to kill every last one of the bastards responsible for what happened to Frank. It was the only thing I had left."

"Vengeance."

"Yes."

He nodded, and it was a relief to know he understood the burning need that had driven her for so long. "Know what I was thinking about when I thought I was dying?"

She lifted her head to look at him, her heart aching at the mention of it. "What?"

"I was looking up at you. You were crying, begging me to hold on, and that look on your face told me you really did care. But I didn't want to hold on. Because I knew if I lived, I'd either wind up behind bars or maybe facing the death sentence. But mostly, I knew if I lived, you'd never be safe."

She drew her head back in shock. "*What*?" What the hell kind of thinking was that?

He nodded slowly, his expression solemn. "It's true. I was on the other Fuentes lieutenants' hit list. If I died, then my enemies would have no reason to target you anymore. You'd be safe. Free." His lips curved in a sardonic grin, a spark of humor in his dark gaze. "But that was before I woke up in the hospital and was told you were actually a badass government assassin."

She couldn't have summoned a smile at that moment if her life had depended on it. Georgia could barely process it all.

She tucked her face into the curve of his neck and took in a shaky breath, inhaling his scent. He was an amazing man, the most complex she'd ever met, a complicated blend of dark and light.

And yet she'd known from the moment she'd met him that he was inherently a good person, despite everything he'd done in his quest for his own brand of cartel justice. An avenging angel instead of a psychopathic serial killer, as the authorities would have everyone believe.

Much like her. And he'd wanted to die to protect her.

"You're shredding me," she whispered, aching inside.

"I don't mean to." He leaned down and touched his lips to hers. The kiss was soft, tender, filled with such caring it made her throat tighten. "I've missed you so damn much."

A rush of tears threatened. In that moment she knew there was no way she could ever walk away from this man. Not after she'd already lost him once. "I missed you too."

"Sometimes I think you're the only thing that got me through my recovery. I thought about you constantly, wondered what had happened to you and where you were, hoped like hell that you were safe."

She swallowed. "I hate to think of you lying there in pain, wondering about me and whether I lied to you about everything."

He shook his head. "Not everything. I knew the chemistry part was real. And I knew that for you to react the way you did when I was dying, I had to mean something to you."

"You do mean something to me." Huge understatement.

He stilled above her, watching her with that intense way he had. "How much?"

I think I'm in love with you.

She would cut out her own tongue before saying that out loud when he hadn't given her anything first.

She shot him a sharp frown. "Enough that I just let you do me against the bathroom wall and have me lying here naked with you now, thereby compromising my objective for the mission I've been planning for almost a year."

A slow, sexy smile spread across his face, full of masculine satisfaction, turning her all mushy inside. But a moment later he turned serious again. "Then don't do this alone. Let me help you with this."

If she was honest with herself, the truth was she'd already changed her mind back in the bathroom. "No, you're right. It's time for me to put my need for vengeance aside. I'll tell Rycroft where the flash drive is. We'll get it together and expose the people involved, make them pay with a life sentence. A bullet through the heart is too easy for them anyway. This way they'll have years of suffering." That and having more time with Miguel were the only things that soothed her stinging conscience.

Miguel let out a relieved breath, cradled the back of her head in one hand and covered her mouth with his. "Thank you."

Georgia twined her arms around his neck and drew him closer, getting lost in the caress of his lips and the erotic glide of his tongue. For just another few minutes, he was hers.

After that she would leave this bedroom and tell

Rycroft what he wanted to know. But if she could have made time stop to stay tangled with Miguel in this bed, she'd have done it in a heartbeat.

Because she already knew that people like them didn't get happy endings. In the end, she'd have no choice but to let him go.

Chapter Fifteen

Nico's attention sharpened when a silver SUV pulled into the bank parking lot. Traffic in and out of the lot had been steady over the past couple hours but had begun to slow in the last little while. This particular vehicle caught his attention immediately.

The SUV had tinted windows, and it pulled right up to the front entrance rather than parking. As he watched, two men got out, mostly blocked from view by the body of the vehicle. From his vantage point Nico could see that one of them had brown hair sprinkled with gray and the other was dark-haired.

Ducking down lower in the driver's seat, he raised his binos to get a better look.

One of the men turned slightly and he immediately recognized Rycroft.

"*Yes.*" Finally.

Switching his focus to the other man, his heart rate spiked when he saw Bautista's profile. Both men were vigilant, scanning the area around them.

Someone else was still inside the SUV, other than the driver. Was it Georgia?

With slow, careful movements Nico reached behind

him to retrieve his weapon. Just as his hand closed around it, a black truck zipped into the lot and pulled alongside the SUV, blocking it completely from view.

Definitely not random. The truck had to be with them.

Cursing under his breath, he shifted to try and get a better angle to see what was happening, but couldn't. Someone popped out of the backseat and Rycroft and Bautista rushed them into the bank.

Had to be Georgia.

His grip tightened around his rifle. For a moment he thought about getting out and circling around the side of the building on foot. There was a tall hedge running along the east side of the parking lot that would offer concealment.

That wouldn't work though. Taking a shot now would only potentially give him one kill. He needed two. And if he shot now, he'd not only give himself away, any survivors would immediately come after him. If he screwed up, he'd be dead.

No. Too risky. Think it through. Bautista had always told him to think it through, be at least three moves ahead of your target.

He'd be better off following them, catching them completely off guard when they least expected it. Maybe disable the vehicle, force them to scatter. Then he could pick his targets off individually and escape.

Nico set his weapon down and studied the black truck, but couldn't see the driver through the tinted windows. Reaching for his phone, he texted Diego.

They're here. Going after them.

It was torture to be this close and have to wait, but his discipline held him in place.

A few minutes later the top of Bautista's head appeared above the roof of the truck as he exited the bank. Moments after that, the SUV quickly drove out of the parking lot with the black truck directly behind it.

They had to have the contents of the safety deposit box. He could retrieve it once he killed them, wrap everything up this afternoon and be on a plane back to Miami tonight.

Excitement flashed through him. This was what he lived for, the thrill of the hunt, his prey wary but not realizing he was so close. Not realizing that their time was almost up.

He waited until a few cars were between him and the other vehicles, then pulled out onto the street and followed. They were headed north out of town, probably about to head back to NSA headquarters in Maryland.

He was going to disrupt those plans indefinitely.

Making a quick decision, he turned right at the next light and sped up a side street. The only highway out of town was a two-lane road. Once they were on it, they'd have to drive another twelve miles before they reached a turnoff. If he could get ahead of them and onto the highway, he could speed ahead, find a place to wait and then disable the SUV.

If they survived the resulting crash, he could pick them off one by one as they crawled out of the wreckage.

****

Georgia plugged the flash drive into the laptop and waited for it to load. She'd placed it in the safety deposit box herself soon after Frank was killed, but there was still a tiny possibility someone else had found out about it and the other backups. She needed to make sure this one was authentic, and still contained the information she'd loaded on it.

To her relief, the files that came up looked right, and the first one she opened contained the pictures she'd taken of the crime scene at Frank's house. Even though she'd been prepared for the sight of it, it hit her hard to see him lying there dead on the tile floor.

His face was cherry red from the cyanide poisoning. He'd ripped open his own shirt during his final struggle to breathe and his throat and chest were covered in scratches made by his own fingernails as he'd clawed for air.

A hand closed around hers, warm fingers enveloping it.

She glanced over at Miguel and squeezed his hand in return, touched by the gesture. There was so much more to him than met the eye.

It was true she'd always miss Frank. But at least now with Rycroft about to take over, she knew the men behind his murder would at least face justice for what they'd done. And Frank would have wanted that rather than her winding up serving a life sentence in some dark hole, or being killed while trying to hunt his killers down.

And now that she'd found Miguel, she wanted to live for the first time in forever.

"Everything looks okay to me," she said to Rycroft, who was swiveled around in the front passenger seat, watching her while Briar drove. Gage Wallace was behind them in another vehicle, for added security on the way back to Fort Meade.

"Good. Pull up the emails you've got on file and let me take a look at what—"

Georgia jumped as something slammed into the front of the SUV. Briar cursed and turned the wheel to correct the sharp sideways lurch and keep them in their lane. "Somebody just put a round through the engine block," she said grimly.

Everyone looked out the window toward the direction where the shot must have come from. "Has to be hidden in the woods," Georgia said.

The glass was bullet-resistant and the body was reinforced, but that didn't mean they weren't in danger of being shot. As Georgia automatically gripped the door handle to brace herself, another loud bang sounded and the big vehicle skidded sideways.

"Shit," Briar muttered. "Tire's blown."

"Where is that fucker?" Rycroft snarled, searching for the shooter. Already the vehicle was slowing. Smoke began billowing out from under the hood.

Briar counteracted the skid expertly, stopping them from flipping over, then wheeled them around to face back toward town and brought the SUV to a plunging, rocking stop on the gravel shoulder, a dozen yards or so from the thick band of forest that bordered the east side of the highway.

Georgia yanked the flash drive out of the laptop and shoved it into her hip pocket, then reached into the back where their weapons were stowed. Miguel was already grabbing his rifle, handed her hers. None of them knew how much time they had before the shooter opened up again, and he or she would be moving toward them right now.

"Everybody out," Rycroft ordered.

Georgia slid out the rear driver's side door after Miguel and hunkered down behind the safety of the SUV's body.

The sound of a racing engine came from her right. A heartbeat later the black pickup roared past them and plunged to a sudden halt, swinging around sideways to block them, giving them added protection close to the tree line.

The truck had barely come to a stop before Gage Wallace popped out of the driver's side door, a pistol in hand, and took shelter behind the cab. "Shooter's somewhere to the northeast, hidden in the trees," he told them.

"Think it's just the one?" Rycroft asked.

"Dunno," he answered, then ducked lower behind his

own vehicle as a shot slammed into the engine block, leaving a good-sized hole where it had entered the grill.

So much for having a getaway car.

A car came around the corner, squealed to a stop when the driver saw the two vehicles, stranded and smoking, in the middle of the road. Rycroft immediately waved them off, shouted at the driver to stay in their car.

Georgia glanced around. Shit. They couldn't stay here, waiting to be picked off, and every second they hesitated was a second the shooter was moving into a better position.

There was no way for someone to cross the highway without them seeing, unless the shooter managed to do it around the curve in the road up ahead. Either the person was maneuvering for a better shot, or they were retreating.

But if it was her on the hunt, Georgia would double back and wait for the right moment to take out her targets.

"I'm going after him," Miguel announced, and began moving toward the back of the truck, heading for the trees.

"I'll go with you," she said. They were all wearing neutral earth tone colors, nothing that would stand out in the woods, except that there was no camouflage to break up the solid blocks of color. Moving was risky. But they couldn't afford to let this shooter go.

He turned his head to nail her with a hard stare. "No. Stay here behind cover."

"Fuck that, I'm not letting you go by yourself." He was good but he was still mortal, and they'd be safer together.

"We'll follow you at intervals," Rycroft said, his gaze pinned toward the area of forest where the shots had originated from.

Miguel's lips compressed into a thin line but he didn't argue further, turning his attention back to the trees. "Stay behind me," he told her.

Georgia didn't answer, watching for any signs of

movement in the forest. He crouched behind the rear bumper and looked back at her. "You ready?"

When she nodded he took off in a blur of movement, disappearing into the trees moments later. She waited a few heartbeats, then followed.

Her running strides ate up the distance between her and the trees. She swallowed a yelp when a tree trunk she passed exploded in a hail of splinters.

Diving to the ground, she kept her head down. *Shit, that was close.* A few inches to the right, and that round would have slammed right into her chest.

Flat on her belly, she took a look around, spotted Miguel hidden behind a group of trees not far from her, his gaze locked on her. Even from her position she could see the fear there.

She did a quick thumbs up to reassure him, began leopard-crawling to the right, stopping close enough to see him easily but not so close that she would accidentally give away his position if the shooter had seen her move.

Glancing his way again, she read the brusque hand signals he gave her. He would go right while she moved left and crept forward, hopefully circling around the shooter.

She signaled back that she copied and began moving left as she crept forward, careful to disturb the undergrowth as little as possible. The surge of adrenaline flooded her system, a high she'd learned long ago how to control.

It felt good to be on the offensive again, and this time, with Miguel at her side, she had the best backup in the business. If the shooter was still in the area, they'd find him.

Five against one, asshole, she thought with grim satisfaction.

Whoever he was, this son of a bitch was going down.

****

You just fucked yourself.

Nico couldn't control the burst of fear that shot through him as he realized his fatal mistake.

He'd missed Georgia by mere inches, and it might have cost him everything.

He should have made his escape the moment that black pickup had swerved in front of the SUV. Now there were five potential hunters out here targeting him, including Bautista.

Just the thought of his idol lurking in these woods sent a wave of terror crashing over him.

He should have run for it when he'd had the chance. There was no way he could take out five trained shooters without giving away his position and one of them nailing him before he got them all. Now his only chance was to disappear into these woods before one of them found him.

With effort he cleared his head. *Think it through. Melissa's counting on you.*

But he was suddenly terrified that he'd never see her again.

No. He knew what to do. *Take control. Clear your head. You're still in this fight. You can still win.*

Pushing the fear aside, he fell back on his training. *Stay low. Move slow. Use the cover around you to conceal your position.*

The scent of the damp earth hung heavy in the air. He used his elbows and knees to propel his body along the ground, pausing behind sturdy tree trunks to get his bearings and listen for any telltale signs that someone was nearby.

But the forest was eerily quiet, only the creak of the branches in the slight breeze filling the silence.

He crept northward, knowing he needed to make the best use of the cover available to him on his way to his rental. If he could just reach it, he could have a head start. Even a minute might make the difference between living to fight another day and taking a bullet.

The quiet snap of a branch somewhere in the brush behind him froze him in place. His gaze shot toward it, his heart pounding at what it meant.

The high-power scope of his rifle showed nothing. No rabbits or squirrels that might have disturbed the underbrush. No recognizable outline of a person hidden in the dense tangle of branches.

But he knew someone was there. Knew they probably had him in their sights.

He was the prey now. And the hunters were nearly on top of him.

I'm not fucking dying this way.

He was too good at what he did, and he wasn't leaving Melissa this way. She needed him, would be devastated if he died and she'd never understand what he'd done, or why. It wasn't too late. If he was careful enough, patient enough, he could still get Bautista and maybe one or two others.

He had to. He'd been waiting for this moment for so long, the chance to take control of his destiny, his future. He fucking deserved that chance after everything he'd gone through in his shitty-ass life.

Nico swallowed, gathered his resolve as he planned his strategy. If he was lucky he could take Bautista out and still get away.

Even as he thought it he knew it was impossible. Not with five of them out there.

The uncertainty clouded his brain, interfered with his concentration. His life was at stake here, and not just because of the people hunting him now. If he failed in this mission… He'd be a liability.

One his uncle would have no choice but to eliminate.

Shoving the chilling thought aside, he grimly turned

and propped the barrel of his rifle on a low, fallen log, set his eye to the scope.

Just give me a damn target.

Calling up an image of Melissa's face for courage, he held onto it and sent up a silent prayer. *God help me.*

He wasn't going down without a fight.

****

Movement at her four o'clock.

Georgia froze, waiting, her attention locked on a bush that was starting to lose its leaves. The damp ground was cold beneath her, the chilly air coating her bare arms below the sleeves of her T-shirt, but she hardly noticed, focused on her target.

A branch close to the bush twitched and shivered, sending more leaves to the ground. She homed in on it. Through her scope she made out the shape of a man's leg as it slid along the forest floor. Camo pants, not black ones, like Miguel had been wearing.

The shooter.

Taking aim, Georgia consciously calmed her heart rate as she lined up the laser dot. She breathed out, waited until all the air had escaped her lungs before squeezing the trigger.

The report rang out a split second before she heard a pained grunt, saw a flash of movement as her target dropped flat to the ground. Allowing herself to breathe normally once again, she waited, knowing Miguel and the others would have heard her shot.

She waited there for a minute.

Two.

Four.

Then the target moved.

She tensed, eye to the scope, ready to fire again, but the leg slid out of view behind a group of tree trunks. But she'd hit him. She knew she had. How badly wounded he was, she didn't know.

Time to move in for the kill. Or capture, if he was still alive and unable to shoot back. Either way, he was going *down*.

Pushing to her feet, she slung her rifle across her back and ran, pulling her sidearm from the holster strapped to her hip.

Miguel suddenly appeared beside her, materializing out of the brush like a ghost. It startled her. No one snuck up on her when she was on her game, ever. Yet he had.

"I got him but he's not down," she called out in a whisper.

"I know. Now stay back," Miguel ordered her, racing past to intercept the threat.

Stay back? Screw. That.

Ignoring the ludicrous command, Georgia ran headlong after him.

He was much faster than she was, pulling a few dozen yards away within the first few minutes, and soon was swallowed by the screen of trees that separated them. She blamed her recent bout of sickness. Gritting her teeth, she chased after him, annoyed at how quickly she became out of breath.

A shot rang out, the report echoing through the silent woods.

Miguel.

Heart in her throat, she put on a burst of speed and ran, dodging trees, logs and bushes. It was maybe only another minute before she reached him but it seemed to take forever, her only thought that he might be hurt, or pinned down.

Leaping over a fallen log blocking her path, she veered around a large boulder—

And skidded to a sudden halt at the sight before her.

Miguel stood unmoving at the edge of a small gulley,

pistol aimed at someone lying at the bottom of it. A burst of relief hit her but the rigid set of his back and shoulders told her instantly that something was wrong. When she drew close enough to see his face, her heart stuttered at his expression.

The look on his face was one of utter disbelief. And betrayal.

She glanced away from him, to the man lying on the ground before them. Young, maybe in his late twenties. Dark hair, golden brown skin, clean shaven. Still alive, though from the looks of it, not for long.

He was half-sprawled on his stomach, rifle cradled in the crook of one arm. His eyes were half open and his lips were parted, a rivulet of frothy blood bubbling out of his mouth to drip into the bed of fallen leaves beneath him.

Either she or Miguel had hit him in the lung. More blood dripped from another wound in his upper thigh.

She must have hit him in the leg then. Miguel had been the one to actually take him down. That might have annoyed her at any other time, but she was more worried about his reaction.

"What's wrong?" she asked him quietly.

He refused to look at her, a muscle jerking in his jaw.

Running footsteps came from behind them, breaking the taut silence. Georgia turned to see Briar, Rycroft and Wallace appear through the trees, racing toward them.

"You get him?" Rycroft called out.

"Yes," she answered. But they wouldn't be able to get any information out of him now. He'd be dead within minutes.

Rycroft stopped beside Miguel and took in the situation with a single glance. "Still alive." He took a step into the gulley.

"Not for long." Miguel's wooden tone and his stiff expression as he stared at the man worried her.

Rycroft handed his weapon to Briar. "I'll take his fingerprints while you guys pull security. Let's see if we can find out who our mystery shooter is."

"Nico Montoya," Miguel answered in a flat voice, still staring at the body.

Georgia looked at him sharply as Rycroft stopped in his tracks.

"You know him?" Rycroft asked, frowning.

Miguel drew a deep breath before tearing his gaze from the dying shooter and looked at Rycroft. The haunted look in his eyes hit Georgia like a punch to the gut. "He's Diego Perez's nephew," he answered, the words clipped. Cold. "And I trained him."

Without another word he turned and walked away, back toward the road, leaving Georgia and the others staring after him in stunned silence.

Chapter Sixteen

S eated in front of a desk in an office at the small airport, Bautista forced himself to look at Rycroft as the man came in and sat on the edge of the desk.

"So. Perez," Rycroft said.

He resented the calculating gleam in those gray eyes when Rycroft said the name, even though he knew Rycroft was a pretty decent guy. Less than an hour ago Rycroft's team back at NSA headquarters had managed to trace the phone calls to and from the cell they'd found on Nico's body.

At first Bautista had assumed that Perez had been using Nico as his new enforcer to fill the void after Bautista had "died". That he'd somehow gotten wind of the things Georgia had uncovered during her investigation, and sent Nico after her.

But it turns out that was only partly right.

He'd sent Nico after *both* of them.

Bautista didn't know how Perez had found out he was alive. Maybe through the cartel network, after the NSA had leaked intel about him surviving. He didn't care how. All he knew was, the evidence was right in front of him. Transcripts of the traced and unencrypted texts from several burner phones, sent over by some analyst at the NSA. And it was irrefutable.

Put them both down.

Those words jumped off the page, sending a wave of cold through him. Perez had said that same phrase to him numerous times while he'd served as Perez's enforcer.

The targets had always been bad men. Killers and rapists, drug and human traffickers, thugs like the ones who had taken his *abuela* from him. Perez had never asked him to go after anyone who didn't deserve to die, and each time Bautista had done the job like a good and loyal little lackey.

They'd shared meals at Perez's dining room table together. Gone on fishing trips together. Spent the holidays together.

But his former boss and mentor had crossed an unforgivable line when he'd targeted an innocent like Georgia, wanting to silence her simply because she could expose his involvement in the murders of Frank and Janaia, who were also innocents.

And then he'd made a fatal error by targeting *him*.

Bautista shook his head at himself. He'd been close with the whole Perez family. Had been treated like an adored relative, had always assumed he'd meant far more to Perez than just a hired thug.

Apparently he'd been dead wrong about that. And it *hurt*.

Finding out someone you'd idolized and protected for the past decade had betrayed you, sucked. He felt bruised inside.

He vividly remembered Perez's words when he'd called to inform his boss he was leaving the game after the Villa op, during the drive down to Key West.

I'll be sorry to lose you. But I understand why you'd want that, and I wish you the best. He'd sounded so sincere. Bautista had believed him, thought he'd be able to get out of the game and start a new life.

Lies. All fucking *lies*.

"You need to let me warn Laura in person," he said to Rycroft. "Whatever Perez has done, she and the kids are innocent. None of them know the truth about him and the things he's done. I want them protected and I want your word you'll let me be the one to talk to her, in person, before I'll give you anything else."

Laura and the kids didn't deserve any of this. He hated knowing how hard this was going to be on all of them.

Rycroft crossed his arms, his expression calm but interested. "Where are they?"

"Vacation house in Destin. Laura always takes the kids there for the week after her daughter Jenny's birthday."

"You're sure about that?"

"Yes." They'd gone every year. Bautista had accompanied them several times over the past few years, as added security.

"And you think Perez is still in Miami and not with them?"

"He never goes. But I can find him." And he wasn't disclosing the possible locations Perez might be until he got what he wanted.

A guarantee of Georgia's freedom.

Rycroft tilted his head a fraction. "He got a mistress or something he's trying to hide?"

"*No*." Twisted and fucked-up as Perez's morals might be, he was a good husband and father. He worshipped and respected his wife, would do anything to protect his family and hide the bad things he was involved with.

No matter what else he'd done, there was no way Perez would ever cheat on Laura. Of that he was certain.

Although he'd been certain of Perez's friendship as

well, so there was a chance he was wrong.

Rycroft didn't look convinced. "Can you do it without Perez being alerted?"

"Yes." He knew Perez wouldn't have told Laura that he was still alive. It would have made things far too complicated for him.

Because she absolutely would have demanded to come see Bautista in the medical facility they'd put him in, and get their lawyers to try and win his freedom. She'd always fussed over him like a mother hen, had invited him on family trips as a guest rather than security because she and the kids adored him.

Yeah. No way she knew he was alive.

"How tight is the security there?"

"I can handle it alone."

Rycroft made a scoffing sound. "Not an option. Either we all go, or we don't go at all."

Bautista fought for patience. The day had started out in the best way possible and quickly turned to shit a few hours ago and he wasn't in the mood to piss around with details. Laura and the kids would be freaked enough to see him, let alone learn what he had to tell them. He needed to be the one to break the news.

"I go in there alone," he insisted, unwilling to budge on that point.

Rycroft's jaw clenched and his eyes cooled at Bautista's tone. "With us standing by as backup and security, and you'll be wearing a wire. And you'll also give me whatever I need to plan an op to get Perez on the way down there."

He inclined his head. "Fine. But there's one more thing."

Rycroft raised an eyebrow. "And that is?"

"I want you to wipe Georgia's record and let her walk away after this."

She'd been fucked over too many times by people

she'd trusted. He now knew exactly how that felt and he wanted her to be free to start over, have a life again.

"She uncovered things that implicate people throughout the cartel, not to mention a certain government intelligence agency. Even if we get Perez and Rossland is taken into custody, she'll still be at risk. You said you wanted to recruit her but you know the only way she'll ever be safe is to get out of the States. She's given you what you wanted. She deserves to start over."

Rycroft's expression turned unreadable. "You realize I don't have to agree to a goddamn thing here, right? That basically you're fucked in terms of options here. You either do what I want or you get locked up until you die."

"Yeah, I know all that," he said bitterly. "I also realize you fucking kidnapped her and have no solid evidence against her in terms of any crimes. And I'll make your life a living hell if I don't get your word you'll take care of it."

The agent drew in a deep breath, let it out slowly. "I'll do what I can."

He shook his head, refusing to give in. "Not good enough."

After holding his gaze for a long moment, Rycroft nodded once, his gaze holding a grudging respect. "All right. I give you my word I'll do everything I can to make sure she's protected. Once this is all over, I'll do my best to see that she's treated fairly. That's the best I can do, because you know that kind of deal isn't up to just me."

He was right. But Rycroft did have major sway in the agency, and was well respected in the intelligence community. Not to mention all the connections he had to draw on. If anyone could help Georgia start over outside the U.S., it was Rycroft.

"Okay. Then I agree."

"Good." Rycroft relaxed his stance. "Briar's

working on getting us a flight to Destin right now and Wallace and Georgia are on their way back with the cleanup crew who'll be taking possession of the body. We need to be wheels up as soon as possible, so you can get the wife and kids to safety before Perez figures out Montoya is dead and goes on the run."

That didn't leave them much time. A matter of hours, probably, if Perez wasn't already aware of what had happened to his nephew. Bautista nodded. He was sure Laura would do what he asked. "I'll be ready."

Rycroft stood, then reached out and set a hand on his shoulder. "I know he meant a lot to you. I'm sorry you have to be the one to do this."

He tensed at the contact. "I'm not." Because the need for vengeance was already burning hot in his veins. "And let's be real, this is what you were hoping for all along. You couldn't have asked for things to work out any better for you."

Rycroft withdrew his hand. "I've got some calls to make," he muttered, and left the room.

Bautista turned his head to stare out the window, watching small aircraft land and take off. What he wouldn't give to be on one of those planes right now, out of the country to start over somewhere else.

He literally had no one now. No one who cared about him or what happened to him. Except maybe Georgia.

Well, he *hoped* Georgia did anyway.

His gaze followed a small airplane as it sped down the runway and lifted off the ground, winging its way into a sky filled with all the brilliant colors of an October sunset.

He'd never be that free again. And even if he was, he wasn't sure if Georgia would want to be with him on that plane anyway.

The door opened again and his heart gave a hard thud when she stepped into the room. Her clothes and arms were still covered in dirt from when they'd been crawling in the woods, but she was still so beautiful.

Jesus, it had scared the shit out of him when that shot had hit the tree next to her as she'd run into the forest. For a moment when she'd fallen to the ground he'd thought she'd been hit. He'd been on his way back to her, going to her despite the danger of drawing the shooter's attention, and had only begun breathing again when he finally saw her move.

She pushed the door closed behind her, concern clear in her expression. "You doing okay?" she asked softly.

He forced a nod even though it felt like his entire world had just been turned upside down. He wanted to pull her into his arms and never let go, take her away from all of this bullshit. But he couldn't. And that ate him up inside.

"Yeah."

"I'm really sorry."

Jaw tight, he nodded. He was still reeling inside, didn't know how to process this. She probably knew how he felt. But he'd be damned if he'd let anyone know how much he was hurting, even her.

Old habits die hard. *Never let anyone see your weaknesses.* "Thanks."

She cleared her throat, suddenly looked uncomfortable. "Listen, I need to tell you something."

The dread in her tone made his stomach muscles clench. His gaze sharpened on her. "What?"

"Perez was the other name on my list."

He absorbed that without reaction, mainly because he'd already figured that out this morning after their talk in bed. It made the most sense as to why she'd needed to get close to him in Miami. Perez was an impossible target that only a trusted insider could get close enough to in order to carry out a hit.

Or a former trusted insider.

He nudged that thought aside for the moment, just glad she was being honest with him now. "And Montoya? Did you know about him too?"

"His name came up during my investigation. I knew Perez was using him as an enforcer off and on this past year. But I didn't realize until this morning when we were talking that he'd done it behind your back."

"Yeah, apparently he did a lot of things behind my back." How had he been so blind and stupid? Him, the cartel's most feared enforcer?

She cocked her head. "Did you know him well? Montoya?"

He shrugged. "I thought I did. But then I thought I knew Perez, too." Because the man he'd thought he'd known would never have lied and hidden something like that, let alone put a hit out on him.

"You said you helped train him."

"After he was kicked out of the Army with a dishonorable discharge, Perez had me work with him to increase his skill level. He was Perez's favorite sister's son. I taught him advanced techniques in stalking, marksmanship, evasion. Basic sniper skills. I honestly never thought anything would come of it. He was too young and inexperienced to be of any real use to Perez, even with my help, and he had a giant chip on his shoulder that made him too much of a wild card."

"Anger issues?"

"Yeah, way too unstable and cocky. He was super competitive, even with me, and it pissed him off that he couldn't beat me."

But he'd gotten the final word on that one, hadn't he? Nico was currently zipped into a body bag because of him and no matter how hard Bautista tried to avoid it, his conscience pricked at him with sharp claws. Nico had been a close part of the Perez family. Bautista had seen him play in the pool with Laura and Diego's kids, be there for parties.

Georgia sighed, rubbed at a streak of dirt on the bottom of one forearm. "Everything's been taken care of with Montoya. They're transporting him up to Langley for the CIA to deal with him."

He frowned. "But that just means it's more likely that whoever's still targeting you will find out."

She nodded, looking a little worried now. "I know. I think that's what Rycroft wants. He's waiting to see if it draws any reaction from the other person I've got evidence against on the hard drive."

"Rossland." He nearly growled the name.

"Yes." She crossed the room to sit in the chair next to his, close enough that he could smell the sweet scent of her shampoo.

He searched her eyes, craving that deep connection he always felt with her. Even early on when she'd begun volunteering at the care home, he'd felt it. She'd opened up to him so much this morning.

He craved her complete trust. Wanted to protect her, claim her and take her far away from all of this, keep her with him always. "Who was he?"

"One of my former trainers. He was tight with Balducci when they worked at the company together. After Rossland left to pursue politics, he distanced himself from him somewhat. And since Balducci was arrested, Rossland's been busy trying to erase any evidence linking him to any of this."

"But he can't erase what you've got on the flash drive."

"Right. And that's why that company hitter was at the cabin the other night."

Bautista rubbed a hand over his jaw, thankful he'd been able to drop the guy when he had. "Tell me you've got other copies hidden somewhere."

She snorted as though that was obvious. "Of course.

And if I die, the whereabouts die with me."

The mere mention of her dying triggered an instant, powerful denial, fueled the anger already beating at him. "You're not going to die," he bit out, a savage rush of protectiveness rising up inside him. "Because anyone coming after you is gonna have to get through me first."

When she stared at him in astonishment he gave her a tight smile. "And it turns out I'm not the easiest guy to kill."

At that her expression softened and she put a hand on his arm, the light contact sending a jolt of sensation through him. He took a deep breath. He was too worked up inside. There was so much anger, so much pain that Perez would betray him this way.

Throughout everything Bautista had been through, he'd always protected Perez, even during and after his recovery and in contract negotiations with Rycroft about joining this team. He'd flat out refused to turn on Perez, had made it clear the man was off limits.

And now he realized his loyalty had been for nothing.

Georgia's fingers wrapped around his arm and squeezed. "I don't want you risking your life for mine. Not ever again."

Her pale blue eyes delved into his with an earnestness he craved desperately. Nothing else in his life was real. Only her.

"Losing you once almost killed me. Don't do it to me again."

The plea in her voice undid him.

Unable to stop himself, he leaned over, cupped the side of her jaw in one hand, and kissed her. Her answering moan vibrated through him, soothing the raw edges of the invisible wound bleeding in his chest.

Pulling back after a long moment, he stared into her eyes. "I'll do whatever it takes to protect you, no matter what." He would uphold that vow with his dying breath, as he had once before.

She opened her mouth to no doubt argue but a sharp rap on the door made them both look up as Briar poked her head in. "Hey," she said, glancing between the two of them as Bautista pulled his hand from Georgia's face and straightened. "Plane's inbound, should be touching down shortly. It's gonna be a fast turnaround, just changing out the crew and refueling. Pilots are already filing a flight plan now. Wheels up twenty minutes after it arrives at the terminal."

"Okay," Georgia responded. When Briar disappeared into the hallway, she looked at him again, her concern as clear as the beautiful ice blue of her eyes. "Are you ready for this?"

No. But he didn't have a choice now. And it would make Georgia safer. That alone was more than enough reason to do it. "Ready as I'll ever be." And he was selfish enough that he was pathetically grateful to have her with him through what was coming. Afterward…

Well, that was another story. And one he already knew wasn't going to end with a happily ever after.

****

Matt signed the second piece of paperwork in the stack that had accumulated over the past few days while he and Blue Team had been on an op in Kentucky, and reached for the next. His eyes were burning from lack of sleep and not just because he'd been on the road for the last four days.

He hadn't heard a word from Briar since she'd left for the op with Rycroft and Bautista, and he was stressed the fuck out over it.

It didn't matter that he trusted her abilities and knew how good she was in the field, or that Rycroft was there to watch her back. The fact was, she was on a dangerous op going after an unpredictable target, with an even more unpredictable teammate and who the hell knew how many professional assassins after them.

Scowling, he slapped the next folder onto his desk and flipped it open. A quick rap at his door interrupted his reading. He glanced over to see Adam Blackwell, one of Blue Team's assaulters, poke his head in, his brown hair wet from a recent shower.

"Hey," Matt said in surprise. He'd thought the guys had all left well over an hour ago, after their meeting.

"Hey." Blackwell stuffed his hands into his pockets. "You busy?"

Matt leaned back in his chair. "Just catching up on some paperwork. You know how much I love that shit."

Blackwell grinned. "Yeah." His smile fell away. "Can I talk to you a minute?"

The tone, his slight hesitation, pinged Matt's radar. He tossed his pen onto his desk and motioned for him to come in. "Sure, have a seat."

Blackwell shut the door behind him, confirming that something was definitely up.

Then he sat in the chair in front of Matt's desk and crossed one ankle over the opposite knee, bounced it up and down while he drummed his fingers on the arm of the chair.

Blackwell wasn't the fidgeting type, and Matt could count on one hand how many times Blackwell had sought him out to talk about anything in private. "What's going on?" Though he was pretty sure he already knew.

Blackwell let out a deep sigh. "You might have heard through the grapevine that uh…things haven't been going so well for me on the home front lately."

The words merely confirmed Matt's suspicions, because yeah, he'd heard. He made it a point to know what was going on with his guys. Not spying on them or prying into their personal lives, but he liked to have his finger on the pulse of the team. Because anything that affected his guys was a potential danger to the others if that team member didn't have his head locked in during a training op or mission.

"Sorry to hear that." He waited, allowing Blackwell to continue when he was ready.

"Thanks." More tapping with his fingers. "So, you know that Summer and I have gone through some tough things over the past two years or so. But now, when things should be getting better between us, they're not." His knee bounced harder. "We've gone to counseling a few times in the past and whatever, but it didn't do much. Our work schedules make it pretty much impossible to be together long enough to try to fix anything."

He paused, cleared his throat, clearly hating to talk about this, and Matt felt bad for the guy. "I'm not sure we're gonna make it. But I can't let things go until I've tried everything I can, you know? And if she still wants to split after that, well then…"

Matt nodded. He did know. He and Lisa had gone through a lot of shit together too. She'd fought hard for them, until it had finally penetrated his thick skull how close he was to losing her. By the time he'd figured that out and everything looked bright again, with a child on the way, he'd lost them both forever.

And not a single day went by when he didn't regret treating her better during those tough times. It was why he made sure Briar knew how much he loved her, that she was a priority in his life.

Blackwell hesitated, looked like he wanted to say something more, but then glanced away. "I need to take some personal time. I wouldn't ask unless it was a last resort. But I don't know what the hell else to do."

Matt hid his surprise. Blackwell was one of Blue Team's longest standing members, and a quiet, efficient operator. All the guys liked him, though he didn't seem particularly close with any of them. He was solid, all the way around. Losing him right now for any length of time would be tough on everyone, but Blackwell's mental health and marriage were more important in the long term scheme of things.

"Okay," he said in a calm tone, wondering how he would fill this hole. "When were you thinking?"

Blackwell's deep blue eyes met his. "The sooner the better."

Hell. "We're already down one member, with Vance's shoulder injury. He won't be back with the team for a couple months yet."

Blackwell nodded. "Yeah, I know, the timing sucks and I'm sorry. But can you see about finding a replacement for me as soon as possible? I don't know how long I'll be gone, but you know I wouldn't ask if there was another way. This is literally a last ditch effort to save my marriage."

Matt held up a hand to stop him from apologizing. "I hear where you're coming from and I'm sorry you guys are going through a shitty time. But I'd rather not replace you indefinitely if I can help it. You're a great asset to this team, especially with Vance missing. It's gonna take me a little time to look into a replacement for you. You think things over a bit more and—"

"I *have* been thinking about it. For months." He shook his head, jaw tight. "My mind's already made up on this one, commander, I'm sorry. I have to do this."

Matt was quiet a moment, watching him closely. It boded well for Blackwell's marriage that he obviously cared enough to take this step. It couldn't have been easy for him to come in here and say any of this. "You still love her?" he asked quietly.

Blackwell drew in a deep breath. Nodded. "Yeah."

"You gonna fight for her?"

Blackwell's smile was weary. Sad. "Been fighting for her, just not the right way. Guess I've just gotta fight harder."

Matt nodded, feeling for the guy. "Okay. I'll find a way to make this happen. You're part of my team and you've been an outstanding operator for us. We'll all miss you like hell, but for now just—"

His cell chirped.

His personal cell.

Matt's heart skipped a beat and he grabbed it from his belt, hoping to see Briar's number on the display. But it was Rycroft's.

Worry hit him instantly and he shot Blackwell an apologetic look. "Sorry. I need to take this." Ignoring whatever Blackwell said in reply, he answered. "DeLuca."

"It's Rycroft. I've got some news."

"Is Briar all right?" he demanded.

"She's fine. We're just about to board a flight."

Matt leaned back in his seat as relief swamped him. Thank God. He drew in a deep breath. "Where you heading?"

"Miami. And you might want to get a team down there to meet us, ASAP."

Matt stiffened. "Why, what's happened?" He was aware of Blackwell watching him closely.

"We're going after Perez."

He blinked. "Diego Perez?" As in, Fuentes's former top lieutenant, whom Bautista had served as the man's personal enforcer?

"That's the one. We've uncovered certain…evidence that suggests Perez was involved with the murder of at least one CIA officer. And he knows Bautista is still alive. He sent a hitter to take out both him and Georgia. We got the shooter this afternoon, and now we're on our way to pay Perez a little surprise visit. I know that's your boys' area of expertise."

And Briar was with them right now, about to head to Miami so they could plan a sting to arrest him.

Matt ran a hand over his face. He fucking hated this, hated not being there to look out for her personally. "What are you going to do?"

"A little recon, first. Bautista's got insider knowledge that none of the rest of us have. He's ready to give us whatever we need and help us take Perez down. Once we locate him, you guys will need to move fast. How soon can you be here?"

"I'm on it." Matt was already out of his chair and pulling open the door, snapping his fingers at his secretary to get her attention. "Get Blue Team on a flight down to Miami, ASAP," he told her. Then to Rycroft, "We'll be there sometime tonight. I'll call you when we get in."

"All right. See you in a few."

Matt tucked the phone back into its holster on his belt, mind racing as he moved back behind his desk and sank into his chair. Perez was a dangerous target. But at least now Matt would be able to see Briar.

He hoped.

"What's up?" Blackwell asked, poised at the edge of his chair, on alert.

"Sorry, but your personal time is gonna have to wait. Blue Team's going to Miami tonight to arrest Diego Perez."

Chapter Seventeen

I'll be waiting right here for you.

Bautista tucked Georgia's parting words away, along with the knowledge that she was positioned below him on the street right now, hidden in the shadows. He'd worked alone for a long time but he had to admit he liked knowing she was here.

Because this was by far the toughest assignment he'd ever been given.

A simple phone call had confirmed that Laura was here, staying under her alias. The security in the building was the same as it had always been, and Laura never liked her security team to stay in the condo with her and the kids. He couldn't believe Perez hadn't taken more measures to protect them after finding out Bautista was alive.

If Bautista were a different kind of man, killing Perez's family would have been all too easy. And that pissed him the hell off.

Timing the sweep of the security cameras attached to the exterior of the building, he gripped the iron bars of the balcony on the outside of the third-story unit and hoisted himself up. He paused in the shadows next to the sliding glass door, shook his head with an internal sigh.

The curtains were drawn over the sliding glass doors but the slider was open a few inches with the screen shut. Because Laura loved to let the ocean breeze blow through in the evenings.

It was something he'd chastised her for time and time again, but she'd always laughed off his concern. She thought she had an alias and security when she traveled because they were wealthy. She didn't realize where most of the money had come from.

He could hear her voice now. *You act like you expect someone to climb up the side of the building and break in from the balcony.*

That's exactly what he'd just done.

At least she and the kids would be safe now, he consoled himself, leaning in to listen at the screen door. Laura wasn't an ignorant or stupid woman. She might suspect that not all of her husband's business dealings were above board, but Perez went to great lengths to hide all his criminal activity from her—from everyone—and project the image of the doting husband and father, the philanthropist and pillar of the community. Hell, Bautista had helped him maintain the ruse.

He could hear the faint sound of Laura's voice coming from somewhere to the far left of the condo. Probably Michael's room. Laura tucked her babies in faithfully every night whether at home or on vacation, without fail, even though Michael was ten and her daughter was almost seventeen.

How Perez had ever been lucky enough for that sweet, devoted woman to fall for him back when he was a struggling, legitimate businessman, Bautista would never know. At least the bastard appreciated her and treated her well.

He picked the lock on the slider without a sound. If

she'd left it open like this, it meant she'd disabled the alarm system too. God, she had no idea how vulnerable she was up here, didn't have any concept of the kind of violence her husband's enemies could bring down on her and the kids.

Pushing aside the edge of the curtain, he checked to make sure the living room and kitchen were empty. He slipped inside, quickly closed the curtain and stood in front of one of the couches in the lavishly decorated room. He'd wait here for her to come out, not wanting to scare the kids.

The murmur of her voice continued to float from down the hall. A few minutes later things got quiet.

The sound of a door quietly shutting followed soon after, then the patter of her bare feet on the travertine tile floor as she came toward the kitchen/living room. Bautista braced himself, knowing Rycroft and the others would hear every word of this exchange via his earpiece.

Laura appeared around the corner a moment later, heading for the kitchen. She put her phone on the counter and turned toward him, let out a yelp as she stumbled back a step, her face paling and her eyes wide with terror.

"Hi, Laura."

The terror faded quickly, only to be replaced by sheer shock. A hand flew to her chest, her mouth open. "Miguel. Oh my God, you're…"

He gave her a small smile. "Still alive. Yeah."

Her face crumpled. She started across the room, picking up speed as she rushed for him, threw her arms around his neck and hugged him tight. Bautista returned the embrace as she started to cry, wished the hell he hadn't come here for the reasons he had.

"How?" she demanded, her slender arms surprisingly strong as she gripped him fiercely. "How did you survive?"

"It's a long story." One he may have to tell her

eventually.

"Mama?"

He looked up to see Jenny and her younger brother peeking around the corner from the hallway. When they saw him their eyes went wide and huge smiles lit their faces. "Uncle Miguel!"

Bautista gently set Laura aside as they raced for him, grunted when they both pounced on him. He caught one in each arm and gave them a squeeze before setting them on their feet. "Hey, squirts." Damn, Jenny was nearly up to his chin now.

"Where have you been?" ten-year-old Michael asked. His namesake. Laura had insisted they name their son Diego Miguel, after their father and their favorite "uncle", who they'd never realized was actually their father's faithful assassin. "Mama and Papa said you went to heaven."

More like hell, until Georgia had appeared back in his life. "No, no heaven for me," he said with a stiff smile.

God, it hurt, seeing those innocent faces beaming up at him. He'd missed them more than he'd realized. And now he was here to end their world as they knew it.

He set a hand on Michael's shoulder. "Sorry I came to visit so late, I know how your mom hates it when the whole bedtime routine gets interrupted."

Jenny rolled her eyes. "Ugh, I know. She's insanely OCD."

He couldn't help but grin. The teenage attitude was still out in full force. "Listen, I need to talk to your mom about something important. You guys go on back to bed, okay?"

Both of them protested with disappointed groans. "Will you come talk to us for a while afterward then?" Michael asked, those big brown eyes pleading. He'd always had a sort of hero worship thing going on with Bautista, and he'd never had the heart to tell the kid he should find a more worthy man to idolize.

He nodded, because there was no way he could refuse that simple request. "Sure. But you two squirts have to go to bed right now then, or no deal."

"Okay," Michael pouted, then turned with his sister and followed her to the hallway.

The moment the second of the two doors shut, he turned to face Laura. She was wiping her face, still smiling, her bright green eyes full of questions. "We have to call Diego and tell him the news. He'll want to know—"

"He already knows."

She blinked at his clipped tone, her smile fading.

Ah, shit, he just wanted this over with. "Sit down, Laura," he said quietly.

Slowly backing up a step she sank onto the couch, her gaze locked with his. "What's wrong?" she asked, her posture stiff.

There was no easy way to say it.

He sank into the easy chair beside the couch, leaned forward to rest his forearms on his knees. "I need you to pack up the kids and leave here tonight." He kept his voice calm, not wanting to scare her even more than she already was. Rycroft and the others would already be on their way up with a team to secure her and the kids.

Her eyes widened. "What? Why?"

"There's a team of federal agents waiting to escort you to the airport." He ignored her shocked gasp, kept talking. "They're going to fly you to an undisclosed location and put you in a safe house with a 24-7 security detail."

She shook her head as the gravity of the situation dawned on her. "Oh my God, what's my husband done?" she whispered, looking stricken.

After a second's hesitation, he told her straight out. "He was involved with the murders of two CIA officers.

And then he sent Nico to kill me."

Laura's already pale face completely blanched of color. She swallowed convulsively, her hands twitching in the folds of her dress, and shook her head. "No…"

"Yes. And now Nico's dead."

"Oh my God…"

Yeah. "I'm sorry, and I wish the hell it wasn't true. You know I wouldn't lie to you about this."

She swallowed again, looking ill.

Reaching out, he took one of her hands in his. Her skin was cold, clammy, and the shock on her lovely face was all too real.

"Laura." She blinked, focused on him again, and there were fresh tears in her eyes. "I need to find him. Tell me where he is." Perez was smart. Though the NSA had been tracking his online activity and listening to phone calls, he'd proven difficult to pinpoint.

Right now they couldn't verify where he was. Bautista knew several places where he might be, and both the FBI and NSA were investigating, but if Laura could give them more intel it would be a major advantage for them.

More tears gathered, brimming on her dark lashes. She shook her head, her eyes pleading with him not to ask this of her. "Please."

He squeezed her hand, feeling like shit. But there were too many places Perez could be and they didn't have time to investigate all of them. He needed her help. "I need to know where he is."

Teardrops spilled over, rolling down her cheeks. "I can't…" She glanced at her phone over on the counter, knew what she was thinking.

"It's too late, Laura. This entire building is swarming with federal agents right now and the NSA is monitoring everything said in this condo, and all calls to and from it."

Her shoulders shook as she fought back a sob. "I

can't."

"You have to," he said, his heart aching for her and the position she'd been placed in. "You have to, for the kids' sake. You're not safe here, and you won't be until Diego is brought in. He's made enemies. Dangerous enemies, and I don't want you to wind up a target." If Georgia had found out about Perez's involvement with the murders, then Rossland might have already sent someone to kidnap or kill Perez's wife and children.

At that she stilled, inhaled a shaky breath. "But what will... What will happen to him if I tell you?"

"He'll be arrested and charged with murder of two federal agents." *If* he went quietly.

She gripped his hand now, her fingers digging into the backs of his. "But they won't...kill him." She searched his eyes, her desperation clear. "Right?"

Not unless he forces them to. And Perez might. "They're going to arrest him," he repeated, unable to tell her the brutal truth. That her husband wasn't even close to the man she'd thought, and he might choose death rather than face a lifelong prison term for his crimes.

He could feel the seconds slipping past as he awaited her answer, the tension growing inside him with every heartbeat. Perez had a lot of money and resources at his disposal. If he'd gone into hiding, it would be that much harder to find him. Even if he hadn't, they still had a number of locations to search. And Perez was paranoid enough to keep moving. They needed to find him before he got nervous enough to go on the run.

"The man in charge of this op—a federal agent— allowed me to come and tell you this myself, but my time's up now. He'll be at the door any minute to move you guys out of here. Before he gets here, I need to know where your husband is. *Tell* me, Laura."

Her lips quivered as she gazed up at him with a heartbroken expression. "He told me he was going fishing for a few days." She hitched in a breath. "That's all he told me. Wherever he went, he left this morning."

He nodded, pretty sure she was telling the truth. But he wasn't willing to bet on it. She'd just been delivered one hell of a shock and would automatically want to protect her husband.

"Okay," he agreed. At least her answer narrowed down their possibilities to places on the water.

He pushed out a sigh. "Come with me." Standing, he pulled her to her feet and she didn't resist. "I promised the kids I'd see them before I left. We'll tell them you're going on another surprise vacation." Jenny was too old to fall for that story, but it would have to do.

She didn't respond, clearly still in shock and struggling to come to terms with everything. Bautista let out a deep breath and pulled her into his arms. *I'm so fucking sorry*, he told her silently.

She leaned into his hold, curled up against his chest in such a lost and trusting way that his gut twisted. "I'm sorry," he murmured against her hair. "But I had no choice."

Georgia was his only motivation now.

Pulling away, he took Laura's hand and led her toward the children's rooms.

****

Using her key card, Georgia unlocked the hotel room door and peeked inside. They'd arrived in Miami a couple of hours ago, after flying from Destin soon after the agents had taken Laura Perez and her children into protective custody. Miguel hadn't spoken to anyone on the way down here, and they'd all given him space. Tonight must have been hard on him.

He looked over his shoulder at her from where he was perched on the side of the bed, the muscular expanse of his back and shoulders illuminated in the soft light from the floor lamp set in the far corner of the room. His dark hair was damp and slicked back from his face, as if he'd just showered.

A flutter started low in her abdomen as she shut the door behind her, but the bleak look in his eyes made her heart squeeze. "Hey. You didn't eat anything earlier, so I grabbed you something at the deli on the corner." She walked over to him, held out the bag when she was directly in front of him. "Turkey on whole wheat with cranberry and Havarti, no mayo. And one of those iced teas you like."

He reached up to take the bag from her, and she was glad to see some of that bleakness fading from his eyes. "Thanks."

She shrugged. "I remembered you used to get them a lot when you came to visit your grandmother."

"Yeah." He tried a smile then set the bag on the floor at his feet, clearly uninterested in food.

Georgia sank onto the side of the mattress next to him, trying not to get distracted by his sexy bare torso. He was hurting bad inside and she was distressed at not knowing how to make it better.

She and the others had heard every word he'd said to Laura and the children. It had been eye-opening for her. Back in Miami, he'd tried to tell her—well, Julia—what he was, that he wasn't a good man.

But she'd already known the truth. She'd seen the goodness in him plenty of times before, in the tender way he'd cared for his incapacitated grandmother, the way he'd treated her when he'd known her as Julia, and when he'd rescued Marisol and risked his life to protect them both.

Tonight, she'd seen another side of him that had made her fall in love with him even more. Laura and those kids clearly adored him, and they'd been his first concern, even more than nailing Perez after what the man had done.

That told her so much about his character. He was loyal and protective, and was willing to put himself in harm's way for the few people he cared about.

A tiny circle she was now a part of.

But now she could feel the clock ticking. Drone and satellite footage had confirmed that Perez was indeed at his place outside Miami.

At that very moment the FBI's Hostage Rescue Team was prepping to serve the arrest warrant. She, Miguel and the others would assist with logistics prior to and during the op, which was planned for tomorrow night.

Once Perez was in custody, she didn't know what fate held in store for her. For them. And she didn't know how she was supposed to go on without him now.

"I'm glad you got to be the one to tell her," she said softly. "It was obvious how much she adores you. Not that I blame her," she added, nudging his thigh with hers.

A sad smile twisted his lips. "She's a good person. I just hate that it came down to this."

Georgia nodded. "Were you that close with Perez?"

"Different than with Laura and the kids, but yeah. I would have walked through hell for him."

"I think you did walk through hell for him," she murmured, thinking of the things he'd done for the man, all the things he'd endured, including nearly dying. "More than once."

And the worst part would come tomorrow, when he helped the FBI capture the man he'd served so faithfully for so long. It didn't matter that she thought Perez was a piece of shit who didn't deserve Miguel's loyalty. It was clear this situation was tearing him apart.

"Yeah. True." He pulled in a deep breath, pushed it out in a long, slow exhale and lowered his head into his hands, looking exhausted.

She couldn't stand to see him hurting like this. If she

could take even a little of the hurt away over these next few hours together, it would be worth it.

Unsure of her welcome when he was so clearly upset, she reached out to brush a short lock of hair off his forehead. He turned his head to look at her, and as their eyes met, the intensity of that dark gaze echoed deep inside her.

Not wanting to ruin the moment with words, she cupped the side of his face and stroked her thumb across his bristly cheek, let her touch speak for her. *I'm here for you. I'm sorry you're hurting.*

In response Miguel reached up to gently grasp her wrist. For a moment she thought he would push her away but instead he turned his face and pressed his lips into the center of her palm. Warmth slid through her veins at the tender caress.

Feeling braver, she inched closer, framed his face between both hands and leaned in to kiss the bridge of his nose. He closed his eyes as though absorbing the kiss, then surprised her by leaning forward, burying his face in her neck and wrapping his arms around her, holding her so tight she couldn't move.

Her heart cracked in two at his unspoken need for comfort.

Without a word she embraced him, folding her arms around his shoulders, one hand cradling the back of his head. He pulled in a deep breath and let it out slowly, then another, as though struggling with himself.

Minutes ticked past. Gently stroking his hair, she held him that way without speaking, then kissed the top of his head, his temple. Miguel raised his head and met her gaze, the pain in his eyes hitting her like a blow. But there was heat too, and an answering rush swept through her body.

When he took the back of her head in one hand and sought her mouth, she kissed him long and slow, took advantage when his lips parted to slide her tongue inside to twine with his.

A low, rough groan eased from his chest and he met every stroke. Her heart pounded, tremors of excitement and need flowing through her. Every nerve ending was alive and tingling.

She let her hands roam all over his bare back and shoulders, across his chest, exploring the hard ridges of muscle that she found so sexy. Needing more, she swung one thigh across his to straddle his lap. The bolt of pleasure that shot through her when her center pressed against the denim-covered ridge of his erection made her moan into his mouth.

That sound seemed to trigger something in him.

Instantly the kiss turned hot and urgent. He shifted her on his lap, one arm coming around her hips to hold her snug to him while he rocked that delicious erection against her.

She broke the kiss to peel her shirt up and off, making short work of her bra before grabbing his face and fusing her mouth to his once more. He made a low sound of pleasure and approval and swept his hand from her hips, up the length of her spine to grip the nape of her neck.

She shivered at the possessive hold, melting inside. But before he could do anything more she pushed at his shoulders. He stilled for a second, eased away to look into her eyes.

"Lie back," she whispered, her breathing as erratic as her pulse.

Holding her gaze, he slowly lowered himself to the sheets and stretched out across the bed. Offering himself to her.

The soft light from the lamp gilded the honed perfection of his body in soft strokes of gold. She wasted no time in pressing her lips to the center of his chest, following every ridge and hollow as her hands slipped down to undo his pants and free his straining erection. His cock popped free, hot and hard.

With a hum of female appreciation, she curled her fingers around his length. Miguel hissed in a breath, one hand sliding into her hair. His fingers rubbed at her scalp, a restless, impatient motion that spoke of his growing need.

A need she was dying to satisfy.

She was so turned on already, her entire body humming with anticipation, and having him lie there, allowing her to please him made her insanely hot. Shimmying down so that her face was eye-level with his cock, she looked up the length of his body at him.

His eyes smoldered down at her, so hot she could feel their touch on her skin. And when she leaned down to tease the sensitive crown with her lips and tongue, he arched his hips, his eyes sliding closed as his rough groan filled the silent room.

She took her time, savoring his every reaction as she eased him between her lips and sucked his straining flesh.

"God," he bit out, eyes squeezed shut and that hand bunching in her hair. "Ah, angel…"

Emboldened, she worked him with her mouth and hand, reveling in the way his breathing turned rough, the way the muscles in his thighs twitched. Another time she might have finished him off in her mouth, but she knew this was likely their last time together and she desperately needed to feel him inside her.

Still working him with her mouth, she shimmied out of her pants. Giving him one last lick from root to tip that made him shudder, she straddled his hips and settled her aching core against the hot length of him.

Immediately he grasped her hips and started to sit up, but she stayed him with a hand on the center of his chest. He froze, watching her.

She trailed her hand up his chest, over his throat and chin to brush her fingers over his lips. "Just let me love you," she whispered, sensing it wasn't easy for him to let a lover be in charge. But she did love him and needed to show him that.

Heat and tenderness flared in his eyes, then he relaxed against the bedding once more. The trust in that one gesture, more than anything else, made her heart tip over that steep edge into free-fall.

Lifting up, she slid along the hard ridge of his cock until the empty ache inside her became too much. He watched her with blazing dark eyes, his gaze scorching her naked body as his hands gripped her hips.

When she at last eased the head of him inside her and sank down, his head tipped back, a groan of raw ecstasy tearing free. Gasping at the thick, hard length buried inside her, stretching her, she sat up straight and began to ride him.

He stared up at her the whole time, lips pressed into a tight line as he strained to hold back, both hands shifting upward to cradle the tender flesh of her breasts. She sighed at the contact, moaned when he began stimulating her nipples, the sensation shooting down to blend with the ache between her legs.

"Stroke yourself," he rasped out, his breathing ragged, all his muscles standing out in sharp relief as he fought to hold himself back.

Holding his gaze, Georgia slipped two fingers into her mouth before sliding them down the center of her body to her swollen clit. Pleasure instantly tightened her muscles, her inner walls squeezing his cock. He filled her so perfectly, hit every sensitive spot.

Miguel groaned like a man in agony and shifted restlessly beneath her, his eyes heavy-lidded with desire. And in that moment she knew he needed her every bit as much as she needed him.

She'd never felt more beautiful, more powerful than she did at that moment. Poised atop her lover, this powerful, complex man she'd given her heart to, giving them both unspeakable pleasure.

She rocked harder, her fingers moving faster over the slick flesh between her thighs. She could feel the peak coming closer, closer with every stroke, each delicious, rocking glide on his cock. It coiled tight inside her, growing stronger with every second.

Staring down into his face, a punch of pure ecstasy arced between them as her orgasm hit. Her own cries echoed in her ears as the waves took her, the feel of his cock inside her intensifying the pleasure, prolonging it.

Panting as it faded, she set her palms on his shoulders to keep from collapsing on top of him, and looked into his face. He was breathing hard, his nostrils flared, eyes glazed with need.

With a naughty smile she shifted her hips to change the angle and took him deeper, slowing her movements. Drawing it out. Making it last, and cataloguing his every reaction.

His hands blindly reached for her hips, his fingers digging in hard. He swelled even more inside her, growing thicker, harder.

She worked him, squeezed him, loving him even more for this gift he was giving her, his surrender. Something she instinctively knew he'd never given anyone else.

Apparently even he had his limits, because he lost the fight to hold still. Fingers biting into her hips, he growled low in his throat and thrust upward, his hips pumping hard and fast, then he arched and froze, shouting as his release hit. She felt him pulse inside her, bathing her with his warmth, and another shiver rolled through her.

Taking his face between her hands she tipped

forward and absorbed his groans of pleasure in a passionate kiss. He relaxed beneath her, his arms sliding up to band around her ribs and pull her to his chest.

She tucked her face into the curve of his shoulder, pressed a tender kiss there. "I love you," she murmured.

It was terrifying to say it aloud, but she couldn't contain it a moment longer and wanted him to know it, especially if this was their last night together. Whatever happened tomorrow, she needed him to know he had her heart.

Miguel rolled them, reversing positions so he was the one on top, cupping her face and staring down into her eyes. "Say it again." His expression was the most intense she'd ever seen it.

The husky demand made her smile softly. "I love you."

With a rough sound he captured her lips with his, devoured her mouth.

Stifling a laugh, she poked him in the ribs and he lifted his head. "And?" she prompted, lifting one eyebrow.

A slow, secret smile curved his lips. "Yeah. I love you back."

Now she grinned, and it was definitely smug. "Knew it."

He laughed and kissed the tip of her nose. "I never knew I could feel like this. You've turned me inside out."

"Right there with you," she admitted.

When he drew back a second later, his expression was troubled. "So what happens now?"

She smoothed a hand up his ribs, over his back. "I don't know," she answered truthfully. All she knew was, she couldn't let him go. Not now. Not ever.

Something like regret flickered in his eyes for a moment, making her heart clench. They both knew that after the operation to arrest Perez tomorrow, their time together would come to an end. His contract with the NSA was over when *they* said it was over. And they weren't just going to let the two of them drive off into the sunset together. Not to mention her future and all the legal ramifications surrounding her case was still a huge question mark as well.

The thought of being torn away from him now was too painful to bear.

"I can't let you go," she whispered brokenly, the words bursting free. "I can't."

His expression turned fierce, so full of love and conviction that her heart tripped. "I won't let you go either."

So what were they going to do? How could they stay together?

Refusing to waste their last few hours alone together dwelling on that disheartening thought, she tugged him down and covered his lips with hers, determined to find a way for them to be together.

Whatever it took to be with him, she'd do it. Because she was never walking away from this man again.

Chapter Eighteen

autista was already wound tight as a wire when the door to the briefing room opened and the HRT guys began to file in. Eight big, muscular men, all of them moving with a confidence that came only from being a seasoned operator.

Supervisory Special Agent Matt DeLuca led the way. His stride slowed a fraction when he saw Bautista standing at the front of the room with Rycroft, but then his eyes shot to Briar and a wide smile transformed his expression.

The masculine rumble of conversation stopped the instant the next guy in line saw him. A big blond guy, who Bautista recognized as the team leader, Tucker.

All eyes were on him as the others entered the room. The second to last one stopped dead in the doorway, their gazes clashing from across the room. Bautista's pulse kicked up.

He knew that face, would never forget it. Dark hair, bronzed skin, light brown eyes. Pissed off expression.

The bastard who'd shot him and then nearly beaten him to death on the deck of that boat in Miami. Ethan

Cruz. Marisol's boyfriend.

The HRT member's shoulders went rigid as he stared at him. "What the fuck is this?" he growled to the room at large.

DeLuca stepped over to him, put a warning hand on his chest. "Cruzie, don't."

Agent Cruz shot an accusatory look at his commander. "Did you know about this?"

"Not until about seven seconds ago."

"Well," Rycroft began in a dry tone. "I guess formal introductions aren't necessary for most of you since you met in June, but for those of you who don't already know who this is, Miguel Bautista, formerly known as *el Santo*, served as Perez's personal enforcer. He also did a long stint in the Army before that, where he served most of his time as a sniper."

The room was dead silent. Bautista hated having all the eyes on him.

"He's contracted under the NSA and working with us on this op because nobody knows Perez, his likely reactions and his properties better than him. I realize some of you have some unresolved animosity going on but as you're professionals I expect you to put that aside for the duration of the operation. You may not like it, but that's the way it's gonna be, so make peace with it."

Cruz shot Rycroft a cool look, then aimed a hard glare at Bautista that said he didn't trust him, but lost the hostile posture. DeLuca lowered his hand to let him step past. When the entire team was seated before them, Rycroft continued.

"Standing beside Briar is Georgia Randall, who you may remember from the Miami op as well."

Bautista watched the men size her up. There was surprise in some of those gazes, but also a measure of curiosity. He didn't like them staring at her, period.

"Briar and Georgia are both going to be assisting

with logistics for this op, and they'll also act as scouts or snipers if need be. They'll be working directly with your sniper team while Bautista and I accompany the assault team into the target building during the breach and subsequent arrest."

Agent Tucker folded his arms across his wide chest and took it all in, his expression calm and focused. Cruz had his arms crossed as well, but his jaw was clamped tight, his eyes trying to bore a hole through Bautista's face. Bautista refused to acknowledge him.

"You've all been briefed on Perez. We were able to confirm that he arrived at the target residence at twenty-two hundred hours last night. Here's what we're dealing with."

Rycroft pulled up aerial photographs and satellite images of the seaside mansion outside of Miami. A three story, fifteen-thousand square foot Spanish-style palace covered with white stucco, set on three acres of ocean-front land, complete with lushly manicured gardens and grounds. It was set back a fair distance from the road, bordered on two sides by forest and the nearest neighbor was over a mile away.

"We have a small window to work with, so we're tight on time to make the assault. It's only a matter of time before he realizes he's at risk, and we need to get him before he gets suspicious and makes a run for it."

He detailed the security situation, the number of guards likely patrolling the property, that Perez would have at least one bodyguard there. The layout, possible entry and exfil points.

"We'll be inserting via helo close to the target for maximum speed, then we'll go in on foot. Now Bautista's going to brief you on the more exciting stuff." Rycroft nodded at him.

Bautista stepped over to the laptop and began detailing what they needed to know. "Of all Perez's properties, this is the one I'm least familiar with. The last time I was there was last May, and it was undergoing major renovations. No matter what the layout looks like inside now, there's going to be a state-of-the-art security system. Motion detectors, pressure sensors leading up to the perimeter, and likely thermal imaging as well. The guards are well paid, and they keep a low profile around the grounds. One of them monitors the security system at all times."

Pointing to the screen with a laser pointer, he detailed what he knew about the location of the security cameras and sensors. "We'll need to cut the power just seconds before we make the breach, and we'll have only seconds more to get inside before the backup generators start it up again." He paused. "Any questions?"

Tucker raised his hand. "Where are you and Rycroft going to be during the assault?"

"Right behind you."

The entire team looked over at DeLuca, who nodded his confirmation. "The assault team goes in with Bautista and Rycroft following directly behind. Bautista knows the area the best, and he's also the only person in this room who's been inside the place. Ordinarily he'd assist from back at the mobile command center with me via comms, but in this situation Rycroft and I felt it was better Bautista be with you for the assault."

Bautista didn't bother looking at the team members for their reactions, mainly because he didn't give a shit what they thought about this. He had a score to settle, Perez was an ongoing threat to Georgia, and he was going to help the HRT make sure the traitorous bastard could never threaten anyone ever again. If that meant using lethal force, so be it. Even if it meant he had to be the one to pull the trigger.

"'Kay," Tucker answered in an even tone, taking it all in stride.

After the briefing and Q&A period, it took a couple of hours for the team to detail a plan, get suited up and ready their equipment. They all rode to the airfield in silence, Bautista wedged into the back of a van between Rycroft and Briar.

He could still feel Cruz watching him from the other side of it and studiously ignored him. Didn't matter if Cruz still had a problem with him. If they wanted to survive the upcoming assault, they'd all need to have their heads on tight and leave personal differences behind.

Truthfully he wasn't too concerned about Cruz staging some kind of "accident" during the op. Cruz was a professional, had to be disciplined or he never would have made the elite unit in the first place.

Two specially equipped Blackhawk helos were waiting for them on the tarmac when they arrived, their rotors turning slowly and the crews ready to go. It felt surreal, like he'd stepped back in time, about to go on a mission for Uncle Sam. Strange, to be working for him again after all this time, on the legal side of things.

Shouldering his assault rifle and gear, he followed the others to the first bird, paused to hang back with Georgia and Briar. They'd be going with the sniper teams and DeLuca to insert at a different LZ, while he and Rycroft landed closer to the mansion with the assaulters.

He flicked a glance at Briar, who must have realized he wanted some alone time with Georgia, because she grinned. "See you when it's all over," she said to him, reaching out to slap his shoulder before walking for the other helo, leaving him alone with Georgia.

With the camo paint covering her fair skin her pale blue eyes were even more startling in the lights of the airport. "Bet it's been a while since you fast roped into an LZ," she teased, a grin curving her lips.

"Yeah. What about you?"

Her smile widened. "Not as long for me as you might

think."

He marveled again at her self-assurance and skill. He could probably spend a lifetime with this mysterious woman and never learn all her secrets.

And damn, he'd give anything for that chance.

Needing to touch her, he reached out to cup the back of her head, her golden brown hair concealed beneath a black knit cap. "You be safe."

It drove him insane that he couldn't be at her side for this, but at least she'd be in the background, providing overwatch and cover and not directly involved with the assault. That eased his worry a little.

Her smile faded. "You too. Because you and I've got unfinished business to deal with as soon as this is over."

"Bautista, any day," Rycroft called out over the rise of the noise as the helos powered up their engines.

Pulling her toward him, he captured her lips in a hard, fervent kiss. "See you soon."

Within minutes he was sitting in the Blackhawk with Rycroft and the HRT boys. They lifted off and flew through the darkness to the target area. Perez's compound was isolated, far away from the other big mansions the area was known for.

That was no accident. He always liked having a buffer of land around his property, to provide extra privacy and security.

The pilots went into a low hover. One by one, they slid down the thick rope to the ground and immediately fanned out into a tight circle to provide security for each other. As soon as Tuck gave the signal, the helo lifted and flew back toward the airport.

When the sounds of the rotors disappeared into the distance, the music of insects filled the vacuum of silence. Bautista focused on the lights of the target property, way off in the distance. He glanced over at Tuck, awaiting instructions.

"Move in," the team leader murmured into his comm.

They moved in two diamond formations, quickly crossing the shadowed part of the lawn toward the main gate. Perez would have motion detectors in place, Bautista just didn't know where.

About sixty yards from the perimeter fence line, Tuck signaled for a halt. Everyone stopped and dropped to one knee, keeping watch around them. Bautista knew they were waiting for word that the power had been cut. His pulse quickened as he waited there, perspiration building beneath his ballistic vest.

Ahead of them, the lights suddenly went out around and inside the building.

Rycroft's voice was clear through the earpiece. "Power's disabled."

"Go," Tuck ordered quietly.

Bautista got up and ran after Bauer, the big former SEAL eating up the remaining distance to the fence. They had ninety seconds before the generators turned on the auxiliary power source.

He scanned the fence line, all his senses on high alert. This was what he lived for. What he craved. The adrenaline high, the thrill of the hunt. It felt good to be in action again, the rush like a drug he couldn't get enough of.

Up ahead he caught movement in his NVGs. Tuck was out front with Evers right behind him. One of them fired, dropping the guard. Two more shots rang out in quick succession as more HRT guys took out some of Perez's security.

Twenty seconds later they were lined up at the entrance they'd chosen. At Tuck's signal Evers blew the charge on the lock and blasted the door open. They charged inside as a unit, fluid, deadly.

Three more targets appeared around the corner. The

HRT dropped them all. They kept moving forward, Bautista directly behind Bauer, and Rycroft behind him.

Where are you, Diego, you piece of shit?

Didn't matter where he'd gone. They'd find him.

They cleared the first room and headed to the next, working their way toward the rear of the house, which faced the ocean.

Shots rang out from down the right-hand hallway, exploding the tile floor and sending up a spray of marble shrapnel to pepper the wall. Cruz took the shooter out.

Their boots barely made any sound on the polished floor tiles. Faint rays of moonlight spilled in through the tall, wide windows overlooking the ocean at the back of the house, off the kitchen/great room.

No sign of Perez.

A warning buzz started up at the base of his spine. Where could he be? There was no way he'd escaped the premises or made it to the water without one of the sniper teams seeing him, and no one had reported any movement.

They cleared the entire floor and were standing next to the office before the lights suddenly came on. Bautista and the others pushed the NVGs up on their helmet mounts, their eyes quickly adjusting to the sudden brightness.

"Moving upstairs," Tuck reported, likely speaking to DeLuca, who was back at the mobile command center.

Where the hell are you, Perez?

Bautista stayed in the office, mind racing to try and figure out where his former boss might be hiding.

And as he scanned the office one last time, he saw it. The corner of an area rug in the office was rumpled.

Bautista headed straight for it.

"What?" Rycroft asked, following him inside the room.

Going with his instinct, Bautista bent and pulled the

rug aside. Sure enough, he found a door beneath it.

"Son of a bitch," Rycroft muttered, then quickly called the team back in. While two guys provided rear security, they assessed the trapdoor and decided to blow it. "Sniper teams, you see anything?"

"Negative," came both replies.

Rycroft and Tuck both looked at him. "You think he's down there?"

"Has to be. He'll be making a run for a boat." It was the only option for escape here.

"Snipers already have that covered," Rycroft answered, then faced Tuck. "I'll let you do your magic."

Tuck took over immediately, coordinating the assault. When everyone was in position, Evers blew the locking mechanism on the trapdoor and they hauled the heavy slab of marble off the opening.

No one fired up at them and no booby traps went off. But Bautista was still uneasy and he knew the others were too. Perez wasn't the type to go quietly. If he was down there, they were in for a fight.

It made him insane to stand there and wait, to have to hang back until the others dropped through. He wanted to be the one leading this charge. He wanted to be the one to apprehend Perez.

When it was finally his turn he squatted down, grasped the edge of the opening and dropped the six feet down into what amounted to a large concrete underground bunker.

An empty one.

His heart sank and frustration pulsed through him as the five other guys who had jumped down here turned to look at him. Maybe he was just being paranoid but he got the sense they all suspected he'd just let Perez slip through their fingers.

On purpose.

"Well," Cruz drawled from behind him, his tone

dripping disdain and sarcasm. "Any other fancy ideas?"

Chapter Nineteen

Bautista resented the unspoken accusation in the other man's words.

"I want him as bad as the rest of you," he shot back. Yeah he was being defensive but he didn't care. The HRT had made it clear they didn't like working with him but they were all on the same side here.

And right now precious seconds were ticking past while Perez made his escape. "Worse," he added to the rest of them. "I don't give a fuck if you believe that or not, just do your job and—"

"Over here."

At Schroder's urgent voice Bautista and Rycroft both whipped around. The team medic was standing over by the far wall, feeling along the concrete surface.

"I feel a seam."

Bautista hurried over and confirmed there was a rectangular-shaped seam in the wall. Upon further investigation he found a slightly recessed area beside it and pressed it. Something clicked and the panel pressed inward, revealing an electronic keypad.

Tuck and Rycroft were right behind him now,

watching his every move, their tension palpable. "Any chance you can figure out that code?" Rycroft asked.

Bautista entered three he could think of offhand, but none of them worked. Not surprising given how paranoid Perez was and how often he changed all his security codes.

He knew Perez liked to use words, usually Spanish words for each property he owned, sometimes the color of it. Since this house was white, he entered the word *blanca*.

The light on the panel flashed green. A moment later the locking mechanism in the door whirred and the heavy concrete slab slid aside.

"Holy shit," Schroder muttered, and stood back for Tuck to assess what lay ahead of them. Another dark tunnel. "It's like a fucking fortress down here."

Yeah, and who knew what else the cagey bastard had installed since the last time Bautista was here? Perez was notoriously paranoid. And he was slipping farther out of reach with each second they stood here.

The darkened tunnel appeared to follow a zigzag pattern. To cut down the possibility of anyone hitting Perez and his security with a shot if an escape became necessary.

"He's going for the water," Bautista said, urgency humming through his bloodstream. "We have to move *now*."

Tuck motioned his team forward. Rycroft was already on comms while the HRT boys stacked up at the first corner. "Sniper teams, be advised. Perez is heading for the water, likely to make an escape attempt via boat." Since there were no boats moored at the private dock on Perez's property, he had to be going for one at a neighboring property.

"Roger that," Georgia's voice came back, loud and clear. "Moving into better position now."

Just knowing she was out there on alert gave Bautista an added sense of peace as he cat-walked behind Bauer down the first leg of the tunnel. No sooner had they reached the first bend when they heard movement.

Tuck stepped out from behind cover, firing as he moved, with Evers at his back, also shooting. The firing stopped.

Suspects down. Evers and Cruz paused to kick the dead men's weapons away from them when they reached the two bodies, but the team didn't stop.

As they turned around the next bend in the corridor, more shots rang out toward them. But up ahead in the distance, through his goggles Bautista caught a glimpse of a familiar silhouette at the far end of the tunnel as the man darted across the small open space.

Perez.

His hackles went up, a punch of adrenaline roaring through his body. He stayed at the end of the line while Tuck and Evers engaged another threat up ahead. Bauer and Schroder engaged another, with Cruz and Blackwell covering them.

Bautista ignored them all. He raced past them on the left to avoid the line of fire, sprinting headlong for his target.

"Bautista!" Rycroft's sharp voice cut through the roar of blood in his ears. But he didn't slow. Didn't hesitate as he chased after Perez, his sole focus on taking the bastard down.

"Two targets just exited the tunnel and are moving toward the water," Georgia reported over the comms. "Moving in to engage now."

The sound of her voice jarred him for a moment before he locked the emotional response away. He couldn't think about her or her safety. Refused to think about anything other than stopping Perez before he could reach the water and the sniper teams waiting to take him out.

Boots thudding over the concrete floor, he ignored Rycroft's angry commands coming at him through his earpiece.

Perez was his mission. *His* right to take down.

The figure ahead of him suddenly appeared against the backdrop of faint light coming from outside at the end of the tunnel. Perez whirled, a weapon in his hand.

A grouping of bullets slammed into the concrete wall inches away from him, peppering his left upper arm with the sharp bite of tiny bits of shrapnel, like a swarm of angry hornets.

He barely noticed the pain, just kept running, his thighs burning as he raced headlong toward the man who had betrayed him.

Behind him he was dimly aware of the HRT guys rushing after him. He tuned it all out, determined to find Perez before anyone else did. Before they reached the end of the tunnel and Perez stepped outside, where Georgia or the other sniper teams might get him.

He's mine.

Bautista kept the butt of his rifle locked firm against his right shoulder, his eyes on its optics, finger on the trigger. Perez disappeared from view before Bautista could get a shot off, then popped his head around the far corner again, fired again and vanished from view.

Mentally cursing, Bautista ran flat out, the growing light telling him they were nearing the end of the tunnel. The others were charging up behind him. He couldn't let them reach him.

Time was running out. Soon someone else would get Perez. Bautista would not let that happen.

No way, asshole. You're fucking mine.

Jaw locked tight, he burst around the final zigzag in the tunnel, determined to take Perez down or die trying.

****

Flat on her belly with Briar beside her acting as spotter, Georgia stared through her scope at the mansion nestled against the shore. Must have cost Perez a freaking fortune, and that's before all the custom security measures he'd put in place.

"All quiet here," she reported to the HRT sniper team, seven guys positioned at various points on the property. One of them had taken out a guard walking the perimeter about three minutes ago and other FBI agents were positioned along the beach in case Perez somehow got clear.

That's not going to happen, she thought grimly.

"Here too," the leader, Colebrook, answered, and the others reported the same.

She let out a deep breath and forced herself to relax. Not easy to do when Miguel was down in a tunnel engaging Perez and his lackeys. She'd rather be there backing him up, giving him what protection she could.

"Wish we were down there kicking ass instead of stuck up here," she muttered to Briar.

"Tell me about it." She peered through her night vision binos, doing a sweep of the grounds. "But this beats being stuck at a desk. I gotta say, I don't know how Matt stands it. He misses the action, I can tell."

"No doubt." It was strange, being here like this with Briar.

Even after all these years they still worked together like a well-oiled machine, slipping back into their routine as though they'd never taken time apart. And Georgia was insanely curious about how Briar had made the transition into a serious relationship with DeLuca after living and working alone for so long, and planned to ask her as soon as this op wrapped up.

That shouldn't be long from now. With Perez

trapped between the HRT boys and the sniper teams positioned around the property, there was no way he would escape.

A sudden movement caught her attention. She shifted her weapon, bringing the scope to the left to focus on an area overlooking the water. Two men burst into view, both carrying rifles.

She couldn't get a shot off from here. They'd have to move closer.

"Two targets just exited the tunnel and are moving toward the water," Georgia said to the entire team. "Moving in to engage now." She requested cover from the other sniper teams, then pushed up onto her elbows and knees. "Let's go," she said to Briar.

"You're clear," Colebrook answered.

"Roger." Together she and Briar burst out of the brush and raced across the manicured lawn, rifles clutched in their hands. Briar sprinted beside her, keeping pace as they headed for the beach.

They had to take out Perez's remaining security and head him off. She wasn't sure what was going on below in the tunnel but one of the HRT sniper teams was moving down to the beach now, converging on either side with her and Briar.

Forty yards from the house, a man popped out from around the corner of the wall. Georgia and Briar instantly dove to the ground on their bellies, but Georgia was the first to get in firing position. She didn't flinch as the man fired at them, his bullets slamming into the ground less than a foot away from her, kicking up grass and dirt.

Eye to the scope, she aimed at his center mass and squeezed the trigger. He fell to his knees but she was already firing again, striking him square in the heart.

This time he fell flat and didn't move.

Georgia tapped her earpiece. "Target down outside the house," she reported to the entire team.

"Clear," Briar murmured beside her.

"We're still in the tunnel," Rycroft replied. "And Bautista's taken off after Perez."

A sliver of unease corkscrewed down her spine, but she quickly dismissed it. *He'll be fine. He has all the backup he needs.*

Except she was suddenly afraid that his need for vengeance would override his training and instincts. She knew all too well how that worked.

Nothing she could do about that now though. And the best way to help him was to get in position and protect him as best she could from the beach.

"Moving in now." A heartbeat later she was on her feet, running toward the walkway that led to the sand, Briar only a few steps behind her.

Five strides in, her right foot landed on the grass and something sharp hit her in rapid succession, in her calf, her thigh. The hot bites of pain had barely registered before a wicked current of electricity coursed through her.

Agony engulfed her.

Her muscles seized. She couldn't breathe, couldn't move.

She fell to the ground and hit hard, jerking uncontrollably like she was having a grand mal seizure. There was nothing she could do to stop the black wave from taking her under.

****

Perez's heart was in his throat as he raced down the final leg of the tunnel. The tactical team was right behind him. Most of his guards were dead, only a few remained, including one of his bodyguards.

They had to get to the boat. It was their only chance of escape now. He'd head for international waters, pray he reached that safe harbor before they caught up to him.

They'll have air support. Satellites.

He shoved those thoughts from his head. All he could do now was run, and he was going to give that everything he had.

His pulse hammered in his ears as he ran, desperation giving him an added burst of speed. Dammit, he should have left this afternoon, when he hadn't heard from Nico.

He'd been suspicious that something was wrong, and when he'd spoken to Laura this morning his gut had confirmed it. Her laughs had seemed forced, brittle even.

Now he knew why. She must have known they were coming after him but couldn't warn him because they had her in custody. God dammit… He never ignored his gut, but he had today, and it might cost him everything.

The tunnel exit was dead ahead. Rather than go through it, he veered sharply to the left and shoved open the secret entrance to the hidden staircase.

The soles of his shoes slapped in a frantic rhythm against the concrete steps that led him down to the small grotto where the boat waited. His bodyguard was already down there, would have it ready.

No one knew about this place but him and his bodyguards, not even the rest of the security staff. From the outside it was completely invisible, camouflaged by vegetation and a few clever tricks to stop the NSA and its prying eyes from finding it. A small access canal led directly beneath the house, hidden by steel panels covered with sand and vegetation so it blended in seamlessly with the landscape. With one push of a button the panels would lift simultaneously, clearing his escape route.

There would be shooters outside though. They'd have to be fast and hope they could make it through the hail of gunfire that was surely coming. But he couldn't think about that now.

His eyes adjusted to the increasing brightness as he neared the bottom that opened up into the grotto. From there it was only a short sprint to the boat.

Footsteps pounded on the ground behind him. Terror forked through him. He whirled to fire again, stumbled as he pulled the trigger, and missed. The man's shadow kept coming, a deadly figure drawing closer with every breath.

Desperate, he turned and ran. They'd want to take him alive, so they could lock him in some dark hole for the rest of his life.

He'd never see his wife and kids again. Laura would never allow it once she learned what kind of man he really was, and the things he'd done.

God. He'd worked so hard at crafting and maintaining a huge cover to keep her safe, to keep her from finding out about the shady and downright illegal things he'd been involved with.

In that moment he realized his life was already over. He'd rather die here and now than face that.

"*Perez!*"

Shock exploded inside him at the sound of that angry roar. He knew that voice. Would recognize it anywhere.

His foot hit the gravel at the bottom of the stairs. He slipped, blindly threw out a hand to catch himself.

His palm hit the rock wall, knocking the pistol from his grasp. It tumbled down the incline, leaving him unarmed and helpless.

The sudden roar of a boat's motor coming to life made him glance to the left. Outside, the panels shielding the canal were lifting. He watched in horror and disbelief as his bodyguard drove it away from him and out of the grotto, abandoning him to his fate.

Fuck!

He whipped around as the footsteps behind him came nearer still.

And found himself staring into the chilling, hate-filled eyes of Bautista. Fear curdled in his belly, turning his legs to liquid.

He fell back a step, automatically raising his hands, palms out.

Bautista had stopped at the top of the stairs, his weapon aimed at Perez's chest. "Stop right there," he snarled, the look on his face making Perez's blood ice over.

"Where are Laura and the kids?" he asked, the slight tremor in his voice betraying his panic. "I know you know." Had he done something to them? It made him sick to even think it. Bautista was a stone-cold killer, but even Perez had a hard time imagining him harming Laura or the kids. Bautista had never killed innocents before, at least not to his knowledge.

"Safe, no thanks to you," was all he said. "Now don't you fucking move." Bautista took a menacing step toward him, the muzzle of that rifle never wavering.

I can't go to prison. I can't live that way. I'd rather die.

As of now he was dead to Laura and the kids anyway.

Despair rose up, compressing his heart and lungs.

The sound of running feet echoed from up above in the tunnel. Perez glanced upward, another bolt of fear slicing through him. The tactical team would be here any second.

He turned back to Bautista, made a feeble but desperate attempt to beg. "Let me go. Please," he added in a ragged voice.

Bautista's lips peeled back in a sneer. "Not a fucking chance."

Faced with the unthinkable and with no other option left, Perez turned and ran.

Chapter Twenty

Bautista couldn't believe it. Well, he could, now that he'd seen the spineless asshole for what he really was, but it was almost laughable to see Perez trying to flee.

He automatically adjusted his weapon to aim it center mass on his target, finger curling around the trigger. But then he stopped, staring at Perez.

A bullet's too fucking good for you.

The thought triggered a sudden bolt of inspiration.

Slinging his weapon across his chest, he reached down and pulled one of his special blades from its custom-made sheath. With the sound of the approaching team's running footsteps growing louder behind him, he drew back his arm and hurled the knife as hard as he could.

The razor-sharp blade hit Perez in the back of the right shoulder blade, burying right to the hilt. An agonized roar filled the air, echoing off the roof and walls.

Perez arched backward and dropped to his knees, his left hand coming up and across his back to grab for the handle. An exercise in futility.

Bautista moved down the remaining stairs, a cold calm taking over him, reducing his rage to a simmer. A wound in the back of the shoulder would hurt like a bitch, probably cause some permanent nerve damage.

The sadistic part of him liked the idea of Perez rotting in prison and having to learn to wipe his ass with his left hand for the rest of his days.

Above him, the team breached the entrance to the staircase. "Bautista! Stand down!" Tuck yelled at him.

He didn't stop. Couldn't. Just kept stalking toward Perez, his pulse thudding hard and the need for vengeance egging him on.

Swearing and grimacing, Perez rolled to his side and scuttled backward. "No more," he panted, his eyes wide with terror. "Please, no more."

Pathetic. The man had ordered the torture and execution of others, and most of them had shown a lot more balls than this when faced with Bautista and his blades.

"Bautista! Stand the fuck down!"

He refused to look back at Rycroft and the others as he closed the distance between him and the man he once would have done anything for. Including dying to help him escape in a scenario just like this. He'd been such a fool.

The thought tumbled through his brain, bringing a rush of incredulity and something like grief. *I would have died for you.*

Perez tried to scramble backward, his gaze locked with Bautista's.

When Bautista reached him he went to one knee before the man, held that terrified gaze for a long moment. Driving the point home that he would take pleasure in continuing this session.

Then, without a word, he reached back and jerked the knife free. The resulting high-pitched scream of agony was music to his ears.

"Leave him! Don't make me fucking shoot you," Rycroft growled from behind him on the stairs.

Satisfied that Perez was suffering and would finally get the justice he deserved, Bautista stood, the bloody knife held in his grip.

Perez's eyes shot from the team back to Bautista, the desperation on his face clear. "Kill me," he begged. "Do it."

The plea surprised him. And so did his response.

At one time he would have done it instantly, without hesitation, his need for retribution overpowering everything else.

But that had been back when he'd had nothing to lose. Now he did, because Georgia had changed that. She'd changed *everything*. And he wasn't willing to go back to prison for killing Perez and live the rest of his life without her, no matter how good it would have felt in the moment.

"Dying's too easy for you," he answered coldly, and stepped back, detaching himself from this man, his former life. "I want you to know what it feels like to lose everything you ever loved."

Like he had. First his mother. Then his *abuelita*. Then Georgia. And finally the man he'd have given his life for.

It was gratifying to know Perez would suffer that same sense of loss. Only in his case, the loss would be permanent, whereas Bautista had somehow been given a second chance. With Georgia.

He watched the words hit home, the resignation fill Perez's eyes before they went blank with the reality of what was coming.

Bautista dropped the knife and raised both hands in a gesture of surrender as the team reached them.

While Tuck and the others cuffed Perez and secured

the area, Rycroft stalked over, his face livid. "What the fuck was that?" he demanded, shoving a hand into Bautista's chest. "You know how close you came to getting shot up in that tunnel?"

"The op was to take him alive. And we did."

Rycroft shook his head, his expression full of frustration. "That was fucking stupid. I thought being with Georgia would have made you realize you've got something else—someone else—to live for."

"It did," he answered flatly. "That's the only reason he's still breathing." He jerked his chin at Perez, standing cuffed with a ring of HRT guys around him and Schroder doing a patch job on the wound in his shoulder. Bautista would rather have left him bleeding.

Rycroft glared at him for another few seconds, then stepped back. "Well I guess that's something, at least," he muttered.

A voice over their comms interrupted him, from one of the HRT sniper team members. "Perimeter is clear, all tangos neutralized. But we've got a problem."

In the pause that followed, something about the man's tone triggered a surge of dread.

"Georgia and Briar are both down. We're moving in to help now."

Bautista jerked to a halt, met Rycroft's gaze. "Say again?" he rasped out, praying he'd misunderstood.

"They're both down," the man repeated.

His heart plummeted into his boots, his entire body going cold. "Where are they?" he demanded, every muscle rigid.

"On the west lawn, near the path leading down to the water."

Panic blasted through him. Without a word he turned and raced back up the stairs, his only thought of reaching Georgia.

****

Something was tickling the side of her face. But it was dark and she couldn't see. Couldn't make her muscles move.

Sounds began to register. The thump of her heart. Disjointed voices, coming through her earpiece.

Georgia's eyelids flickered open. She was disoriented, confused and weak. Her cheek was pressed against something damp and ticklish and it smelled like…grass.

Groaning, she forced her stiff muscles to obey her and rolled stiffly to her side. Her rifle lay on the grass beside her. What the hell had happened? Something had hit her in the left leg, then electrocuted her.

As soon as she glanced down, she saw why. Three barbs attached to wires protruded from her camo pants. A fucking Taser.

No, some kind of fucking pressure sensitive or laser-activated Taser system. She'd either landed on a pressure plate or triggered some kind of invisible tripwire.

"Sonofabitch," she muttered, gritting her teeth as she pulled them out one by one. When she flung them aside, she caught sight of someone lying on the grass close to her.

Briar. And she wasn't moving.

"*Briar*," she said sharply. Alarmed when her teammate didn't respond, Georgia scrambled over to her on hands and knees, rolled her into recovery position on her side.

She wasn't breathing. A press of two fingers under her jaw told her the worst part.

No pulse.

Georgia immediately rolled her to her back and checked her airway. Nothing was blocking it. Maybe that Taser had stopped her heart.

No. No, you can't die on me.

Briar had risked so much to find her, help her. She couldn't die. She had so much to live for now. Georgia had to save her.

Stacking her hands on Briar's sternum, she began rapid compressions. "Briar's down," she forced out between compressions, knowing the team would hear her as she cast a frantic look around. "She's not breathing and there's no pulse. I'm doing CPR now. Get a medic up here *now*."

Briar still hadn't responded in any way and there was still no pulse.

Swearing, Georgia performed a jaw thrust and gave her two breaths, then immediately resumed the quick compressions.

"Come on Briar," she gritted out, sweat beading her brow, the muscles in her back and shoulders already burning. "Don't do this to me. You have to breathe."

****

She's not breathing and there's no pulse.

Those terrible words echoed in his ears like a death knell.

Bent over the desk, hands gripping the edge of it, Matt stared at the screens before him. One showed a live feed of Tuck's helmet cam down in the underground grotto. The other, a feed from one of the snipers.

The latter were running across the lawn. He saw Briar lying on the grass on her back, Georgia bent over her doing chest compressions.

Raw terror exploded inside him as he faced his ultimate waking nightmare.

Briar!

Her name was a silent scream searing through his brain. Every muscle in his body tightened like steel cables, about to snap.

Matt turned and tore out of the mobile command center, racing through the brush that filled the most direct path to her. His heart slammed sickeningly against his ribs, his throat so tight it felt like he was slowly choking.

Images flooded his brain, dredged up from the vault where he'd locked them in his head.

Lisa lying on her back beside their pool, her skin turning purple and then blue as he desperately tried to revive her. Watching her die right in front of him, helpless to do anything but hold her as her body grew cold.

Grief clawed at him, a strangled moan getting trapped in his throat. He couldn't lose Briar too. Just couldn't. There was no way he could bear that.

He leaped over a tall hedge that marked the edge of the lawn, his boots pounding over the short grass. Up ahead he saw Georgia working on Briar, someone else running flat out toward them. Schroder.

The medic dropped to his knees, ripped open a medical bag. "What happened?" Matt heard him ask.

"Some kind of Taser," Georgia answered, panting from the exertion of the continual compressions.

Matt skidded to his knees beside them and reached for her. "Briar." His voice cracked. She was so still, her skin already turning purple. He shoved Georgia aside and started compressions, not stopping even as Schroder cut her shirt and bra away and placed the automated defibrillator pads directly against her skin. "How long?" he rasped out.

"Just a few seconds," Schroder answered, all his attention on what he was doing.

It was agonizing. Every second felt like an hour, and he swore he could feel her skin growing colder beneath his hands.

"*Briar*," he said hoarsely, his heart cracking into a thousand pieces. "Come on, honey, hang on. Come back to me."

No answer. No pulse.

Just like Lisa. She's going to die right in front of me and there's nothing I can do to stop it.

The tears flooded his eyes and there was no stopping them. He was so fucking scared, couldn't even face the thought of being without Briar.

"Clear," Schroder commanded.

It killed him to lift his hands, to lose that contact with her, but he forced himself to let go. Schroder hit the button and her torso jerked with the force of the current. They both reached for her carotid pulse at the same time.

Come on, baby, come on, he prayed, his face wet and his heart bleeding.

A faint throb pressed against his searching fingertips.

"God," he cried and grasped her face, desperate to reach her while Schroder checked her airway. "Briar. Briar, *please…*"

Her chest moved. It fucking moved as she inhaled.

Drawing a slight amount of air into her lungs all on her own.

A sob broke free, torn from the depth of his chest. "*Yes*. Come on, baby. Breathe for me and open your eyes." He'd give fucking anything for that.

"Pulse is getting stronger," Schroder said, giving him an encouraging half-smile. "Come on, Briar, do as the man said."

Matt stared at her face, praying, taking every shallow breath with her. "Can you hear me?" he asked her. "I'm right here, honey, just open your eyes and look at me."

That's all he wanted. He refused to even contemplate that she might have brain damage. *God, just don't take her from me.*

Her eyelids moved. Her lashes fluttered.

And then her eyes cracked open. She blinked, looked up at him and a little frown creased her forehead. "Matt," she said weakly.

"God. Oh *God*," he cried, wrapping his arms under her shoulders, one hand supporting the back of her head as he lifted her against his chest.

He felt her hands lightly touch his back and he lost it completely as he held her tight. So tight his arms shook.

He was vaguely aware of Georgia placing a hand on his shoulder and then rising, aware that they'd drawn a crowd and he was still crying, shaking, but he didn't care about any of it. All he cared was that Briar was alive and he was holding her.

He didn't know how much time had passed before Schroder put a hand on his shoulder to get his attention.

He looked up to find all his guys kneeling around him, relieved smiles on their faces. Even that bastard Bautista.

Unable to stop touching her, Matt cupped the side of her face as Schroder spoke to her and checked her out. He wiped the heel of his free hand over his face, struggling to get his breath back.

A tissue appeared in front of him. He glanced up to see Georgia holding it out to him. There were tears in her eyes. Bautista was there beside her, wrapping an arm around her shoulders. "Thanks," he murmured, then mopped one-handed at his face.

"I'm guessing it was a close call," Briar murmured weakly.

The sound of her voice nearly made him lose it all over again. Matt drew in a shuddering breath and nodded. "Yeah. Way too fucking close."

"Good thing I'm stubborn."

At that he cracked a grin. She *was* stubborn. Sometimes it drove him crazy, like the way she refused to talk about getting married even after living together for almost a year, or having a family one day.

But right now he was so fucking grateful for her bull-

243

headedness and the sheer determination she possessed. "Yeah."

"I knew you secretly loved it that I'm stubborn."

He let out a watery laugh and bent to kiss her again. He planned on kissing her a lot over the next few days, just to reassure himself that she was still here. "Stop talking. No more talking until Schroder says it's okay."

"It's more than okay," the medic said wryly. "I prefer it, actually. We've gotta keep her alert until the EMTs get here."

Briar scowled. "I don't need EMTs. I'm fine now."

Matt shook his head at her, loving her so damn much it hurt. He was a fucking wreck, this op the last thing on his mind. Perez was in custody, and all that mattered was that Briar was alive. Screw his responsibilities, screw his job. Screw everything but her.

"You're as bad as them," he said, nodding toward his team.

She closed her eyes as though the conversation exhausted her, but there was a little smile on her lips. "It's cuz I'm badass."

"You sure are," he told her, giving her another kiss. When he raised his head, he searched out Tuck and Rycroft. "I'm done," he said simply, knowing they'd understand what he meant. "Can you guys take over from here?"

"Of course, man, no worries," Tuck said as Rycroft nodded. "You just go take care of your girl."

"Thanks." Because there was no way he was leaving her side for the rest of the night at least.

Or maybe ever.

Chapter Twenty-One

"That was so damn scary."

Bautista wrapped his arms around Georgia from behind as they watched the EMTs load Briar into the back of a waiting ambulance. They'd been on scene within minutes of Schroder arriving at her side. "You did great."

"God, I never want to have to do that again for someone I care about. Poor guy," she murmured, watching as DeLuca climbed into the back. Bautista saw him take Briar's hand an instant before the rear doors closed.

"He'll be fine now that she's gonna be okay."

Georgia nodded, the softness of her hair snagging on the whiskers on his chin.

He turned her, took her face in his hands. Those pale blue eyes stared up at him in the moonlight, hypnotic in their power.

Look at you, waxing all fucking poetic.

He mentally shrugged at the cynical voice because she did that to him. Made him see life in a way he never had.

"I've never been scared like that before. Not like

that." Not even when he'd walked in to find his beloved grandmother lying bleeding on the kitchen floor. "When I heard that sniper say you were down…"

He let the sentence trail off because he just couldn't finish it. Couldn't even put into words what he'd gone through in those few minutes between hearing the news and seeing her alive and well, working on Briar. So he could only imagine how DeLuca had felt.

Rather than tell him he was being ridiculous or shrug it off, she smiled, sheer joy making her eyes sparkle. "I'm glad you love me that much."

"I do," he vowed. "I'd do anything for you."

"I'd do anything for you too." Then slowly her smile faded, doubt creeping into her eyes. "So now that this op is over, what does that mean for us?"

He cupped the side of her face in one palm, cherishing the feel of her soft skin against his hand. God, he'd give anything to be with her, but he just didn't see how that was possible. "I don't know. But even with Perez gone there's still a risk to you. I'd feel better if we got you out of the country."

She shook her head, her lips pressing together in a mulish expression he was coming to understand meant *no way in hell*. "Not without you. Never again, I already told you that."

He opened his mouth to argue but in his peripheral he saw someone moving toward them. Automatically he moved in front of her, shielding her. But it was only Rycroft.

"Got some news," the agent said as he strolled up, glancing between them. "This a bad time?"

"No," they answered in unison, and both of them sounded a little defensive.

"Good. So I just got off the phone with the Director of the CIA." He paused a beat, looking at Georgia. "Rossland's in custody. He didn't go quietly, but the point is he's taken care of, and with the evidence I sent out to my various contacts, there's no way he'll ever get off.

"Oh, and the former CIA hitter at the cabin? He's the one who poisoned you with the botulism toxin. The media's already been alerted and the President is being briefed. I know you wanted to be the one to bring him down, but you did, even if not physically. And this way you get to stay out of prison," he added with the hint of a grin.

"Bonus," she muttered, completely unmoved, and Bautista loved her even more for the little show of attitude. His woman was intense.

"As for Mr. Perez," he continued, "he's off to a special holding facility. In your old room, actually," he said to Bautista.

Bautista watched as Bauer and Cruz led Perez, in cuffs, to another ambulance. He hoped the medics didn't use any freezing when they sewed him up. He did feel sorry for Laura and the kids though. "Just wish his family didn't have to go through what's coming," he said.

"They'll be better for it in the long run," Rycroft answered. "But yeah, it sucks. Hopefully that tears him apart for the rest of his days."

Bautista hoped so too.

He stood there and watched the HRT members shove Perez up into the back of the ambulance, almost smiled at the cry of pain that came from across the lawn. Perez would never be a free man again, and he'd hurt just as much inside as he was hurting on the outside right now.

That had to be enough.

"Funny, that you'd tag Perez in that very spot on the back of the shoulder," Rycroft mused, his expression conveying suspicion and something else Bautista couldn't put his finger on.

Bautista shot him a frown. It was funny?

"In any case, you two have earned some time off. I'm

going to be busy with interrogations and paperwork for a few days. I'll see you—" He stopped and pulled out his phone, answered it and walked away without looking at them.

Bautista stared after him, stunned. He'd been bracing for a verbal tear-down, or maybe an assault charge for it. Not this. Back in that cave, Rycroft had been royally pissed at him. He'd assumed he'd be facing some sort of disciplinary measure—if not jail time.

And that comment about the shoulder thing seemed so random, yet Rycroft wasn't a random kind of guy so he had to have said it for a reason…

He went still, felt Georgia stiffen in front of him.

"Did he seriously just…?" Georgia whispered, as if she was afraid to say it out loud.

"I think he did, yeah." He turned around to face her, met her eyes. "His endgame must have been for me to help them get Perez. So I guess for now, we're off the hook." That felt…weird, but incredible, the prospect of freedom exhilarating.

She raised her eyebrows. "Any chance you still have a knife on you?"

Yeah, as a matter of fact he did.

Seizing her hand, he led her into the shadows created by the ornamental shrubs and plants next to the west side of the house. He had the advantage of knowing where all the security cameras were now, knew the exact blind spots that would help them hide. And Rycroft had obviously known it.

When he was sure no one was paying attention or had seen them creep in here to hide, he tugged on Georgia's hand and followed the path he'd picked out. Within minutes they were down at the beach. He was careful to avoid the sand so as not to leave any obvious footprints, finally coming to a stop beneath the shade of a tree positioned close to the bank.

Reaching down, he pulled out his remaining blade and hit the switch. The blade sprung free, gleaming silver in the moonlight. He held it out for her.

She took it, but gave him a hesitant look. "You sure about this?"

"I trust you." He gave her his back, something he never did. But he would for her.

She began feeling around his right shoulder blade with her fingers. "How big is it, do you think?"

"Small. Real small." Otherwise it would have been too easy to detect.

She made a frustrated sound. "I don't feel anything but muscle and scar tissue. Man, you've got a lot of scars back here. This obviously isn't the first time you've felt a blade back here. I—" She stopped, her fingers stilling against his skin. Then she probed harder. "I think I feel something. It's small, about the size of a grain of rice. More scar tissue?"

Only one way to find out. "Get it out of me." He couldn't wait for it to be gone. For *them* to be gone, far away from here. Together.

"Okay, stand still. I mean it, don't move."

"I won't."

The tip of the blade touched his skin. He could feel how gingerly she moved it. It sliced into his skin, a clean cut because the edge was so sharp.

"I think I've got something." She dug around with the tip. "Sorry, I'm being as gentle as I can."

"It's fine." The pain was nothing, just a little sting, and he'd bear far worse for the chance of a future with her as a free man.

"Got it." A moment later she stuck her hand out, palm up, revealing something in the center.

In the little pool of blood that had gathered around it lay a tiny microtracker. "I'll be damned," he murmured.

She handed it to him. "I don't suppose you've got a

bandage on you?" She pressed his shirt against the wound to stem the bleeding.

"No. But don't worry, I clot fast."

She snickered. "That shouldn't be funny, but right now it is."

He grinned. "It's been that kind of night."

A minute later she let up on the pressure. "I think it's stopped bleeding mostly. Sort of." She came around beside him, looked from the transmitter to him, her eyes full of hope. "Now what?"

In answer he drew his arm back and threw the tiny device as far as he could. It landed in the water without so much as a ripple and was swallowed up by the waves. If the NSA or anyone else tried to track the transmitter now, they'd be disappointed.

Georgia wiped his blade clean on the inside of her shirt and handed it back to him. He took it, stared fondly at the weapon.

"What?" she asked.

He shook his head once. "Just ironic."

"What is?"

The blade twinkled silver in the light as he twisted it from side to side. "I used this on men to mete out justice, but in reality it made me a prisoner." Perez's slave. "And now it's set me free."

Her gorgeous, soft lips turned up in a gentle smile. "It's set us both free."

He looked into her eyes, lowered the blade. "Yes." And now they finally had a chance to start fresh— together. How amazing was that?

Putting the knife back into its sheath, he grasped her hand, laced their fingers together. Excitement pulsed through him, the anticipation so heady he felt half-drunk.

"So. You ready for this?" Asking her to disappear with him was asking a lot, he knew that. But he would spend the rest of his life doing his best to be the man she deserved, and love her with everything in him.

She squeezed his hand, looking both excited and nervous. "Where will we go?"

There was a marina a couple miles to the south. They could steal a boat, make it out into international waters within a couple hours. He'd done it before, knew how to disappear. And so did she.

"Cuba, at least to start." It was relatively close, his grandmother had been born there and he was a native Spanish speaker. "From there we can pick a non-extradition country. And if you're worried about money or how we'll live, don't be. I've got funds the government has no clue about. We can easily live off that for the rest of our lives without either of us ever working another day."

He'd buried the offshore account so deep it would take a team of investigators months, maybe longer, to uncover it all. And given the way Rycroft had hinted about the tracking device and pretty much just given him the opportunity to run, he doubted the NSA would have enough interest in him to fund that kind of effort.

Georgia shot him a cocky grin. "Nice. But I've socked away quite a decent little nest egg myself, so I don't need or want your money." She wound her arms around his neck. "Only thing I need is you."

It shouldn't have mattered, but it felt like his heart expanded three sizes in response to those words. "You've got me. All of me. Forever."

"Then let's go," she whispered, and leaned up on tiptoe to seal their secret contract with a kiss.

Bautista led the way, still holding her hand. Together they climbed over the rocks, using the smaller ones as a bridge to the water. Georgia's steps were nimble, her grip on his hand solid, steady.

On top of the final rock, he paused and looked back at her, poised on the larger rock behind him. One good jump from where he was standing, and they'd be on their way to their new life together.

It was more than a jump, it was a leap of faith. One that required the utmost trust between them.

"Ready, angel?" he asked, his heart beating faster. She was so gorgeous standing there on that rock, her golden brown hair blowing in the breeze and a smile on her lips.

She nodded, her eyes shining up at him with pure happiness. "Ready. Let's do this."

Turning back to face the water, he let go of her hand and jumped. His boots and lower legs plunged into the chilly waves, the water rushing around his calves.

Before he could turn around, Georgia was there beside him, grabbing his arm to steady herself.

She gave him an impish grin. "Race you." Without waiting she turned and began running through the waves, following the shoreline toward the marina up the beach.

Bautista followed with his heart full to bursting while the waves lapped against the shore, erasing their steps forever.

****

An arrhythmia.

That's what had almost killed her. The powerful Taser's charge had knocked her heart out of rhythm, then stopped it completely.

Her chest was covered with black and blue bruises and her lungs hurt, she might have a cracked rib or two from the chest compressions, but none of that mattered now.

She was lucky to be alive.

It was a sobering thought, and one Briar had had ample time to think about while the doctors had run a battery of tests. Her heartbeat was once again strong and normal, but the arrhythmia was still there, having gone undetected until now.

But nearly dying had put a lot of things into perspective. She'd been holding back. Not consciously, but she had nonetheless. And Matt deserved better than that.

The curtain was pulled aside and he stepped through as though he'd read her mind. His beloved San Diego Chargers hat was nowhere to be seen, probably still back somewhere between the mobile command center and the place he'd found her on the lawn.

He gave her a gentle smile and came around to sit in the chair beside her bed. "Everything looks great but they want to keep you overnight just to be safe, and so they can monitor your heart rate."

She nodded, reached for his hand. He curled his fingers around hers, his grip warm and strong. Steadfast. Exactly like the man himself. "I haven't been fair to you," she began.

He frowned in confusion, tilted his head a fraction. "What do you mean?"

"I mean about us. I've been lying here thinking for the past few hours. This was a giant wakeup call for me."

God, when she thought of what he must have gone through in those few minutes when he'd been racing to her, watching her lying there lifeless and doing CPR just like he had with Lisa, her heart broke. She knew how badly his first wife's death had scarred him.

That he'd almost had to go through that a second time tore her up inside. And she knew that had the roles been reversed, watching him go off and take unnecessary risks with his life would have made her nuts.

"I've been selfish. And a coward," she continued. "No," she said, holding up a hand when he would have argued. "It's true. You've given me all of you and I was still holding part of myself back. I'm sorry I did that. But

I won't anymore."

She gripped his hand tighter, didn't even try to fight the tears that pricked her eyes. "I love you. More than you even realize. I've been selfish in wanting to keep playing at being a Valkyrie."

"You're not *playing* at anything. And I love that you're a Valkyrie."

"But I don't need to live like one anymore." She pushed out a breath, winced as it put stress on her cracked ribs. "I'm going to tell Alex that I want to move into an analyst position, rather than be a field agent."

Matt stared at her for a long moment, his surprise clear. "You sure?"

"Yes," she said, already feeling better just having said it aloud. "It's time. I can still back him or another team up if necessary, but I can help from behind the scenes too." The next part was hard for her because it made her feel unbearably vulnerable, but she trusted him and it needed to be said. "And I want to get married."

At that his eyebrows shot up. "Wait, what?"

"I know, you've been asking me if I want to for months and I've always made up some excuse or another. But I'm ready now."

Now he looked concerned as he glanced at the IV stand next to her. "What the hell are they giving you?"

"Saline. Straight saline," she snapped impatiently. "Now pay attention, I'm baring my soul to you here. And I'm not saying any of this because I had a near death experience."

His gaze swung back to her, and he gave her his whole focus.

That was better. Looking into his eyes helped combat the slight edge of fear inside her at saying all this out loud. "I love you and I want to be your wife. And I do want a family with you someday. Not right away," she clarified when his eyes bugged out in shock, "but one day. Maybe in another couple years. I don't want to wait too long though."

When he didn't say anything, just kept staring at her like he couldn't believe what he was hearing, she got nervous. She cleared her throat. "So, you wanna get married when I get out of here?"

His lips twitched and his eyes twinkled. He leaned forward, his voice a husky murmur. "Wait. Did you just propose to me?"

Face flushing, she nodded. The man was making her sweat after everything she'd been through today? "Yeah. So will you?"

With a muffled chuckle he slid a hand around her nape and bent to kiss her. "Honey, you know I'd marry you in a heartbeat. But when we actually get engaged, we're doing it the old-fashioned way. A romantic setting. Me on one knee in front of you when I ask. A diamond ring. No hospitals involved."

"Oh…" It sounded magical, like something out of one of those fairy tale books she'd read as a kid. More than she'd ever hoped for. And she knew without a doubt he'd make it the most special moment of her life. Matt was more romantic than even she'd realized.

"Oh," he agreed, then sat back up, still grinning, still holding her hand tight. "I'm not going to tell you until I do it, either. I want it to be a complete surprise."

How the hell did she get so lucky, to catch a man like him?

She cleared her throat, changed the subject before she gave into the urge to cry. "Any word on Georgia and Bautista?"

"No. But I'm pretty sure they're on their way out of the country."

"You think Alex let them go? Just like that?"

Matt shrugged. "Rycroft got what he wanted out of whatever deal they'd made. With Perez taken care of, I guess he decided to look the other way and let them go. Not that I'll ever pretend to understand the way the NSA operates, but I don't think Bautista is a threat to national security and he's clearly devoted to Georgia."

Yeah, she could see that. Finding love was a miracle, she knew that better than anyone, and her old friend deserved happiness. And Bautista wasn't a bad guy once you got to know him. As long as you didn't cross him or someone he cared about. "I know he'll treat her well." Georgia certainly couldn't have asked for anyone more protective than him.

"He'd better," Matt grunted.

She grinned. "Still don't like him? Even after he gave us all the intel we needed, helped your boys and stopped Perez?"

"I like him *better*," he clarified, looking like he'd just sucked on a piece of lemon.

She chuckled. He was so black and white. She loved his moral compass and sense of loyalty. "I love you."

"Love you too, sweetheart. Now get some rest."

"You won't leave?" she asked, not wanting to be alone here. Hospitals gave her the creeps, even though she'd never admit it aloud.

"No," he answered with a shake of his head, his eyes warm with understanding. "I'm staying until I get to take you home where I can have you all to myself."

With a little smile on her lips, she closed her eyes and allowed herself to drift off.

Epilogue

Three months later

Setting down the full-to-bursting grocery bags she'd just walked home from the market with, Georgia dug out her key and opened their mailbox at the end of their road. There were a few bills inside, along with the long-anticipated package containing the specialty dark chocolate bars she was forced to order from the States because she simply couldn't get them down here in Cuba.

Diplomatic relations might be thawing between the two countries but they were far from anything she'd consider to be normal. She was always careful about having things shipped here though, never using the same name twice, always using a different credit card.

Old habits die hard.

A gust of warm ocean breeze ruffled her hair and the deep blue sundress she wore as she walked the final block home. It was early evening, the sun about to set into the ocean. Turning the corner of the secluded lane, a feeling of calm overcame her when their house came into view.

Nestled against the sea and surrounded by lush

vegetation, the two-story golden yellow stucco house seemed to glow in the waning light. Lemon yellow rectangles of light spilled from the windows at the front, emphasizing the cozy feel. This was home now. Adjusting to life here had been relatively easy and her Spanish was getting better each day. Miguel spoke it exclusively to her three days per week, to help her become fluent.

At the gate she paused to slide her hand into the fingerprint scanner, waited for the two beeps that signaled an all clear and the latch unlocked. Their house was a veritable fortress, complete with a state-of-the-art security system they'd designed themselves, including several biometric scanners and a panic room.

Her pistol remained firmly against the small of her back as she moved up the front steps. Neither of them ever went anywhere unarmed, even here, where it would be easy to lapse into a false state of security.

"I'm back," she called as she swept into the front foyer. Something delicious and spicy wafted from the kitchen.

A moment later Miguel appeared in the far doorway, wiping his hands on a kitchen towel. He gave her a slow smile, his gaze sweeping over her figure appreciatively. "Hi."

"Hi," she answered with her own smile, and sighed when he took the bags from her with one hand and used the other to curl it around her nape and pull her in for a slow, deep kiss. Just when she was tingling all over and melting against him, he eased back.

"You get the peppers I asked for?"

She blinked, then snorted. "Were you thinking about that the entire time you were kissing me?"

"Not the entire time."

The teasing gleam in his eyes made her shake her head. "I had no idea you'd turn into a raging foodie once we got settled down here."

"Well, you know how much I love to work with knives, and this gives me my fix in a non-violent way." He pulled a wickedly-sharp knife from the butcher's block and did a fancy twirling thing with it in his fingers that she found ridiculously sexy, then raised a dark eyebrow. "Having regrets so soon about going on the run with me?"

"No, never." With a grin she slid her arms around his waist and leaned in to nip gently at his lower lip. "I love seeing you this happy. And I'm not even complaining about the fifteen pounds I've packed on since we got here." She patted her stomach and hips, which were a whole lot rounder than they had been a few months ago.

Though starting over in a foreign country had its own set of challenges, the new lifestyle had been the best thing for them both. Miguel was a totally different person here. Calmer, far more relaxed than she'd ever seen him, and he'd gained back all the weight and muscle he'd lost with daily runs and swims in the ocean.

Not to mention all the sex they'd been having.

His hand skimmed over her back to grab her butt and squeezed, his voice dropping to a seductive rumble against her ear. "You needed it. And I like having something to hold onto when I'm deep inside you."

She scowled playfully at him. "Tease. You know damn well you have no intention of following through with this seduction until you've finished whatever it is you're making in the kitchen."

He tucked a lock of hair behind her ear, his touch sending a shiver of delight along her skin. "Seduction should be done slowly, so it can be savored, angel," he told her.

She made a sound of irritation. "Hurry up and finish dinner then."

He smirked. "Come keep me company then, and I'll be done that much sooner."

That sounded good to her.

She perched herself on the center island while he chopped and peeled and stirred, making sure the hem of her dress rode up her thighs as she crossed her legs. Legs that were now golden brown and more muscular than before from all the time they spent outdoors.

Over at the stove stirring a pot of something, he dragged his gaze from her legs up to her face, narrowed his eyes at her. "I'm going to remember that for later."

"Please do," she answered, knowing the payoff would be worth it, and plucked the mail out of the bag. Setting the bills aside for later, she opened the plastic wrapping on the box. "My chocolate finally came."

He huffed out a laugh. "You're such a chocolate snob."

"Guilty. And I regret noth—" She stopped dead, staring at the envelope that fell out of the box when she opened it.

Miguel turned to look at her, glanced at the envelope and frowned when he saw the look on her face. "What?"

She stared at the handwriting on the front that simply read *Georgia.*

No one down here knew her real name. And for that letter to have been slipped into the package meant it had to have been done in the States.

You both got too complacent. Dropped your guards and now you're going to pay the price.

Her heart rate shot up as she tore it open. A legal document was tucked beneath a hand-written note.

Took us a while to find you. Should have figured out sooner that you wouldn't be able to stay away from your secret addiction for too long.

You'll be pleased to know that Perez has been extremely helpful in divulging more secrets, all in the hopes of a reduced sentence. We've already arrested four others involved with Fuentes's crimes.

Hope all is well. If you ever need anything, you know where to find me. Say hi to Miguel for me.

Love always, Briar

(P.S. Alex sends his regards too)

Georgia stared at it in disbelief.

"What?" Miguel said impatiently, grabbing it from her numb fingers. His eyebrows crashed together as he read it. Then he turned the page to the legal document, started reading, and his face went blank with shock. "Holy shit."

"What? What is it?" Had relations between the U.S. and Cuba normalized already? Were they being extradited back to the U.S.?

"It's a full legal pardon. For me," he said, his voice full of awe as he looked at the final page.

Georgia crowded in close to read the signatures at the end of document. Rycroft. The head of the NSA. Someone from the Department of Justice. *Whoa.* "Just letting us know they've pinged us, but that you're officially a free man." That didn't make sense though. She looked up at him, confused. "Why bother tracking us down at all if you're free?" Because she couldn't imagine it was simply to mail him this pardon.

He lowered the pages in his hand, met her gaze. "Because it leaves the door open if they decide to ask us back for consulting work later on."

She frowned. "You think?"

"Yeah."

He sounded so certain about that but she wasn't convinced. It unsettled her to know the NSA and whoever else had been spying on them without them having a clue for God knew how long.

"Hey."

A large hand curled under her chin, lifted it. She fell into that black gaze, felt an answering flash of giddy excitement flare to life inside her when she saw the look in his eyes.

Joy. Pure, undiluted joy.

The smile that spread across his face was the most beautiful thing she'd ever seen. It transformed his features completely. In that instant he looked a decade younger, all the worry and stress falling away. "It's over. I never thought it would actually happen, but it did. I'm finally a free man again."

Her throat tightened in relief. She wound her arms around his neck and held on tight, savoring the moment. "I can't believe it." It felt so surreal. "So...we're free to go wherever we want?"

"Yes."

"Maybe back to Miami?" She knew how much he missed being able to visit his grandmother.

His eyes warmed. "Maybe, yeah. Would you prefer that?"

"I'll go wherever you want."

Setting the papers on the island, he captured her face in his hands, searched her eyes. "You're the only one I would ever want to spend the rest of my life with."

A tremulous smile curved her lips. "Same goes." He was so good to her. They were good for each other. "I love you so much."

"Love you too." He cocked his head. "Feel like getting married this week?"

Her eyes widened. "Are you serious?" She'd just never thought it would ever be an option. Not while his future was up in the air.

He nodded once, that intensity radiating from him making her heart pound. "I want to make you mine in every way possible."

Dammit, now her eyes were stinging. She was already his, and he had to know that, but... That tiny part of her that was still the lonely orphan had always dreamed of finding a man to love her enough to want to marry her.

Of building a life together. Maybe even having a family together one day. "I would love to marry you," she whispered, her voice rough.

He gave her a slow smile, his eyes heating. "Okay then." With one hand he reached behind him to turn off the burner the pot was cooking on top of. "I think dinner can wait for a bit while we celebrate, don't you?"

Her insides went liquid at the promise of pleasure she read in his eyes. "Oh hell yeah," she muttered, jumping up to wind her legs around his waist and finding his mouth with hers.

With a low chuckle he cradled the back of her head with one hand and locked his other arm around his hips as he headed for the stairs that led to their master suite.

We're free, she thought dizzily, hardly able to believe it. Free to do whatever they wanted, free to spend the rest of their lives together as husband and wife. They would belong to each other forever, and nothing would ever tear them apart again.

It was an unexpected gift beyond measure, and one she vowed to never take for granted as long as she lived.

—The End—

Thank you for reading BETRAYED. I really hope you enjoyed it and that you'll consider leaving a review at one of your favorite online retailers. It's a great way to help other readers discover new books.

If you liked BETRAYED and would like to read more, turn the page for a list of my other books. And if you don't want to miss any future releases, please feel free to join my newsletter: http://kayleacross.com/v2/newsletter/

Complete Booklist

Paranormal Romance
Empowered Series
Darkest Caress

Historical Romance
The Vacant Chair

Erotic Romance (writing as *Callie Croix*)
Deacon's Touch
Dillon's Claim
No Holds Barred
Touch Me
Let Me In
Covert Seduction

Acknowledgements

Many thanks to my team for helping me with this story! Katie, Deb, Joan and my long-suffering DH. Couldn't do this without you guys!

Can't believer we're almost at the end of this series.

About the Author

NY Times and USA Today Bestselling author Kaylea Cross writes edge-of-your-seat military romantic suspense. Her work has won many awards and has been nominated for both the Daphne du Maurier and the National Readers' Choice Awards. A Registered Massage Therapist by trade, Kaylea is also an avid gardener, artist, Civil War buff, Special Ops aficionado, belly dance enthusiast and former nationally-carded softball pitcher. She lives in Vancouver, BC with her husband and family.

You can visit Kaylea at www.kayleacross.com. If you would like to be notified of future releases, please join her newsletter: http://kayleacross.com/v2/newsletter/